BUTTERFLY WINGS

A NOVEL

JORDAN FORD

～

ISBN: 978-1-99-103477-9 (Kindle)
978-1-99-103478-6 (Paperback)

Forever Love Publishing Ltd
www.foreverlovepublishing.com

For lovers of Beauty & the Beast

There is beauty in all things... even when it's hard to find.
Anyone can be transformed by the power of love.

THE BROKEN BOY

Once upon a time there was very handsome boy who was broken. He lived a life of privilege and wealth, yet he was empty and poor. And then he met a beast... who would show him the true meaning of beauty...

I'm a beast.

That's what they'll call me.

It was what they always said when they saw Grace's face.

Her fingers curled into fists as she stared out the window. The world was flashing by in a blur, her mother taking advantage of the open road and flooring it. She didn't usually speed, but this time was different.

She wanted to get to Connecticut as fast as she could.

She needed to settle. To meet her new boss. To start over.

Grace blinked and tried her best not to cry. Tears had

been spilling out of her eyes at random moments throughout the trip, but she didn't want to burden her mother with them.

~

"After all I've sacrificed for you!" her mother said. "How could you do this to us?"

Her father huffed. "I didn't mean to fall in love, Leola. This is why I wanted you and Grace with me."

"No, you didn't!"

"I asked you to come, and you wouldn't!"

"Only because you wanted to hide our daughter."

"I didn't want to hide her!" Dad's voice rose to a thunder. "I was trying to do her a favor."

"Covering her up with makeup isn't helping her, Irvin! Don't you see? It's like you're ashamed to be around her. She's beautiful just the way she is!"

Silence.

That always hurt the most. People were only silent when they didn't know how to rebut the truth.

Eventually, her father sighed, "I'm not ashamed of her. I just hate the way people stare."

"That's their problem! Grace is gorgeous."

"She's scarred." Her father's voice broke apart like maybe he might cry. But then he sniffed. "Don't look at me that way! You know I'm only telling the truth."

"She's not scarred where it counts." Her mother's voice hitched. "Her heart is pure and beautiful, and if you could just accept her for who she is, then it will stay that way. I couldn't follow you around from one movie set to the next knowing that

you'd be constantly pressuring her to cover up. All you're doing is making her embarrassed of her appearance, and I won't have it!"

Grace squeezed her eyes shut, resting her forehead against the wall and trying not to make a sound. She was tucked out of sight. She couldn't even see her parents. But every word of their argument was crystal clear.

"And now it doesn't matter." Her mother's voice turned wooden. "You love someone else, and what we had is over."

"It was over a long time ago," Dad muttered. "I never cheated on you. My heart just moved on, and now my body is ready to do the same."

Silence.

Again.

It was thick and suffocating, and Grace couldn't take any more.

She crept up the stairs, crawled under the covers, and wept like she was a little girl.

But she wasn't a little girl.

She was sixteen, old enough to cope with all of this. Apparently.

"You okay?" Her mother sucked on her Big Gulp straw, then passed it over. Her eyes were a nutmeg brown, just like Grace's. They were similar in so many ways—the same heart-shaped face, the same fine hair, the same—

Grace internally cringed.

They weren't the same. Not by a long shot. Her mother was beautiful. She radiated sunshine and warmth.

Her smile was perfect, her lips plump, her face symmetrical.

She didn't have ugly scars pulling her skin in odd directions, marring what used to be a smooth, unblemished complexion with jarring red lines that made people's faces bunch in disgust. She didn't walk around wishing the ground would swallow her, all the while pretending that she wasn't affected every time she looked in the mirror.

Grace took a sip of the drink and avoided answering her mother.

"It's okay to feel sad and unsettled, Gracie. This is a big change, and I'm sorry that we have to make it. But it's for the best."

Grace clenched her jaw and tried to smile.

Her mother glanced at her, reaching out to brush a finger down her face. "Beautiful girl. I know it sucks. Parents are supposed to stay married forever. Walking away hurts me too."

"I know." Grace's voice was rusty from lack of use, and she cleared her throat. "This is a chance for you to start fresh. I get that. I'm just nervous, I guess."

She was always honest with her mother. There was no point in lying. The woman had an astute ability to read her like a book.

"Nerves are natural. You're moving miles away from the only home you've ever known. You're starting a new school, and that's a big, scary thing. But you're strong enough to do this."

They're going to think I'm ugly.

They'll either hassle me or treat me like I've got the plague.

It'll be a nightmare.

Grace didn't bother saying those things out loud. Her mother always hated it when she did.

Brushing her finger across the scars running from her right eye down to her chin, she traced the gnarled pattern, knowing it by heart.

How many times had her fingertips mapped the distortions on her face?

"You are beautiful. You are worthy. You are enough." Her mother repeated their mantra, and Grace nodded, trying to believe it.

She did. Logically, she did believe it. Someone's appearance had absolutely nothing to do with who they were as a person. But the way she felt didn't always match that logic. The way society was wired didn't always support that theory. And it left her mind and her emotions at war. She so wanted her mother's absolute truths to win every day, but life was never that fair.

"Walk into this new chapter with an attitude of gratitude. Seize opportunities to bless those around you. To serve. To love. To give." Her mother's voice wobbled as she repeated the words that seemed to keep her going. Grace always knew she was struggling when she started getting preachy like this. She had a series of quotes she'd spit out on repeat, and they seemed to soothe and motivate her.

And sometimes it worked on Grace too.

But not today.

How was she supposed to be grateful for this?

What opportunities could she possibly seize?

It was going to be all about survival.

"Gratitude," her mother murmured under her breath. "Serve. Love. Give." She swallowed, brushing a finger under her eye. "That's how we're going to survive this."

Reaching out, Grace rubbed her mother's shoulder. "You're doing great, Mom."

Her mother's smile was forced at first but then became genuine. "I love you so much, my precious girl. You are the best thing in my life."

"Ditto." Grace grinned, trying to absorb her mother's praise and affection.

It usually boosted her, but the effect seemed to lack its usual luster.

She'd faced her fair share of challenges. Ever since she was a little girl, she'd had to live with the stares, gasps, the odd look of horror, and the numerous gazes of sympathy. All were painful in their own special way.

She'd overcome each one, found a "sort of" place in her high school in Burbank, but this was different. She was about to start attending Lincoln Academy. A rich, elite school. The pictures on the website made it look as if beauty was a requirement to attend—shiny, styled hair, straight white teeth, pristine uniforms. She'd never worn a uniform in her life.

Her mother told her not to worry, to take one step at a time. But each step seemed like a giant leap. Panic pinched her stomach as she gripped the edge of the car seat and felt her throat swell. Her mother took the turnoff to Darien, slowing the car to match the speed limit.

Grace glanced at her, wondering why she was suddenly deciding to obey the road rules. There was a curious smile on her mother's face, and she let out a sigh, like she was starting to relax.

Grace's brow puckered.

"We're nearly there." Her mother grinned. "Oh, Grace, I've been waiting for this moment since—" She pressed her lips together, and Grace knew she was going to say, *"Since I found out your father doesn't want me anymore and I started hatching an escape plan."*

The first thing she'd done after that awful night was call her childhood bestie, Millie. She'd been living in Darien for a few years and worked for a wonderful man— Timothy Griffin. Thanks to a little sweet-talking, she'd managed to convince her boss to hire Grace's mother as the new housekeeper. Not only that, she'd lined up accommodation at the Griffin mansion, plus arranged for Grace to attend Lincoln Academy with Beau Griffin, the billionaire's only son.

Grace crossed her fingers, rubbing the two digits together and silently praying that Beau was nice. Maybe he was a little odd and quirky or had some kind of outcast qualities. That would make life easier. She'd love it if he were some nerdy genius or maybe walked with a limp or something.

That was probably an awful thing to think, but Grace was desperate for any small connection that would have her feel less like a freak.

You're not a freak!

Grace closed her eyes, reminding herself of this fact.

You are beautiful. You are worthy. You are enough.

Repeating the words over and over, she muttered them in her mind as they drove through the quaint town of

Darien with its tree-lined Main Street and historic buildings. It was stunning, picturesque, the kind of place Grace would usually love.

But she was struggling to muster a smile.

She felt like she was driving down the Main Street of Doom.

Holding her breath, she tried to quell her overactive nerves as her mother turned out of downtown and headed for Five Mile River Road. She'd Googled it. The street was one luxury home after another, and they were moving to the nicest of them all.

It was a far cry from the two-bedroom bungalow they'd shared in Burbank, California. Even though her father kept a steady stream of work as a Hollywood makeup artist, her mother never worked. Not after the accident. She immediately quit and started taking care of Grace, helping her through the recovery and then home-schooling her until the end of middle school. Finally, Grace took the plunge and started public high school. It was a nightmare. Or an opportunity to build resilience, as her mother liked to call it.

She certainly grew over that time, but sitting in this car, Grace felt pretty small again. Tiny and vulnerable.

"Here we are!" Her mother's voice was bright. Maybe too bright.

Grace glanced at the steering wheel, checking for white knuckles and a taut grip.

Yep. There it was.

She forced a smile, and her mother reached over and patted her leg. "We can do this, kiddo. Leo and Gracie, the ultimate team, right?"

"Right," Grace croaked, but she *did* manage to form a genuine smile. She loved it when her mother made her feel like the two of them could take on the world no matter what it threw their way.

The moment they reached the end of the long driveway and the house came into view, her smile fled.

"Oh my gosh," she whispered.

"Wow," Mom agreed.

Grace blinked, gaping at the stunning mansion. It had a castle quality to it, but in a modern way. Layers of roofline crossed over each other, cascading down the property and around to the right. The stonework—that obviously spared no expense—adorned different parts of the exterior, making Grace feel like she'd stepped out of time or country. The entrance looked Disney inspired with an oak door and stained glass window. The red rose in the glass caught her eye, and she stared at it while her mother parked in the turning bay.

"One step at time," Mom murmured. "All you have to do right now is exit the vehicle." Her mother's laugh held a nervous edge, the giggle a little high-pitched.

Grace swallowed, her fingers shaking as she pulled the handle and stepped out of the car. Side by side, they walked down the path, Grace keeping her eyes firmly locked on the glass rose.

Sharing a meaningful look, the duo held their breath while Grace's mother rang the doorbell and they waited.

It didn't take long before a gray-haired woman pulled the door open. She smiled at Leola before turning her attention to Grace. No one missed the small flinch. No matter how quickly she produced that polite smile, it was impossible not to notice. After years, Grace was still hyperaware of people's first impressions. She acted like she didn't see it, shaking the old housekeeper's hand and being ushered inside.

"Welcome. It's so nice to meet my replacement," the woman gushed. "Millie has told Mr. Griffin nothing but good things about you. We've all been very excited for your arrival. I'm Talia, as you already know. Come in, come in."

"It's fantastic to be here," Mom said, following the cheerful woman into the entranceway.

"How was your trip across the country?"

"Long but smooth." Mom tucked a lock of hair behind her ear.

"Did you check out any sights along the way?"

"Not really. I was pretty keen to arrive and get started."

"Well, I appreciate it. I can take a day to show you the ropes, and then I'll be out of your hair." Talia extended her arm to lead them out of the high studded entrance. "Please, come through to the den. Mr. Griffin would like to meet you."

Grace couldn't stop gaping as she trailed the women. The house was unbelievable. She'd never been in anything so lush and could only imagine how much this place cost. It was so grand it had a magical quality to it, and she could picture elegant women in ball gowns descending the stairs while men in tuxedos drank glasses of malt whiskey and smoked cigars.

Stepping down into the den, she scanned the pristine wooden interior, the expensive furniture, and—

"Please, take a seat." Talia smiled at her and pointed to a plush armchair.

Grace was almost afraid to sit on it, hoping her pants were clean enough as she perched on the very edge. Everything was so immaculate and in its perfect place. Grace felt like she was sitting inside a glossy *Luxury Home* magazine and not someone's actual house.

"I love the floors." Her mother pointed to the shiny black wood floors they'd clipped over.

"Everything's so... sparkly," Grace whispered.

Her mother giggled. "I've got my work cut out for me."

Grace bulged her eyes at her favorite person and was about to reply when footsteps approached.

She spun in time to see a tall, handsome man in a suit and tie. He had a very neat, short beard and walked with the poise of an aristocrat. "Ms. Bellamy. Welcome."

Her mother didn't correct him on her surname, and Grace wondered how long she planned on carrying her soon-to-be ex-husband's name. The divorce would be finalized by the end of the summer. It was still five and a half months away, but that felt quite quick to Grace.

She crossed her arms, pressing them into her stomach and trying to ward off that sick sensation she got every time she thought about it.

"And you must be Grace." The man gazed at her with a kind smile.

Wait. No flinching?

Had she missed it?

Or had he already seen pictures of her?

She quickly ditched the questions swirling through her brain and stood to shake the man's hand. "Hello, sir."

"Oh please. Call me Tim. 'Sir' makes me feel ancient." He chuckled and leaned his head out of the den. "Honey, Leola and her daughter have arrived."

"Coming." The voice filtered down from upstairs.

"Make sure Beau comes down too."

Grace tensed. This was it, the moment she'd been waiting for...

Trying not to shuffle her feet, she gripped the sleeve of her light sweater and fluctuated between dread and hope. The sounds of footsteps on the stairs were panic inducing, curiosity scorching her as she held her breath and waited.

And then there he was.

Appearing in the entranceway like a vision.

Grace's lips parted, her stomach twisting into a painful knot.

The fragile optimism she'd been clinging to disintegrated, and her heart stuttered while her insides seemed to fill with an unfamiliar heat that bloomed throughout her entire body.

He was gorgeous.

Beautiful.

Human perfection.

Chiseled features, unblemished skin, sapphire eyes, and perfectly styled hair. His mother appeared beside him, and the resemblance was uncanny. Wow, he really had no shot but to be gorgeous. The entire family looked like they belonged on the cover of *Vogue*.

Grace was so busy admiring them that she would have missed "the flinch" if it hadn't been so obvious.

Mrs. Griffin's nose wrinkled at the edge, her forehead

creasing with despairing sympathy before glancing away like she couldn't handle the ugliness before her.

Beau just stared. His frown lacked sympathy, and his expression was the picture of repulsion. Those eyes were cutting right through her, making her feel like a piece of dog turd that needed scraping up and disposing of immediately.

Grace had seen it before, but somehow his reaction was like a slap across the face.

Why it hurt more than usual, she wasn't sure.

Or she didn't want to acknowledge it.

She rejected that flash of attraction that shot through her when Beau walked into the room. It was probably a good thing he was so obviously rude. It would make it easier not to like him.

2

FRANKENSTEIN

Hideous.

It was a cruel thing to think, but it was the only word circling Beau's brain as he stared at the girl standing in his house.

Long dark hair with a subtle wave curled down past her shoulders. That wasn't so bad. Her figure was pretty decent too—a sweet curve to her breasts and a narrow waist. Her legs were lean, and he wondered what her skin was like beneath those fitted jeans.

But that face. How could he possibly get past that face?

Jagged scars ran across her cheek, starting at the edge of her mouth and running up to the bottom of her eye. It looked like Wolverine had taken a few successful swings.

Had this family never heard of plastic surgery before?

Beau was baffled. If he looked like that, he'd never leave his house, yet there she stood, gazing back at him like she was normal.

Her brown eyes studied him, and for some reason, he couldn't hold her gaze.

He looked to the floor and sniffed, sliding his hands into his pockets and dreading Monday morning.

"Grace and Leola, I'd like you to meet my wife, Celine." Dad pointed at Beau's mother, who gave the new pair a serene smile. It was her closed-mouth one that Beau knew all too well. It was her "I'm smiling because I have to be polite to you" smile.

He rolled his eyes behind his father's back.

"And this is my son, Beau." His father grinned and tipped his head—a silent command to use some manners.

Beau reluctantly stepped around his father and nodded. "Hi."

His eyes darted over the scars, and he couldn't help cringing when his father kept talking. "Beau will be driving you to school on Monday. He'll show you around Lincoln Academy and make sure you're well looked after."

Grace's forehead crinkled like she was worried, but she managed to iron out her expression pretty quickly and put on a smile. "Thank you."

Her voice was soft, sweet almost, but all Beau could see was the way Grace's mouth pulled out of shape when she smiled. Her skin kind of puckered at the edge.

Frankenstein.

That was what they'd call her.

Beau winced, running a hand through his hair and wondering how he was going to pull this off.

His friends would never be able to cope with him driving into the parking lot with Grace in the passenger seat. They'd annihilate her.

They'd annihilate *him*!

"Beau is a top student at Lincoln." His mother started her usual spiel about how amazing he was.

Beau clenched his jaw and glanced at his father. The man looked straight ahead, his cheeks puffing out like he'd heard it a million times before and was over it.

"He got the lead role in the school play. *A Midsummer Night's Dream.*"

"Oh wow." Leola's face lit up. "We love Shakespeare, don't we, Gracie?"

Grace nodded, her smile growing. *"Midsummer Night's Dream* is one of my favorites. Which part are you playing?"

Her eyes skimmed over him, and Beau had to clear his throat. "Oberon."

"That's a great role," she murmured, her cheeks splashing pink.

Great. Another doe-eyed girl to stare at him.

He was used to the attention. For some reason, his particular look seemed to appeal to a lot of people. Flirty smiles and pink blushes were the norm. It didn't matter who seemed to be looking at him—everyone had some kind of reaction.

But he couldn't stomach the idea of this beast falling for him too. That was the last thing he needed.

Gritting his teeth, he was seconds away from fleeing the room when his mother rested a hand on his arm and continued gushing. "He's perfect for the part." She beamed. "Tall, handsome, in command. We couldn't be prouder."

Beau's father looked to the floor like he was bored

with the conversation. And was that an eye roll? Beau's shoulders stiffened, his insides clenching when his father cut off his wife's spiel.

"Grace is also an A+ student." He smiled at Scar Face. "Your mother tells me you are quite a talented artist."

Grace blushed, this one a softer shade, as she looked to the floor.

Her mother grinned, genuine pride shining from her eyes as she brushed her daughter's hair behind her shoulder. "She is."

Beau's stomach hurt.

He frowned and pulled the phone from his pocket as an excuse to get away.

Flicking his thumb over the screen, he texted an SOS to Julius and was relieved to see an instant gray bubble appear.

Julius: Do you need me to call you?

Beau: No. Just give me an excuse to get out of here.

Julius: Ouch! I'm guessing our hopes of a hottie moving into your place are a no-go?

Beau: More like a beast. Get me outta here, man!

Julius: Okay, chill, dude. I've got you. Tell your olds that the greatest person you know needs help with an assignment or something.

Beau snickered and started tapping back. Normally, he'd take the time to reply with some derogatory comment at Julius's expense, but he was desperate to get away, so he kept it simple.

Beau: Let's shoot some hoops at the court.

Julius: See you in ten.

Beau slipped the phone back into his pocket just as his father said, "We're so happy to have you in our home. Talia will spend the day showing you the ropes. Grace, feel free to explore. I'm sure Beau can show you around town if you'd—"

"Sorry. I've got plans." Beau pointed over his shoulder. "I'm meeting up with Julius. He needs help with an assignment."

"Well, Grace can probably join you—"

Beau was already shaking his head while his mother stepped in to rescue him. "Oh, he's such a studious boy. Say hi from me, darling." Her smile was so bright and shiny, sparkling the way it always did when Beau mentioned his friendship with another one of the richest families in town. His mother knew how to stay in good with the right people.

Beau gave her a closed-mouth smile, then glanced at his father when he huffed and bulged his eyes at him. "You can't take Grace with you? I'm sure she'd love to meet your friends."

Old man, you are delusional!

Beau couldn't help a soft scoff, which scored him a glare from every adult in the room. He refused to look at Grace when he adapted his lie to fit. "We're gonna shoot hoops after we're done. I doubt she'll be into that."

He stepped out of the room before anyone could tell him he was wrong, rushing for the stairs.

His father huffed the way he always did, and he heard the soft murmur of an apology. Gripping the handrail, Beau took the stairs two at a time. He couldn't get out of this house fast enough.

There was only so much of his plastic-coated gushing mother and unimpressed father he could take in a day. Ten minutes of their bipolar company was enough to drive anyone insane.

3

JUST ONE THING

Grace's new room was twice the size of her old one. It smelled fresh, no doubt enhanced by the citrus candle burning on her dresser. Everything felt so new and expensive, yet it looked like it'd been carefully selected from an old province in France.

Her suitcase zipper sounded loud in the quiet space. She flipped the lid and gazed out the window, enchanted by the greenery and the river beyond. Talia had shown them to their rooms about ten minutes ago.

"Unpack your things, and then you can explore." Her mother winked at her, then followed the housekeeper back upstairs to no doubt get inundated with all the things she'd need to know to keep this stunning estate pristine.

If Mrs. Griffin was anything to judge by, the house had to stay pretty much perfect, pretty much all the time.

Grace sighed, her eyes tracking over the corner of the pool before landing back on her feeble suitcase. Her clothes seemed dull, the colors so plain, the fabrics so cheap.

With a frown, she took out her favorite T-shirt and held it up. She couldn't imagine Beau ever wearing this color. And plain cotton? Ugh, had something that common ever touched his skin?

His perfect, beautiful skin.

His friends were probably all the same. Made from expensive DNA with perfect features and pristine bodies.

They're not better than you, Grace!

With a huff, she snapped her eyes closed and tried to remind herself that wealth didn't equal value.

"You're enough," Grace murmured, folding her shirt back up and opening the second drawer down.

She unpacked her clothes, taking her time to order her things the way she liked them and then moving the candle to arrange her most precious items.

A photo of her mother sat front and center, next to a framed picture of her father. It was her favorite image of him, holding her when she was only four. She had ice cream smeared across her perfectly formed face. Her skin was smooth and scar-free, but the best thing about the picture was the adoring look in her father's eyes.

She couldn't remember the last time she'd seen it.

Ever since the accident he'd made himself so busy that he barely had time to look at her.

"I miss you," she whispered, brushing her fingers over his face. A tremble rippled through her body, her eyes starting to sting before she squared her shoulders and sniffed.

Nope. Don't go there.

Moping didn't heal anything.

Resentment didn't solve problems.

Go and do something productive. Distract yourself.

Pausing, she drew in a calming breath, closing her eyes and holding it. She then let it out, nice and slow, repeating the practice three times before sending up a quick prayer.

"Help me understand Beau so that I can handle being around him." It hurt to say it, but she knew the best way to cope with anyone was to try and find something—even the smallest sliver—that she could appreciate about them.

And for Beau, it couldn't be how insanely gorgeous he was.

Her body flushed with another wave of heat, and she frowned at her reflection in the mirror above her chest of drawers.

"Don't." She pointed at herself. "Do not be attracted by that guy. He's got 'rich bully' written all over him. Why would you even want to crush on someone like that?"

Her best line of defense would be to avoid him altogether.

"But that will be impossible." Closing her eyes, she let out a long sigh, her shoulders slumping. "Your only other option is to become his friend."

He's not going to let you do that! And again... why would you want to?

Okay, fine... but she had to find something likable or sympathetic about the guy or this year would be a nightmare. Every person had one good thing inside them, didn't they?

She just needed to find his.

Remember, hurt people hurt people.

Maybe if she could find the source of his pain, it would help her forgive his disgusted looks and aloof behavior.

Surely it wasn't just a snobbery thing. Surely he had a few layers she could peel back. There had to be something likable inside him... didn't there?

By the looks he was shooting his father earlier, she could immediately tell something was a little off between them. Maybe that could help explain why he was so grumpy and rude in the den.

Or maybe he just hates the look of your face.

Maybe he didn't want to invite you to shoot hoops because then he'd have to look at you!

The familiar taunts always came so easily.

Her shoulders slumped, and it took maximum effort to pull herself up tall and try another prayer. "Just... help me be around him without feeling any kind of attraction... or despair... or hatred. Please, just... give me a way to cope with all of this. Let him see past my scars... and maybe I can see past his perfect veneer."

Her insides quivered as she fought her doubts.

How would he ever be able to do that?

He was obviously disgusted by her. He didn't want to drive her to school. He wanted to escape her.

She pictured him playing basketball with his friends, no doubt complaining about the beast who had just moved into his beautiful home.

Monday was going to be awful.

"Or it's going to be amazing." She tried to bolster her spirits but could barely muster a smile.

With a huff, she spun on her heel, heading for the

door. Beau had squealed off in his car nearly twenty minutes ago. Exploring the house wouldn't be quite so intimidating knowing she couldn't accidentally bump into him.

Padding down the carpeted hallway, she walked up the stairs to the main entrance, then turned left, her socks nearly slipping on the polished dark floors. Righting herself, she gazed around, wondering which way to turn. The stairs leading up caught her eye, and she quietly ascended, her ears straining for noises around her.

There were female murmurs coming from the kitchen. Her mother. She relaxed, comforted by the sound. Stopping at the landing, she listened for the Griffins, but all was quiet. She took her time, pausing by the bay window and gazing out at the scenery. It was so picturesque, she felt like she'd stepped into the pages of a book or something. Her imagination ran wild, picturing a brave knight riding along the waterline on a white steed. She waved to him, pretending to be Rapunzel in her tower... or maybe Juliet... or Titania—the beautiful fairy queen.

"Who fell for an ass." Grace snickered and shook her head.

How fitting.

No. Not fitting.

She wasn't falling for an ass.

Clearing her throat, she walked away from the window, shaking the images of Beau from her mind. What kind of fool would she be if she let that spark of attraction turn into something more? A person's personality outweighed their looks. Grace wasn't stupid.

"But imagine if he was kind too." Her voice held a

dreamy edge, but she quickly blinked, snapping herself out of it.

With a huff, she picked up her pace and turned into the first room—a large drawing room overlooking the river. There was a fireplace to her right, and above it sat a painted portrait of the boy she was trying to forget. Drawn toward it, she stopped and stared, studying the oil-painted lines and admiring the skill it must have taken. As she followed the brushstrokes over Beau's smooth features, she came to rest on his bright blue eyes, noting for the first time how sad they were. Not even subconsciously sad… just empty maybe.

He was hurting.

"Help me see why. Help me to be kind," she whispered again, crossing her arms over her chest and walking out of the room. She found it the best way to cope with a bully. Try to see them, figure out their backstory… put some sort of meaning behind their behavior. It helped to stand against it somehow. And responding to their cruel venom with kindness often seemed to throw them. It didn't always deter them, but at least it tripped them up for a minute.

She'd been able to withstand many taunts with the help of her mother's advice.

"Pity them, Grace. The fact that they have to belittle you in order to feel better about themselves is just sad. How can they not show kindness? What's stopping their flow of compassion? All we can give them is our sympathy and our grace."

Her mother would always smile, loving that her daughter's name was also such an important virtue in her life.

She wondered if she could extend grace and sympathy to Beau. After staring at his painting, maybe she could. She'd have to guard against her attraction, though. Attraction so easily became a crush, and that was the last thing she needed. It shouldn't be too hard since Beau obviously didn't want to be around her. As much as she needed to understand him, she also wanted him to stay aloof.

A sound on the stairs caught her attention, and she quickly ducked into the next room. Easing the door shut behind her, she spun... and lost her breath.

"Oh, what is this beauty I see before me?" Grace's awestruck words were broken apart by a soft giggle.

Stepping farther into the room, she did a slow spin and drank in the walls of books.

"A library. They own a library." She'd never seen so many leather spines in her life.

Skipping over to the shelf on her left, she ran her finger across the expensive volumes. Surely most of them were first edition!

She couldn't believe it.

Her smile grew wide as the pads of her fingers skimmed classic titles—*Huckleberry Finn, 1984, The Great Gatsby*. Then she reached a new shelf dedicated to her favorite wordsmith of all time.

"Shakespeare." She breathed the name as if it were sacred, then carefully slipped a copy of his comedy plays out from the shelf. Brushing her hand over the hard leather cover, she hugged it against her chest and wandered to the cushioned seat in the bay window.

The spine creaked a little when she opened the book, as if she were the first to read it. Surely not.

She blinked and shook her head, then flicked through the pages, stopping on *A Midsummer Night's Dream*.

Now, fair Hippolyta, our nuptial hour
  Draws on apace. Four happy days bring in
  Another moon. But, O, methinks how slow
  This old moon wanes! She lingers my desires
  Like to a stepdame or a dowager
  Long withering out a young man's revenue.

Grace leaned her head back and grinned. Shakespeare always had a way of making her smile. His words were like written art—ethereal, slipping off the tongue with a magical quality.

Closing her eyes, she imagined how she would paint Theseus and Hippolyta, picturing them first in fifteenth-century clothing, then changing them to modern-day attire.

She loved to play with famous stories that way, twisting the imagery to capture something new.

"Grace."

She jumped at the sound of her name, jerking out of her seat.

"Uh, he-hello, Mr. Griffin." Standing tall, she tugged down the edge of her shirt and cradled the book in her arm. "I'm sorry. I hope you don't mind me—"

"Of course not." He grinned and looked around, his smile turning sad. "It's nice to see the library in use."

"So many books. You never read them?"

"I simply don't have time. I set up this space for Beau to study in, but..." His voice trailed off, and he ended with a shrug and a sigh.

Grace stepped around the glossy oak table in the middle of the room, gliding her fingers over the smooth surface before stopping by the large globe of the world.

"This is a beautiful space. I would happily study in here," she said. "Although, I'm sure I'd find the surrounding walls very distracting."

Mr. Griffin laughed. "The space is all yours, my dear. Use it as much as you like. Take any of the books. Read them all if you want to."

"Really?" Her heart took flight. "Thank you so much."

His warm gaze was heartfelt as he studied her. Grace didn't know what the man was thinking, but his expression beamed with kindness.

"When Millie told me about you and your mother, I... I can't even explain it, but I knew hiring her, bringing you two here, was the right thing to do. I know change can be a scary thing, but... I hope this transition isn't too hard for you."

Grace's throat swelled, and she looked down at the table. "I'll try to make the most of this opportunity."

"I'm sure you will."

She looked up when he didn't say anything else, and she thought she saw a flash of desperation.

"You'll be good for my boy." He said the words so soft and fast, she nearly missed them.

And then he was walking out of the room.

Grace watched him go, hugging the book to her chest with a small frown.

Grace couldn't get the look on Mr. Griffin's face out of her head.

What was wrong with Beau?

What could she possibly do that was good for him?

Why did Mr. Griffin look so helpless?

She mulled over it, tossing and turning in her bed. It was hard not to miss the sounds of Burbank, the smell of her old bedroom, the feel of her old bed. She curled on her side, listening to night birds calling from the trees and the soft rustle of water.

She wanted it to soothe her to sleep, but it took hours.

When she woke the next morning, she was blurry-eyed and hardly in the mood for company, but her mother had the day planned.

"Sunday is my only day off. We have to make the most of it."

She dragged Grace around the small town, oohing and aahing over the quaint shops. Grace kept the large sunglasses firmly on her face, but it still didn't stop the stares. She held her head high the way she was taught, but by lunchtime, she wanted to crawl into a hole and hide.

"Gracie! Oh my gosh, my beautiful girl!" Aunt Millie came rushing toward them, arms outstretched.

She wrapped Grace in a hug, kissing her cheeks before enveloping her best friend.

"I'm so glad you're here!" She laughed against Leola's hair and swayed side to side as they held each other. "This is going to be the best! Two of my favorite people, finally living so close!"

She touched Grace's cheek and then took her hand, pulling them into a small café and then peppering them with questions about their drive across the country. Grace let her mother do the talking, taking the chance to hide behind the menu.

It didn't take long for it to be snatched away from her, and then she was exposed again.

She ate in silence until the two women wouldn't let her anymore.

"Um... no, I'm good," she answered Aunt Millie's question. "They have an amazing library. Mr. Griffin said I could use it whenever I want."

"He's such a sweet man. I mean, he can be gruff and scary when he needs to be. You know, at work. He can slay a business meeting, but he's a marshmallow."

"And... what about his wife and son?" Leola's voice was measured, but Millie saw straight through it.

She rolled her eyes. "Sorry. You'll just have to deal with Mrs. Plastic and her arrogant kid. From what I gather, they're not around much anyway, so it shouldn't be too hard."

"He's supposed to be driving me to school every day," Grace murmured.

"Yikes." Millie made a face. "Well, at least it's only a ten-minute ride." She winked and grinned at her. "You'll be fine. Lincoln Academy is an amazing school with so much to offer. The arts program is phenomenal. This is a wonderful opportunity, and if anyone can make a success of this, it's you. You have a strong spirit, and your heart is made of pure gold, Grace McKenna Bellamy."

"That's right." Grace's mother nodded. "I have total faith in you, *papillon*."

Aunt Millie beamed at her, and Grace was soon basking in the warm glow of the two proud women.

She put on the smile they wanted and bobbed her head, choking out the words, "Yeah, it's gonna be great."

4

SHE KNOWS HOW THESE THINGS WORK

This is a nightmare.

Beau slid his hands into his pockets, clenching his jaw and waiting out one of his father's rants. At least they were relatively quick. His father didn't waste time when it came to words. He was brief, cutting, precise. A small litany of opinions and he could leave someone feeling ripped to shreds, slain and bleeding.

"You will do as I tell you, Beau Griffin! And you will not embarrass me."

Beau kept his eyes locked on the wall behind his father's shoulder.

He shouldn't have said anything.

But after hanging with his friends all weekend, he realized that driving Grace to school the next morning would slay him. He couldn't do it.

"Oh, Timothy, don't be too hard on him," Beau's mother jumped in, her voice gentle with persuasion. "You're asking a lot."

"I'm asking him to drive a kindhearted, sweet girl to

school!" His arms rose, then slapped back down against his thighs.

"Yes, but you need to think about how it will look." Mom made a face, her blue gaze flicking to Beau's before attempting to calm his father down. "She's a... well, she's an ugly little thing."

"That is not her fault!" his father roared. "And if you even spoke to her for two minutes, you'd realize how beautiful she is. Where it counts." Tapping his chest, he impaled Beau with a judgmental look that made his skin crawl.

He rolled his eyes in time with his mother.

"Stop it! Both of you!" Dad thundered, pointing between them. "You're as bad as each other. This is an opportunity for us to help these people."

"Look, if you want to ease your conscience with a little charity, that's fine, but you don't have to bring me into it." Beau met his father's incredulous gaze head-on.

The sparks flying between them were hot with fury, but neither backed down.

Stepping into his space, Beau's father told him for the last time, "You are driving Grace Bellamy to school. You will take care of her and treat her with respect."

Beau scoffed. "Or what?"

"Do you really want to do this?" His father's voice took on a cool, dangerous edge that made Beau stiffen. "Who pays for your life, Beau? Tell me that. Who pays for your car? Your games? Your clothes? Where do you think that money comes from, huh? It's not like you work for it!"

Beau ground his teeth together.

"I can take it all away." His father snapped his fingers. "Just like that."

"Timothy, you wouldn't!" Mom gasped. "Don't be so cruel."

"Celine! He needs to learn." Dad silenced her next protest with a pointed finger, looking back at Beau and making his warning abundantly clear. "I know thinking of others is an impossible feat for you, so I'll put it in terms you can understand. You will do as I tell you, or I will systematically take away everything in your life that matters. We'll start with your car. If you're not willing to drive Grace to school, then she can have it and you can walk!"

Beau's lips parted in horror. Over his dead body! His 2019 Aston Martin Vanquish was a prized possession. He'd gotten it for his sixteenth birthday—a lavish gift arranged by his mother—and no one but him had ever driven it. He wasn't about to let some beast jump behind the wheel.

"I mean it!" His father's look of warning was too adamant to ignore.

Beau couldn't even find the words to argue, so he pressed his lips together and gave a quick nod.

His mother tutted in disgust, shooting his father daggers before storming from the room.

Dad closed his eyes with a heavy sigh, dipping his chin and cupping the back of his head.

"Why do you look so defeated?" Beau snarled at him. "You just won!"

He stormed out of his father's office, slamming the door behind him. Hurrying to his room, his slammed that door for good measure, too, then slumped onto the end of his bed and let out a frustrated yell.

Why his father wanted to torture him this way, he didn't know. What had he ever done to deserve it?

Squeezing his eyes shut, he stamped his foot on the ground, the sour taste in his throat enough to choke on.

So freaking typical.

Dad always loved his stupid charity cases more than him.

After a night of tossing and turning, then giving up and flicking through TikTok videos for a few hours, Beau got up in a foul mood. His head pounded, and the black coffee he was guzzling like water wasn't easing the ache at the base of his skull.

"Can I get you anything else before you go?" Leola's voice was bright and perky, way too cheerful for the early hour of the day.

"No." Beau dumped his mug on the kitchen counter and unwrapped a piece of gum, leaving the trash next to his dirty cup.

"Okay. Well, Grace is just getting her bag. She'll be up in a second. Thanks so much for taking her to school. It's nice to know she has someone watching her back." Leola's eyes landed on him, the unspoken message abundantly clear—*please take care of my girl.*

Beau turned his back on her, mumbling an excuse about getting his own bag organized.

Five minutes later, he reluctantly walked down the

stairs and found Grace waiting for him in the entrance-way. Her new uniform was pristine. Paid for by his father.

Beau's upper lip curled before he could stop it. Grace wasn't facing him, so he took a moment to study the back of her. She had nice legs, and her butt wasn't bad either. The navy-and-burgundy tartan skirt she was wearing accentuated the curves of her body. Too bad the jacket hid the top half.

She turned as if sensing his perusal, and he internally sighed.

Too bad the jacket can't hide her face.

"Come on," he muttered. "Let's get this over with."

Grace blinked at him, then bobbed her head with an accepting smile. "See you later, Mom."

"Bye, baby." Her mother rushed into the entranceway to give her a hug. "I love you."

Grace hugged back like it wasn't a chore.

Pulling away from her daughter, Leola touched her face, smiling at her. The gleam in her eyes told the world Grace was her precious jewel. "You can do this. You're beautiful. You're worthy…" Her mother paused, raising her eyebrows.

After a beat, Grace softly murmured, "I'm enough."

"Yeah, you are." Her mother winked and laughed, kissing Grace's scars and giving her one last hug.

Beau watched the exchange in utter confusion.

He'd never heard words like that. He didn't even know the last time his father had looked at him with pride or his mother had hugged him. Sure, she talked him up like he was the most amazing son on the planet, but that was only ever in front of other people.

Clenching his teeth, he took the stairs to the left, heading down to the large garage beneath the house. They had to walk past Leola and Grace's downstairs wing, and he couldn't help a quick glance down the hallway. For some bizarre reason, he was curious to know what Grace's room looked like.

What is wrong with you? Stop thinking, you idiot!

Grace followed in his wake, gasping softly when they entered the large four-car space.

Beau couldn't help a little smirk. It was kind of impressive. Between his James Bond car, his mother's custom-painted Audi, and his father's Tesla, it was quite the display. His father's old Harley Davidson was also parked in the corner, but Beau couldn't remember the last time he'd seen his old man rumbling away on that machine. All he ever seemed to do was work and complain.

Beau yanked his door open, still simmering over their argument from the night before. He'd barely got a word in, which pissed him off. His father was usually a little slower with the threats, and Beau could drop a few caustic quips of his own before his mother jumped in to protect him. But last night, his old man had been fired up and on a roll. There'd been no stopping him.

Damn his stupid threats. He looked 100 percent serious about them, too, and Beau wasn't willing to risk his ride over it. He'd just drop Grace off outside the school gates or something.

He slipped behind the wheel and noticed her still standing there. "Are you coming, Beast?"

She flinched like he'd just slapped her. And then she started blinking.

Shit! Why the hell did you say that out loud? If she starts crying now, you're screwed. If she runs upstairs and tells on you, you lose your car. Just keep your mouth shut!

Clenching his jaw, Beau gripped the wheel and wondered if he should apologize, but he couldn't seem to make his lips move. He stared at the garage door while it slowly whirred up and was just waiting for the rush of retreating footsteps.

But they never came.

Much to his surprise, the passenger door clicked open and she slipped into the car. She didn't look at him. Didn't say a frickin' word. She just sat there, staring calmly ahead and waiting for him to drive her to school.

He revved the engine and accelerated away from the house, watching her from the corner of his eye. Her brown hair was clipped up on the side so it was out of her face, but as he drove them through the gate, she slipped the clips out of her hair and fluffed her locks so they hid her scars a little better.

He nearly said, "Good idea," but managed to stop himself.

Seriously, man. Check yourself!

Touching the screen, he got some music playing. He didn't really care what song came through the radio; he just wanted something to cut through the awkward silence. He wasn't in the mood to talk to Grace or get to know her. He didn't care that his father thought she was kindhearted and intelligent. He'd been going on about how he'd found her reading Shakespeare in the library.

Who freaking does that?

Yeah, he was acting in a Shakespeare play, but not because he loved the playwright. Lincoln Academy was all about celebrating the arts. Being in the school play helped his social standing, plus it got him out of class for extra rehearsals. It wasn't all bad that some of the hottest girls in school were acting right alongside him either.

His lips rose with a smug smile as he pictured Colette and Ella. They'd moved into his friendship circle when their bestie started dating one of his friends. Amell and Zari—the epitome of couple goals. He rolled his eyes, swallowing down that little bit of puke that always rose up his throat when he thought about how sappy they were together.

He couldn't complain too much, though. Zari brought her friends along for the ride, and hotties hanging at his table could only be a good thing. They were pretty decent girls. Ella was about as smart as a bag of bricks, but her body sure made up for it. Colette could be a first-class bitch, but again, with a body and face like hers, he could tolerate a little cattiness. If he got bored with her gossip, he'd just turn away and start talking to Julius or Etan.

Yeah, he was rich when it came to his circle of friends. They were his family.

He was rich when it came to a lot of things.

He glanced at the girl in the passenger seat and winced. He wasn't rich in *all* things.

When they reached the school gates, he slowed, nearly stopping to let Grace out, but then she turned to him with a nervous look and asked, "Where do I go? To get my schedule and stuff."

She looked so terrified that he eased his foot off the brake and, for some reason, continued rolling into school. "The main office. It's down that way." He pointed to the pathway and could tell that Grace had seen the sign, because she relaxed a little.

"Okay. Thanks. You can let me out here."

He braked and mumbled, "You don't want me to walk you in?" His eyes darted toward her.

She shook her head with a resigned sigh. "I know that's what your dad wanted, but I'm sure you'd rather crawl into a hole and die than be seen with me at your school. I'm guessing you're one of the popular kids, and I'm not stupid. I know how these things work." She cast her gaze to the dashboard and pulled in a breath, like she was summoning her courage. "I don't want to torture you. I really appreciate the ride here, and if you want, I can wait outside the gates after school so your friends don't see me get into your car."

He blinked, gaping at her for a moment.

Trying to absorb everything she just said.

Trying to figure out why he wasn't sagging with relief.

It was bizarre. She was giving him exactly what he wanted, yet it felt... awful.

He shook his head. "I'll wait for you in the parking lot."

Why did you just say that?

"Are you sure?" She glanced back at him, her eyes kind of daring him to tell the truth. He was surprised her pretty gaze had any effect on him, but... her eyes were a soft brown, almost nutmeg. And they seemed to hold a spark or... something. When they looked straight at him that way, he felt...

He didn't know what he felt.

He nodded. "I'm sure."

"Well, thanks." Her smile grew, and he glanced away from her puckered face. "Have a good day."

She slipped out of the car before he could say anything, and for a second, he just sat there watching her walk away.

Who was this chick?

A car honked behind him and he jumped, accelerating forward way too fast and then having to correct while still looking cool. He skidded around the lot and found a spot away from the trees so his car wouldn't get pooped on by the birds.

The music cut off along with the engine, and he glanced up in time to see Colette and Ella walking toward him. Their curious faces and concerned frowns told him all he needed to know.

He muttered an expletive under his breath, grabbing his bag and slipping out of the car.

"Who was that?" Colette asked.

"Huh?" He raised his eyebrows, trying to play the innocent.

"The girl." Her disgusted expression gave her usually flawless face an ugly quality. "The one who just got out of your car."

"Uh…" Beau scraped the toe of his shoe on the ground. "Nobody. Just my dad's new charity case."

"Ugh." Colette stuck out her tongue while Ella made a face of her own. "Was she put through a blender at birth or something? What is up with her face?"

"I don't know." Beau shrugged. "I haven't heard her story."

"So, why was she in your car?" Ella asked.

He closed his eyes, wishing he didn't have to explain.

Julius loped over and caught the tail end of the question. He laughed and slapped Beau on the shoulder. "Oh, they've seen the beast."

Colette giggled. "Good name for her."

Beau wished he'd never said it, but he'd been too busy venting when he was shooting hoops with Julius to think about it... and then he'd gone and said it again, *in front of her*, which was an idiot move.

His friend slung his arm around his shoulders. "Yeah, our boy Beau has to live with her."

"What?" The girls bulged their eyes.

"The new housekeeper comes with a kid!" Julius kept explaining, obviously delighting in being the one to tell everyone Beau's sad news.

"Why is she coming here?" Etan joined the group as they strolled to class. He'd obviously overheard everything as he walked across to them. Julius's voice always carried.

Beau cringed. "My father arranged it. Charity case. You know how it is."

Colette scoffed in disgust. "I don't see why our parents have to involve *us* in their stupid whims. Why are they always so compelled to do this stuff? It's like they feel guilty over making too much money or something. It's stupid. My brilliant mother"—Colette rolled her eyes—"wants me to go through my closet and bundle up a bunch of stuff to give to a clothing bin. As if I want to see some homeless person walking around in Chanel and Louis Vuitton. Puh-lease."

Beau was used to Colette's stinging remarks. She had the sympathy of a tiger shark, but for some reason, it was bothering him today.

"So, what's the deal with this chick anyway?" Etan asked, his smile growing as he wiggled his eyebrows in Beau's direction. "You gonna score a little something with the help?"

"Ew, no!" Colette answered for Beau. "If you'd seen this girl, you would *not* be saying that."

"What do you mean?" Etan looked around them. "Is she fat or something?"

Julius cracked up laughing and squeezed Beau's shoulder. "Dude, should we keep it a surprise?"

Beau shook him off and glared at his friend.

"What?" Julius was so genuinely startled by Beau's dark look that he stopped walking for a second.

Everyone picked up on the vibe, and Beau had to quickly cover for himself.

Shaking his head, he forced a smirk and muttered, "I don't think she's your type, Etan. Trust me on this one."

Everyone started howling with laughter, and then Ella opened her stupid mouth, sealing poor Grace's fate with a comment that made Beau's insides crawl.

"Unless you're into vultures and mole rats, I'd listen to Beau." Her singsong voice and giggle were the ugliest sounds Beau had ever heard.

He didn't even understand why he wasn't laughing along, but something about their teasing grated him. For the first time, he felt a surge of rebellion against his friends. It was such an unexpected sensation that he had to shake his head.

What the hell is wrong with you? These are your people, the only ones who get you. They make life bearable. Stop acting like an idiot and frickin' laugh already!

But he couldn't do it.

With his foul mood a few shades darker than when he woke up, he shoved his hands into his pockets and stalked to class, silently willing his friends to shut the hell up every step of the way.

5

A SEA OF SHARKS

Grace's insides shook as she found her way to the office.

You can do this, kiddo.

Her mother's voice rang inside her head, spurring her forward. Somehow she managed to make it from Beau's car down the concrete path. She kept her eyes on the ground, admiring the vibrant green grass and homing in on the sounds of birds twittering in the trees. She tried to block out the two gasps, the one gag of disgust, and the crescendo of laughter that seemed to hit her from every point of the school.

Eyes were on her with every step. She could feel each look from curiosity to sympathy and disgust. None of it was new, yet she felt stripped to her bones by the time she finally walked into the main reception area. As she approached the counter, the word "Beast" was circling her head like a taunting vulture.

You're a beast! A beast! A BEAST!

"Good morning, how can I…?" The woman's voice

trailed off, but she quickly found her smile and finished. "How can I help you today?"

For a moment, Grace wondered if she'd even be able to answer. Her throat was clogged up tight, and it took one deep breath and a full swallow before she stepped forward on shaking legs and softly murmured, "My name's Grace Bellamy."

Her voice was so tiny, the receptionist had to strain to hear her.

What is wrong with you? You've been called worse things than "Beast" before. Just put it out of your head and focus on what you can control!

Clearing her throat, she lifted her chin and tried to sound more confident than she felt. "My name's Grace Bellamy. It's my first day here."

"Of course. Welcome to Lincoln, Grace. It's wonderful to have you join us." She started looking up something on her computer. "You're staying with the Griffins, is that right?"

"Yes."

"Mr. Griffin phoned last week to set this all up for you."

Tap. Tap. Tap.

Her manicured nails clicked on the keyboard, and then the printer started to whirr.

"Now, let me just see if the principal is free. She wanted to meet you and walk you to class."

"Really?" Grace squeaked. "Why?"

The woman chuckled as she collected a few sheets of paper off the printer and handed them over. "Ms. Hatler likes to meet every student personally."

"Oh." Grace nodded, nerves scattering though her stomach like a blown grenade.

The receptionist gave her a kind smile. "It's nothing to worry about. She'll just say hi and walk you to your homeroom."

Grace took the paperwork, the sheets vibrating in her trembling fingers.

"That's your class schedule and the Code of Conduct, although I'm sure you've already read it." She winked, and Grace couldn't help a smile.

"I have actually."

The woman's grin grew. "I thought you may have. You look like the type of student we just love having at this school."

An office door to the right opened, and a middle-aged woman in a tailored pantsuit walked toward Grace with the confidence of a king.

"Grace Bellamy," she said, her voice deep and in charge.

"Hello, Ms. Hatler." Grace shook her hand. "Thank you for having me."

"We couldn't reject a student with grades and talent like yours. I can't wait for you to meet Mrs. Gold. She's our art teacher."

Grace's insides started to settle, hope rising in her chest.

Art—painting, sculpting, photography—things she could get lost in. Safe things that wouldn't judge her or stare at her. It was a place where she had full control.

"But first, homeroom."

The hope in Grace's chest wilted. She put on a brave

smile and nodded, following Ms. Hatler's clipped steps down the corridor.

The sharp sound of her sensible heels on the tiles echoed off the high ceilings and empty hallways. All the students were already in class, and Grace took a moment to look around. The school reeked of wealth and privilege. Even the dark green lockers were shiny, as if they underwent a weekly polish to rid them of finger marks and smears.

"You've been allocated a locker in the junior corridor. Here's the code." She handed over a printout with three digits on it. Grace quickly memorized the numbers as she hustled after the woman. Two turns later, Ms. Hatler stopped and pointed to the brass numbers at the top of a narrow locker door—23C.

Grace opened it and found a padlock inside. She wasn't sure what she'd need for class, so she took the padlock out and secured her locker without placing anything inside.

"And you'll be in Mr. Martin's homeroom. He's the Biology teacher—a very intelligent man with a passion for science." She grinned and Grace tried to reciprocate, but her smile didn't have time to form before the door was pulled open and she was met with a room full of beautiful faces—perfectly styled hair, pristine uniforms... unblemished skin.

She swallowed and forced her chin up, trying to walk with an air of self-assurance. Every step was a battle. It was like a piece of string was attached to the bottom of her chin and someone was yanking on the other end, trying to force her chin to the floor. But she fought the sensation and stared at the back of the classroom when Ms. Hatler introduced her to the class.

"As we do with all students at Lincoln, I expect you to make her feel welcome." She turned to smile at Grace. "You have a wonderful day."

With that, she left, and Grace slowly pivoted to scan a sea of sharks before looking to what she hoped would be a lifeboat.

Mr. Martin was blinking, nodding his head, his eyes darting to her scars before he put on a bright smile.

"Why don't you take that spot in the front right?" He pointed to the empty seat.

Grace obeyed, grateful when he didn't do that painful thing where he asked her to tell the class "a little about yourself."

She didn't get so lucky in AP English, where she had to tell everyone where she was from and what brought her to Connecticut. She fudged her way through a story about her mother needing a change of scenery. When she mentioned that her father was a makeup artist and worked on movie sets, someone called from the back, "So, why doesn't your dad help you out? Doesn't he work with prosthetics?"

The remarks scored him an instant detention from the teacher, whose face bloomed red. "Etan, get out of my class!" She pointed at the door, and he slowly collected his stuff, strutting into the hallway with a smirk.

Grace ignored the laughter and the sympathetic winces from the girls in the front row.

Insides on fire, she took the class novel from the

teacher's hand, grateful she'd already read it. At least the schoolwork would be easy.

That was about the only thing that would be. Between overly friendly teachers, gaping stares, flinches, snickers behind her back, and a very lonely, hungry lunchtime in the library, Grace was thoroughly done with her day. She just couldn't face the cafeteria, and the safety of nonjudgmental books in a quiet corner beat out her growling stomach.

As much as she tried, she lost her battle with her chin, and it spent most of the day dipped to the floor. It didn't rise again until she entered her final class of the day—art. She walked into the spacious, well-lit room with strains of ethereal music floating through the air and felt like she'd found home. Inhaling the smell of paint and clay, she couldn't help but smile.

And then she met Mrs. Gold.

The short woman had a round, merry face and inquisitive eyes, and her bright, colorful dress and green head tie gave away her African ancestry. Within two minutes of meeting the art teacher, Grace knew she was talking to a kindred spirit.

Leading her to an easel and blank canvas, Mrs. Gold handed Grace a pencil and said, "Tell me your story." She tapped the canvas, winked, and then walked away.

Taking in her first full breath, Grace closed her eyes and pictured her life—flashes of color, pain, joy, laughter, tears, triumphs, and failures. Absorbing it all, a picture began to form in her mind's eye, and her hand took over from there. Pencil strokes, fluid and swift, formed on the canvas, developing a face that was both beautiful and terrifying, strong and weak.

Her soul flew into the canvas, pulling her out of the real world and letting her float and disappear, shutting everything else out and giving her a small reprieve.

When the bell rang to end the day, Grace actually jumped as if she'd just reentered the universe, becoming aware of her surroundings and feeling the weight of reality again.

Mrs. Gold came around to stand behind Grace.

"Wow. I can already see where this is going, and I cannot wait." She beamed. Pointing at the canvas, she followed the curves on the right side of the face. They were distorted, the shape taking on an alien-type form. "What does this represent?"

Grace smiled. She could tell from the look on the teacher's face that she wasn't referring to Grace's scars. "My father's a makeup artist. He's a part of me and should be represented in my story."

"Very good." Mrs. Gold smiled and tipped her head. "Has he taught you much about movie makeup?"

"A little. I know basic makeup skills, plus he's shown me how to work with prosthetics and make someone look completely different. I'm not very good at it yet, but I'm learning." Grace's shoulder hitched, and she tensed for a question similar to the one she'd heard earlier today.

Why didn't he help you out?

Grace closed her eyes, wondering if her father was right all along. Sure, it'd take hours every day, but she could probably do a pretty good job of hiding her scars so well that people wouldn't even know she had them. She just hated the feel of makeup on her skin.

And her mother didn't want her to hide.

You're beautiful. You're worthy. You're enough.

"Grace? Did I say something wrong?" Mrs. Gold sounded concerned.

Grace opened her eyes, forcing a quick smile and shaking her head. "Not at all." She scrambled for a quick cover. "Actually, I was just thinking about how much I enjoyed watching him. He used to let me be on set sometimes, and I'd practice there. Sometimes he'd let me work on him, and as I got better, I was allowed to do touch-ups on the extras. It was always fun. A face is just another blank canvas, right?"

Mrs. Gold grinned and nodded, her eyes narrowing as her smile grew. "There's someone I'd like you to meet."

Grace gave her a nervous wince.

Mrs. Gold laughed. "His name's Mr. Lassater, and he's the head of drama. He's directing the school play, and I know he could really use your talent behind the scenes. Are you interested?"

Yes! That sounds amazing!

Grace swallowed.

But the school play? Was that the one Beau was in?

She bit her lip without meaning to, and Mrs. Gold gently nudged her. "Do you mind if I just make the decision on your behalf? I think this would be really good for you and our school, so I must insist you join me." She tipped her head. "Come on."

Grace looked at her watch. "I'm supposed to be meeting my ride in the parking lot."

"I'm sure they can wait a minute for you."

Grace didn't want to argue with her, so she followed the enigmatic teacher down the hall, studying her bright dress and the way the fabric moved as it swished around her legs. Nibbling the inside of her lip, Grace worried that Beau might be annoyed if she made him wait.

Maybe he'll just leave, and I'll have to walk home.

The idea fluttered through her brain, but the pang of panic quickly subsided.

Actually, walking home might be a nice reprieve.

Even if it would take her an hour, even if she did get lost, the idea of getting a little time on her own sounded divine after a day full of open-mouthed stares and background snickers.

6

IT'S LIKE A CAR WRECK

Beau was in a foul mood, and he didn't even know why. The day hadn't been awful.

Or maybe it had.

The thought of hearing one more insult about Grace's face and then trying to answer why she looked that way made his head ache. He didn't know what had happened to her! Birth defect?

Quite possibly. That was what happened to the kid from *Wonder*, right? Maybe she had the same thing he did.

Whatever it was, he didn't want to know, and he definitely didn't want to answer any more freaking questions about it!

The niggling irritation in his gut had been chewing his insides raw, and he couldn't wait to get to rehearsal and just switch off. He could step into Oberon's shoes for a while. Forget about school and hang out with some hot little fairies.

A smile toyed on his lips as he sauntered through the hallways, heading for the drama department. Girls smiled at him, a few said flirty greetings, and he lapped it up. Guys raised their chins or eyebrows. He acknowledged them all but kept his pace steady, not faltering as he headed for his target.

Drama.

Escape.

No Grace!

He never thought he'd be into drama. He'd planned on having nothing to do with those artistic douchebags in the arts department, but Mr. Lassater saw something in him, and two years ago, when the star of the show broke his leg, the drama teacher wouldn't stop pestering until Beau eventually gave in and agreed to show up for his stupid play. Apparently he had the perfect look for the part, and then he went and surprised everyone with an acting ability not even he knew he had.

He stole the spotlight, and in spite of initial teasing from Etan and Julius, he ended up being the heartthrob of the school. That shut his friends up real fast. He'd gone from being in the popular crowd to ruling it. He was a shoo-in for prom king. Everybody knew it.

Ever since then, he auditioned for everything and always won a main role.

This play, however, he hadn't auditioned for. In fact, Mr. Lassater gave him the role without even asking him. To Beau's drama teacher, it was a no-brainer. Beau was tall, handsome, and could pull off anything. Last year, he got to play the villain in *Little Shop of Horrors*—the sadistic dentist. He'd had so much fun with that part.

But Shakespeare was a beast of its own, and he didn't want to admit how much he was struggling with the lines.

When Colette got the role of Titania, he figured they could have a little fun together, but Shakespeare was not fun. It was damn confusing.

"Hey, Beau, wait up!"

Beau turned at the sound of his name and spotted Colette chasing after him. Reluctantly slowing his pace, he waited for her to catch up, and they fell into an easy step beside each other. She didn't say anything, which was helpful, because Beau's insides were already clenched.

What would she come out with next?

She always had to bitch about something.

He felt a little rude walking next to her in silence, but he really didn't want to start up a conversation. Instead, he glanced down at the script curled in his hand and read over the lines at the top of the page.

Having once this juice,
I'll watch Titania when she is asleep
And drop the liquor of it in her eyes.
The next thing then she, waking, looks upon
(Be it on lion, bear, or wolf, or bull,
On meddling monkey, or on busy ape)
She shall pursue it with the soul of love.

Beau was pretty sure he understood all of that. Basically, Oberon was tricking the fairy queen into falling in love with a beast. It was pretty funny actually. He wouldn't mind having a potion like that. Imagine stuck-up Colette falling for some science nerd or that outspoken guy on the debate team. Ugh. Shaun Hinkleman. What an irritating know-it-all.

"So, I'm thinking makeup better do a damn good job with us. I've been searching up ideas." Colette opened her phone and started thumbing through her Pinterest "Titania" folder. Beau gave it a cursory glance and nodded the way he knew he should.

"Isn't that gold pretty?" Her big eyes demanded attention, response, something more than a nod.

Beau cleared his throat and nodded again. "Yeah. Looks really cool."

"I'm gonna make sure that chick who's really good with the makeup does mine. What's her name again?"

Beau shrugged. He didn't know. He didn't care.

What the hell was wrong with him today?

Usually he'd be flirting up a storm with the hottie beside him, angling for some action after rehearsal. But after a day of listening to her biting comments about his new housemate, he just couldn't bring himself to do it.

Which was bizarre. Why did he care what Colette thought of Grace?

Pressing his lips together, he turned the corner and walked through the double doors at the back of the theater. He'd normally take the back entrance, but this one was closer, and Colette was talking again. Something about the evils of chemistry and how she was going to fail because the teacher hated her.

Shoving his hands into his pockets, Beau picked up the pace, and they were soon climbing the stairs on the side of the stage and joining the rest of the cast. They dotted the polished wood—clumps of humans softly talking among themselves.

Beau was about to join Cassidy and Marcus, dropping his bag onto the floor next to them, when he spotted Mrs. Gold floating in from backstage. And right on her heels was the last person he expected to see.

In fact, if they'd stuck to his original plan, she would have been waiting for him in the parking lot. He'd forgotten about rehearsals when he'd said that to her but figured she wasn't stupid. She would have heard the notices and worked it out, then either waited for him in the afternoon sunshine or walked home.

He frowned. He'd been looking forward to rehearsals. It was a chance to get away from the Grace-Face drama, and yet it freaking followed him here.

A few murmurs rippled from one group to the next as Grace was spotted. Her eyes grazed the room, and when she saw him, she actually flinched. Beau stared back at her for a moment, his forehead wrinkling before he glanced down at the stage floor.

"Mr. Lassater, I've found you another makeup artist," Mrs. Gold called across the theater. "You were saying you need one more, yes?"

Grace shrank back, but the art teacher wouldn't allow it. Laying her hand on Grace's lower back, she pushed the girl forward.

Mr. Lassater spun from his conversation with Puck, climbing the stairs at the side of the stage with a beaming smile.

"Welcome!" he boomed, his long legs dodging bags and students' feet as he walked over to Grace.

She gave him a shy smile, her face scrunching awkwardly on the side.

Mr. Lassater shot out his hand. "It's nice to meet you..."

"Grace." Her voice was soft, but Beau noticed her steady handshake.

"So, you enjoy makeup?" His face flickered with brief confusion, and then he grinned. "But you're not wearing any."

She swallowed, gripping her bag strap and nodding. "I don't like wearing it, but putting it on other people is fun."

Colette scoffed and muttered under her breath, "Doesn't like wearing it. If anyone needs it, it's her." She bulged her eyes at Beau, obviously wanting a swift nod or some follow-up comment.

But he looked away, focusing on his drama teacher instead.

"Well, that's fair enough. I'm looking forward to seeing what you can do. The makeup for this play should be a fun experience."

"Most definitely." Grace smiled as if she didn't know she was doing it, her face lighting up. "*Midsummer Night's Dream* is one of my favorite plays."

"A Shakespeare fan?" Mr. Lassater's eyebrow rose, and everyone could see how impressed he was.

Grace nodded. "His comedies are my favorite."

"My kind of student." Mr. Lassater patted her shoulder. "It's great to have you join us."

"You haven't even seen what she can do yet," Colette complained, and Beau wanted to shrink into the woodwork.

All heads spun toward them, and Beau had to pull his shoulders back, pretend like he agreed with Colette.

"Let me assure you, she will be perfect for the job." Mrs. Gold shot them a pointed look. "Her father is a makeup artist for Hollywood, and he's taught her everything she needs to know."

"Doesn't look like it," Colette muttered, raising her eyebrows at Beau.

He clenched his jaw, refusing to react, annoyed that she was pulling him into her bullshit. Yes, Grace was ugly, but did she have to down the girl in front of the teachers? She was making him look bad!

"Trust me. This girl is going to be magic." Mrs. Gold shot Mr. Lassater an eyebrow wiggle, and he shared a quick wink with her.

"Natural talent. I love it. Come with me, my dear. I'll introduce you to Essie. She's in charge of costumes and makeup."

"Why's he doing that?" Colette made a face, obviously trying to be funny. "He should be casting her in the play, right? I'm sure there's some ugly, gnarled tree she could play." She giggled, the cute sound in perfect contradiction to the harsh words coming out of her pretty mouth.

Zari laughed, but then her cheeks flamed red as if she didn't mean to make that sound. She looked to the floor, and Beau had to force out a laugh of his own. Colette's sharp look demanded one.

As Grace followed Mr. Lassater backstage, she smiled at something he said, and Beau couldn't help wincing at the weird shape her face made. But her eyes. Those brown eyes. They shone with a unique beauty that he'd never seen before.

"Why are you staring at her?" Colette snipped.

Beau flinched and glanced down at his friend, scrambling to come up with a plausible reason that wouldn't get him scoffed or laughed at.

After a shrug, he softly muttered, "It's like a car accident—you just gotta look, right?"

Ella giggled behind them. They both turned, only just noticing she'd arrived.

Colette winked at her bestie, and then they both grinned at him.

He forced a smile back, his eyes darting to the doorway Grace had just walked through. He couldn't help wondering what did happen to her. Did she used to be beautiful, or was she born with those scars?

And if she didn't have them, what would he think of her?

7

HIS BEAUTIFUL FACE WOULD BE RIGHT THERE

Essie was a sweet human being. That became clear the moment Grace stepped backstage and peered down at the senior who might be short in stature but made up for it in personality.

"Very cool to meet you." She pumped Grace's hand up and down. Two firm shakes before spinning away and obviously expecting Grace to follow.

Throwing a glance over her shoulder, Grace gave Mr. Lassater a questioning frown, but he just grinned and pointed after Essie. "Better move fast. She's a pocket rocket, that one."

Grace hopped to it, rushing between racks of costumes and popping out into a well-lit makeup area.

"This is where you'll be working." Essie's petite fingers danced as she flicked her hands around, indicating the way she'd set up the area. "I'm so excited that you're joining us."

Grace caught a glimpse of herself in the mirror. The scars running up her cheek seemed more prominent in this light. She glanced at Essie, waiting for some kind of reaction, but the girl was busy explaining her systems with a flair and obliviousness that made Grace's shoulders relax.

Either she didn't notice Grace's face—highly unlikely.

Or she didn't care—nicely refreshing.

Grace let herself smile as she drank in Essie's words and familiarized herself with the costume and makeup department.

"Can you sew?" Essie asked, her big, bright eyes giving her an expectant look.

"Um… not really. My mom can. She's pretty good, but I never really picked it up. I'm a fast learner, though."

Essie grinned, revealing two deep dimples. "I can tell." Her eyebrows wriggled while her big hoop earrings swayed like they were trying to match her beat no matter what she was doing. "I can't tell you how stoked I am to have someone who knows a thing or two about acting makeup. It's a completely different thing to the normal makeup you'd wear into town, you know what I mean? And we've got *Midsummer Night's Dream*! I am so excited!" she squealed, dancing on her toes before spinning and beckoning Grace with a flick of her hand. "Come on, let me show you my ideas."

When Grace didn't move fast enough, Essie shot back and grabbed her wrist, hauling the new girl to a cluttered desk in the back corner. Rifling through a stack of sketches, she pulled out a drawing of Titania. "I was thinking greens and blues, you know? With flecks of gold that will dance under the stage lights. I want to go for a really ethereal look but have those earthy foliage tones as well."

"That's going to look amazing." Grace took the sketch, her mind's eye embellishing it a little more. "We really want to make her eyes pop," she murmured, then began describing her idea for the eyeshadow and how she could work the eyeliner.

"Yes! That's what I was thinking." Essie jumped up on her tiptoes. "Colette is going to look so amazing, with her blonde hair and those big blue eyes. She's already so stunning, it's like enhancing beauty itself."

Grace swallowed, choosing not to say anything. She wasn't exactly sure which one Colette was, but if it was the mouthy, insulting girl standing next to Beau, then she silently prayed Essie would ask someone else to do her makeup.

"And then we have Oberon." Essie handed over another sketch.

Grace gazed at the costume, a beautiful match to Titania, but with a more kingly appearance. She really liked the simplistic lines that were made rich with a foliage pattern on the fabric.

"This is so cool." Grace couldn't help but feel a zing of excitement. Essie's designs were phenomenal.

"I've already found the fabric too." Essie spun, pulling out a big swatch. "Isn't it gorgeous?"

Grace fingered the silky material, tracing the outline of the leaves and nodding with a grin.

"And for makeup, I was thinking you could highlight his cheekbones—you know, put some shadowing around here." Essie used her pinkie finger to indicated the lines on the face.

Grace nodded, her stomach dropping when she pictured using Beau's face as a canvas. That was what she'd be doing if she agreed to stay and help out.

She'd be touching his skin, leaning in close to apply those finer details. His beautiful face would be right there. Those chiseled cheekbones, the perfect jawline... those cold eyes.

Her stomach jerked and trembled. Maybe she could get someone else to do his makeup too. Maybe she could just stick with the background extras.

And rob yourself of the chance to do Oberon makeup? Or even Titania makeup?

Don't you dare!

Battling an internal maelstrom, she stood her ground, begging herself not to let her fears win.

Focus on the makeup. The chance to shine in all the right ways.

Mr. Lassater, Mrs. Gold, Essie—they were all expecting her to use her skills, and she couldn't just deny them because the thought of getting up close and personal with Beau freaked her out. She'd just have to get over herself and hope that Beau wouldn't mind such an ugly beast touching him.

She swallowed, dipping her eyes to the ground and reaching for her mother's words.

I am beautiful. I am worthy. I'm enough.

"This is going to be so much fun!" Essie touched her arm. "Come on, let me show you what you've got to work with.

I'm hoping it'll be enough. I've spent quite a bit on material, and there's not much left in the budget for anything else. Mr. Lassater gave me free rein." Her smile took on a wicked, mischievous edge. "Something he may come to regret."

Her giggle was adorable, and Grace couldn't help joining her.

"But if I go too much over budget, big trouble."

Grace kept laughing, because the expression on Essie's face was so funny.

"I'm gonna love working with you," Essie said. "I can just tell."

"Me too." Grace's heart gave a little trill and stayed pretty upbeat for the rest of the afternoon.

Time flew as they went through each costume design and took notes, Grace adding ideas Essie hadn't thought of. By the time she walked out of the backstage area, she felt energized and ready to face a trip home with Beau. She could do this. She could be kind and focus on all the good things that had happened in her day.

Walking to the edge of the stage, she noticed no one was on it, so she peeked her head around the curtain... and found the entire theater was empty.

"Oh crap." Hurrying up the aisle, she raced outside, not wanting to keep Beau waiting.

But she didn't have to worry. As she ran down the concrete path to the parking lot, she spotted Beau's convertible pulling out of its spot. It was loaded up with his friends, all laughing and talking at the same time. One of them noticed her and drew their attention.

Grace stopped walking, her shoulders curling in as every eye in the car hit her like a laser beam.

She couldn't meet their gazes, looking down at the plush grass until her flesh was burning. Then came the squeal of tires.

"Looks like you're walking home, Beastie!"

She didn't know who shouted the words, but she stayed rooted to her spot until the roar of Beau's engine was far enough away.

"People who treat you badly are unhappy and have a lesser life. Every time they're mean to you, they're giving you the chance to show dignity and grace."

She let her mother's words spin around her head a few times, forcing herself to repeat them, trying to push the word "Beastie" out of her brain and focus on the things she could control.

Like walking home.

Didn't she think earlier that it would be a nice thing to do?

Looking up to the sky, she forced a smile. It was a beautiful day, the sun was shining, and the walk would do her good.

"Exercise always makes you feel better, right?" she murmured to herself, pulling out her phone and bringing up Maps.

She studied the blue line on the screen and nodded, then opened Spotify and put on some tunes. With a soft hum, she started the trek back to the mansion, forcing herself to notice every lovely thing she could—the vibrant green of the grass, the birds flittering between the trees, the melodies keeping her company, the feel of her voice as she softly sang along, the air hitting her skin, and the steady beat of her slow march back to her mother... her safety.

8

RENDERED SPEECHLESS BY THE BEAST

Beau's music was blasting as he pulled into his driveway. A heavy rock beat pulsed through him as he took the long, narrow road to his front door with a grin. Dropping off his buddies after a day that felt kind of shitty had ended up putting him in a better mood. Julius had spent most of the trip embellishing his story about Ms. Wiltshire's straining zipper and the way the buttons on her shirt were looking ready to pop off. They laughed along with him, and then Colette cranked the music and they sang like idiots, scaring a couple pedestrians and cracking up laughing at their shaking heads and angry shouts.

No one mentioned his beast of a houseguest, and it'd been a nice reprieve.

Until now.

He spotted Grace just ahead of him and slowed, his grin disappearing. The guilt he'd been dodging all afternoon slammed into him with the force of a wrecking ball.

With a sharp sniff, he pulled his shoulders back and tried to ignore it.

He shouldn't feel guilty. He'd just saved her from a car ride with his friends. That would have been hell for her. If anything, he did her a favor.

Braking near the garage, he chose to keep the car outside in case he needed a quick escape later. When he dropped Colette off, she gave him a flirty smile and said she was free for a study date later. That was code for "hot make-out session," which he wouldn't be totally opposed to taking her up on.

They had an understanding. No strings attached, just some scorching hot kisses and whatever that led to. It relieved a little tension and then they were back to being buddies again.

As he cut the engine and was drenched with the silence that followed, he nearly turned the key right then and there. Screw later. He needed that now.

But Grace's soft footsteps approached, the gravel crunching beneath her feet, and he turned to glance at her.

She gave him a pensive look as he got out of the car. An unnerving sensation worked through him as he clicked his door shut and faced her.

She was still staring, her gentle brown gaze studying him like she was trying to work out a cryptic crossword.

"How was the walk?" It felt like a stupid question, but anything to break the silence, right?

She didn't say anything for a long, painful beat. Instead, she extracted the phone from her pocket and turned off her music before squinting up at the sky and softly replying. "The sun is shining, and there's a nice breeze. I needed the exercise, so I'm gonna say good."

His face bunched as he hitched his bag onto his shoulder. "Look, I'm sorry for—"

"No, you're not." Her gentle voice made him pause. "And it's not okay, but I understand why you did it."

His lips parted while hers rose into a sad smile. That was all she said before brushing past him and walking into the house.

Never in his life had he gotten a reaction like that. His father would have given him a stony glare cold enough to freeze magma. Colette would have bawled him out, foul words spitting out of her, and Ella probably would have cried. Etan would have made some sneering, sarcastic joke, and Julius would have called him a first-class douchebag.

But Grace just gazed at him with a serious lack of disparity and then stated the truth—plain and simple.

Who was this chick?

She sounded sincere, genuine... like she really *did* understand. But it wasn't okay. She basically told him off without making him feel like the scum of the earth. Just a soft reprimand to put him in his place.

He'd never met someone with such dignity.

What the hell was he supposed to do with that?

Part of him wanted to be pissed off, but how could he be when she was so obviously wronged and didn't retaliate in any way?

He shook his head, more confused than ever as he trailed her into the house.

The wide front door clicked shut behind him, an eerie echo bouncing off the walls as he walked across the polished tiles and into the kitchen.

Leola was busy preparing dinner, asking Grace about her day with an enthusiastic smile that Beau didn't even recognize. She genuinely looked interested in Grace.

He stood quietly in the archway, watching the girl move with an elegance that seemed mismatched to the gnarly scars on her cheek.

Why would they be?

Scars didn't take away someone's elegance.

You're such a prick.

The thought made him jolt, and he actually flinched when his mother swanned down the stairs, drawing his attention.

"Beau, darling, how was school?"

Her loud greeting drew the attention of everyone nearby, and he winced when Leola and Grace both looked at him. Spinning around, he faced his mother, noticing her friend—the tall brunette with the high cheekbones and model pout. He couldn't remember her name but was polite enough to smile at her before answering his mother.

"Yeah, good."

"Rehearsal went well?" His mother turned to her friend before Beau could even answer the question. "Beau's the lead in the school play. He didn't even audition, but the director sought him out. He knows Beau's the most talented actor in the school."

She was always showing him off, and he tried not to mind it, but Beau couldn't help squirming under everyone's watchful gaze. He could feel the eyes behind his back and wondered what they were doing. Were they rolling? Were Leola and Grace sharing a quick look of disdain?

"Impressive." The taller woman gave him a thin smile before looking past his shoulder. Her eyes zeroed in on Grace like she was a duck during hunting season. Again with the thin smile, her red lips tipping at the edges. "You must be Grace. Celine has told me all about you."

Beau turned to see Grace doing a little squirming of her own. Beau could only imagine what his mother must have said.

Those critical eyes were taking in every one of Grace's scars. "How was your first day, dear?"

Did the woman actually care?

Beau glanced between them, trying to read the vibe in the room. Was it tense?

Something felt off.

He adjusted his tie, anything to ease the agitation skittering through him. He didn't remember injecting ants into his bloodstream, but there they were. Scurrying around, making him itch and glance at the front door.

Escape.

Leave now.

"I really enjoyed art class."

Grace's sweet voice distracted him, and he turned back to face her. The way Mrs. Gold had raved on, she must be pretty good. He wondered what kind of art she did, if she'd ever let him see one of her pieces.

Hold up. What? I don't want to see her artwork!

"Well, that's lovely." Celine's voice dripped with a coating of thick honey. "It was so nice of Beau to drive you to school. I hope you weren't too bored waiting for him to get out of rehearsal."

He stiffened, the ants forming a solid mass that clumped in his stomach.

Was he about to get seriously dumped on?

In front of his mother's rich friend?

She would not tolerate that.

He held his breath, scrambling for an excuse, when Grace spoke up, her voice steady and sure. "Not at all. If anything, Beau had to wait for me in the end. I got talking to the head of costumes and makeup. She wants me to help backstage."

"Oh, that's wonderful." Leola's voice was so bright and genuine. She drew Grace into a hug. "You'll be such an asset. You talented thing. I'm proud of you."

"Backstage," his mother cooed. "Sounds like the perfect place for you."

The words could have been construed in a few different ways, but Beau couldn't miss the slight bite. There was something in his mother's plastic smile that gave her seemingly benign comment a darker edge.

Leola raised her chin, brushing Grace's hair back as she spoke. "You're so right, Mrs. Griffin. Grace is a very talented artist, and the production crew is lucky to have her."

Beau couldn't help but be impressed by the way she took control and turned what could have been an awkward insult into a compliment that made Grace's pale cheeks blush a pretty red.

His mother gave a delicate sniff. "Exactly." And with

the dignity of a queen, she turned away from the conversation and ushered her friend to the front door.

Beau remained in the kitchen archway, his arms crossed over his body as he watched the woman leave. Turning back for a moment, he saw Grace give her mother another hug, her smile brightening at whatever Leola was saying. He couldn't hear the whispered words, but he knew they were good. They were no doubt genuine and reserved just for Grace.

Why hadn't she told on him?

It would have been the perfect payback, but instead she didn't say a damn thing.

Leola's arms encircled Grace yet again, the loving smile on her face filling Beau's mouth with a sharp tang of jealousy. His mother never touched him unless for show, and his father seemed allergic to affection.

It was a wonder Beau was ever born.

9

PINS AND NEEDLES

Grace didn't know how she was doing it, but by some miracle she was surviving... just.

It'd been two weeks since starting school, and in spite of the constant stares, titters behind her back, and nasty comments she caught in the hallways, she was managing to keep her head up... sort of.

Except that she wasn't.

If she was truly honest with herself, she felt like she was drowning. It was taking every ounce of willpower not to fake a sicky and hide away from the world. But it wasn't like staying at home felt any safer. Living with Beau was hard work. He usually ignored her, but sometimes she felt his gaze tracking her as she rushed through a room he was in. And he was always so impossibly hard not to look at.

It seemed monumentally unfair that he was so incredibly beautiful. Shouldn't those kinds of looks be reserved for people who were actually nice?

Driving to school with him in the morning was frosty and painful. For the first week, she'd tried to be kind and make conversation, but his answers were short, terse, and screamed "Stop talking to me, Beast!" so she quickly gave up.

Every day when they arrived at school, she couldn't get out of the car fast enough.

For the first time in a long time, she was fighting an internal battle that she was struggling to win. Life sucked. Plain and simple.

But she didn't want to be pulled into a puddle of self-pity!

If she did that, all the people determined to taunt and bully her won.

And so she spent every spare second she could in the art room, drawing strength from the things that filled her soul.

It had become a haven—the only place she could forget about the world around her. The story Mrs. Gold had asked her to paint was complete and had earned her high praise from the art teacher. She was then assigned a new medium—sculpture. This wasn't her forte, but she was having fun reinventing her painting in a new way. Trying to tell her story in 3D was a lot harder than she expected. Her insides were a torrent of emotions she didn't understand, and she fought to finish the piece with some semblance of calm. It was hard to perfect a sculpture that she wanted to punch off the stand and stomp with her foot.

Why couldn't she get it right?

Why did it make her feel so horrible?

Clay was still caked under her fingernails as she crouched in front of Colette, pinning the bottom of her Titania dress and willing her hands not to shake so much. The girl was gossiping with her friend about how fat Allie Barker had gotten over Christmas.

"She still hasn't lost the weight. I don't even think she's trying. Whale is obviously some trend she wants to set for the summer, but we all know that'll be a fail."

Her friend started giggling. "Allie's Whale Fail."

Collette joined in on the giggle-fest, and Grace had to resist the urge to shove the pins into the mean girl's ankle. They were so horrible about other people. How would they like it if someone stood there critiquing every little thing about them? Who were they to judge what was beautiful and what was ugly?

Fat wasn't ugly.

Allie Barker was probably a sweetheart, and these skinny sticks were nothing but nasty nettles who loved to sting and burn.

"Would you hurry up down there," Colette snapped. "I have a life outside school, you know." She flicked her foot out, only just missing Grace's chin.

Grace leaned back, holding her breath and riding out the storm within. She could do this. She could be polite, calm, dignified.

Her stomach rebelled, but she gritted her teeth and went back to work in silence, refusing to go any faster because it might ruin the delicate fabric of the dress.

Colette tutted. "Maybe Beastie here is a little... you know..." She pointed at her head and mouthed the word "slow" so obviously that it would have been impossible to miss.

Grace clenched her jaw a little harder.

"Honestly," Colette continued, "it's impossible to find good help these days. Mr. Lassater took one look at your face and decided to make you his next charity case. I admire the guy's spirit, I guess, but he could have at least taken pity on someone with a little talent."

Okay, that's it.

Grace had sat through the entire rehearsal, sacrificed her time to be there watching Beau and all his beautiful friends act like they were God's gift to man. She'd listened to their heartless comments about Allie (whoever she was), and now she was being insulted for working too carefully.

Her trembling fingers found a strength of their own, and before thought could stop her, Grace jammed a pin right into Colette's anklebone.

"Ow!" The girl screamed as if Grace had just started open heart surgery without anesthesia. "What the hell is wrong with you!" Her foot shot out, catching Grace on the shoulder and kicking her back.

Grace landed with a thump, pain firing from her shoulder to her butt. She blinked, sucking in a breath through her nose.

Her brain was struggling to put together the words she knew she should say.

I'm sorry.

But she was positive Colette deserved that little sting.

It wasn't your place to give it to her.

Guilt swamped her, and Grace closed her eyes with a sigh. "I'm sorry."

"Oh, you will be!" Colette stepped off the dais and towered over Grace, her pretty face made ugly by a frightening scowl. "Not only are you the ugliest thing I've ever seen, but you're worthless too! You can't even pin a freaking dress! Why are you here? What good are you to anybody?"

"Colette!" Mr. Lassater's voice was a boom that Grace had never heard before.

She flinched, while Colette actually jumped and Miss Giggles let out a terrified little yelp before they all turned toward the drama teacher.

His expression was cool, his dark eyes leaving no room for argument. "That's enough." Although the words were said softly, every person in the room seemed to be holding their breath. "You need to apologize."

Colette looked incredulous. "I don't think so. She totally dug that needle into me! And I bet it was on purpose! It hurt."

"I'm sorry." Grace repeated her apology, annoyed with herself. She shouldn't have behaved that way. She was better than that.

"You don't talk to people like that." Mr. Lassater's voice rumbled. "I don't care what she did."

Colette worked her jaw to the side, shaking her head.

Mr. Lassater crossed his arms, his eyebrows dipping. "You apologize, or I'm finding a new Titania."

The girl's blue eyes bulged in outrage. "You wouldn't!"

"Try me." Mr. Lassater crossed his arms, glaring down

at her like a formidable statue. He really was tall, and with that look on his face right now...

"Oh for—" Colette flicked her arms in the air, biting her lips against what was obviously a string of curses. After a few moments of fuming, she turned and pasted on a plastic smile. "I'm sorry for yelling at you."

Before Mr. Lassater could give her another instruction, she spun on her heel and raised her voice. "I'm getting out of this costume and going home. Rehearsal is over for the day!"

The drama teacher didn't argue with her. Instead, his face dropped to a sad frown as he watched her stomp away. The awkward stillness seemed to lift, the other students softly murmuring to one another and moving away as Mr. Lassater gazed down at Grace.

"Are you okay?" His voice was soft and warm, a complete contrast from only moments ago.

"Yes." Grace nodded, getting to her knees to collect the pins that had spilled across the floor.

Her ears felt hot. She could sense people's stares and wished they would all just go away. Keeping her head down, she kept busy, focusing on the clean-up and silently begging the ground to open up and swallow her.

It didn't.

It never did.

Footsteps finally started to move behind her, and she stole a glance over her shoulder. Mr. Lassater was walking away, shaking his head. The rest of the cast trailed behind him, except for Beau. He stood there, staring at Grace with a troubled frown she couldn't decipher. Was he mad at her for hurting his friend? Was Colette his girlfriend or something?

She didn't know.

She didn't *want* to know.

Turning back to her job, she felt the burn of tears in the back of her throat. She blinked a few times and quietly sniffed as she hurriedly packed her things away.

Essie tried to talk to her on the way out, but Grace made an excuse about her mother waiting and fled the building, running until she was well past the school gates.

The walk home was the calm she needed after her horrible day. She was glad Beau hadn't caught up to her and offered her a ride. He'd reluctantly asked a few times throughout the week, but she could tell he didn't want to. She had no idea why he was even asking and she always said no, much to his obvious relief. She liked the walk. It was good exercise, the air was fresh, and it gave her time to compose herself before seeing her mother.

Mom was so desperate for this to work. She didn't need Grace's sob stories at the end of each day. She needed the wins. The walk home allowed Grace to come up with all the good things from the day.

But this afternoon, she was struggling.

Picking clay from beneath her fingernails, she ambled along at a snail's pace, desperately trying to dredge up something positive. Unfortunately, the day hadn't had much. Colette had been the icing on a very sour cake.

The rumble of an engine made her step to the side of the road, and she didn't look up until the car was right beside her. She recognized it before her eyes even landed on the driver, and she instantly tensed.

"Hey." Beau slowed to her walking pace, and she wished he wouldn't.

Just go! She wanted to point down the road and beg him to leave her alone, but the words wouldn't come, so they ambled along in silence, her shoes scuffing the ground, his engine obviously confused by the slow speed.

Grace gave the Aston Martin a sideways glance. "I don't think your car likes going this slowly."

Beau grinned. "Well, get in and it won't have to."

Her head whipped to face him before she could stop it. She gave him a confused frown.

His eyes narrowed back at her and then he looked away, a muscle in his jaw moving when he clenched it. "Come on, let me give you a ride. It's what I'm supposed to be doing anyway."

She swallowed and looked straight ahead, confused by this entire conversation. Why was he doing this?

Did he want to torture her some more?

Tell her off for jabbing his girlfriend or something?

The thought made her insides flail, and she stepped away from the car, crossing her arms and mumbling, "I'm good. I want to walk."

Beau revved the engine just a little. It honestly sounded like the car would stall or something if he didn't get moving.

Glancing at her again, his lips rose into a half smile. "Please. I want to give you a ride."

No, you don't.

She shook her head, planting her feet so he could move along and leave her be.

But then he went and braked.

After an awkward beat that was all things painful, he finally sighed, tapping his thumb on the wheel. Grace fought the urge to turn and face him properly. Instead, her peripheral vision got the workout of its life.

"Look, don't take everything Colette says to heart, okay? She's a real drama queen."

Grace clenched her jaw. Was he seriously standing up for that witch right now?

Her stomach curdled.

"She wouldn't have meant everything she said. You don't need to be afraid of her."

"I'm not." She said the words too quickly and then had to wonder if maybe she was a little afraid. But why should she be?

Uh... because she kicked you and then belittled you in front of everybody.

"Are you sure I can't give you a ride?" Beau asked again.

Grace's throat was burning, and she was frustrated by the unexpected tears. With tingling nostrils and stinging eyeballs, she shook her head and managed to say, "Just go. Please. Go." Her voice cracked on the final words, and Grace was sure Beau noticed.

He hesitated for a moment more before taking off down the road. Grace watched him drive away, wishing he wasn't so handsome. Wishing he hadn't tried to be kind to her. She wasn't even sure why he did.

She didn't want to be confused by him. She didn't want to spend a second of her brainpower on him.

It was so much easier when he was aloof and grumpy.

That way her heart could stay in the right place and avoid that fluttery feeling.

She didn't want to like him at all.

She didn't want to feel anything!

Unfortunately, her heart wasn't made of stone. It was soft, squishy, and vulnerable. She desperately wanted to protect it, but betrayal seemed imminent somehow.

"Not if you fight it," she whispered, crossing her arms and trying to ward off the stupid moments of weakness that caught her off guard. When she let her mind wander, she'd sometimes find herself in a fantasy where Beau was sweet, where he smiled at her and sought her out. Where he held her hand and protected her from the bullies.

But as if!

They could never be together. He was too beautiful, too cold, too selfish.

Why would she even want that?

Anger bubbled up, the frustration from her day forcing the tears to the surface. She brushed them away with an irritated growl. The scars beneath her fingertips taunted her, and she didn't know how she was supposed to own them today.

She didn't want them!

She wanted to be normal, invisible—anything but the school's pet beast!

As soon as she walked through the door, she shot up to the library. She couldn't see her mother in this state, and doing her homework might give her a chance to compose herself. Pulling out the heavy wooden chair, she thumped into it and slapped her books onto the table—thud, thud, thud.

The book covers were whipped open and pushed aside to allow room for her laptop. Swiping the last of her tears away, she sniffed and tried to focus on her work.

But her brain wouldn't play fair.

The text on the page blurred, the screen seemed to fuzz, and no matter how much she blinked and berated herself, she couldn't stop reliving Colette's scathing words. She could feel the foot on her shoulder, the slaps of abuse thrown down at her.

"Why are you here?"

"What good are you to anybody?"

Grace couldn't even answer those questions. And everyone just stood there watching. It was so humiliating. No one fought for her, stood up for her. Not even Essie.

Sure, Mr. Lassater did, but he had to. He was the teacher! No student stepped forward to shut Colette up. Grace should be used to that. She didn't need anyone, but...

She sighed, sniffing another tear away.

"It'd be nice to feel cared for," she whispered.

"Grace?"

Flinching at her mother's voice, she sat up straight, wiping her face clean and pasting on a smile before her mother appeared in the doorway.

"Hey, sweetie." Her warmth emanated throughout the room as she bustled in with a tray of food. "I didn't even realize you were home until I saw Beau a few minutes ago. He didn't know where you were, but I knew." She grinned, setting the tray down and lightly running her hand over the back of Grace's head. "My little book bug would be in the library."

Grace forced a soft laugh. "Thought I'd get my home-work out of the way early."

"Good idea." Her mom sat down, leaning her arms against the table and watching her daughter with a careful eye.

Grace swallowed and reached for the grapes. "Yum."

Popping one into her mouth, she tried to avoid eye contact but was forced to look up when her mother gently placed her fingers beneath her chin and turned her head.

"Why didn't you come find me when you got home?"

There was no point lying. Her mother always knew. She saw her daughter like no one else did, and Grace would be a fool not to let her only ally in.

Her lips wobbled as she forced out the truth. "I had a rough day. I thought homework might distract me, give me some calm before I saw you."

"Aw, baby. What happened?"

Grace's shoulders slumped forward. She felt defeated and could feel her armor slipping as she asked, "Do you want everything or just the worst parts?"

"You know I always want every detail." Her mother's soft smile and kind gaze pulled the words out of Grace.

She ended up confessing more than she planned to, and by the time she was done, tears were running down her cheeks. Her mother now knew it all, from that first horrible day through the two heinous weeks and the catastrophic afternoon she'd just had.

"I didn't mean to hurt her," Grace blubbered. "I don't know what came over me."

"She was being mean, and you are human." Her mother

ran a comforting hand down her arm, obviously annoyed by Colette's behavior. But then—like she always did—she took the higher ground. "But, Gracie, you're a better human than her, and I don't want you to do that again, okay?"

"I won't." Grace's lips twitched. "Even though it was just a little satisfying."

Her mother tried and failed to suppress her giggle. "You're better than that, young lady."

"I know," Grace whispered. Picking up her pen, she beat it against the side of her book.

"I'm sorry it's been such a rough start. We both knew it wouldn't be easy, but I didn't realize it was quite so bad. You should have come to me sooner."

"I didn't want to burden you or make you feel bad about this big shift. I know how much you need it. I want it to work out for you."

Her mother's affectionate smile filled Grace's heart. She was loved with the same amount of strength she loved with. They were a team, and it was nice to not be doing it alone.

"It's going to be okay. You will get through this, because you're strong and beautiful and—"

"I'm not beautiful, Mom." She shook her head. "I have to accept that."

"Hey." Her mother frowned. "Yes, you are."

Grace wrinkled her nose as tears flooded her eyes. "I know I am on the inside. I know that counts for more, but the reality is that the outside matters too. To these people I have to be around all the time, it matters!" She shuddered and swiped a hand under her snotty nose. "But I don't want to have to plaster makeup on my face every day. It's exhausting."

"And you shouldn't have to. I don't want you hiding behind a mask. People need to love you just the way you are."

"But they don't!" Grace's voice pitched. "And maybe I don't need them to, but maybe I do! You know? I'm trying so hard to do everything you told me to. I'm trying to be grateful for what I have. I'm trying to tell myself that I'm enough, that I'm worthy, that I'm beautiful just the way I am, but it's not working! It's not making me feel better, because it all feels like a lie!" Her chest started heaving and she gave in to the tears, covering her face and weeping like a lost child.

Arms encircled her, holding her tight. Her mother's words came soft and calm. "It's not a lie. Don't buy into that. You are beautiful and worthy. You're enough."

"Why can't I feel that?" Grace whimpered.

"I know. Baby, I know. But the feelings follow, I promise."

"Why does it have to hurt so much? It makes me feel unlovable."

Her mother shifted, crouching in front of her and forcing Grace's hands away. She looked up at her daughter with a tender smile. "You're not unlovable. You're the most wonderful person I know."

Grace scoffed and shook her head.

"Don't fall into despair, my love. Keep practicing what I've taught you. Don't let yourself believe anything but those truths. Even on the days they don't feel real to you. You have to hold fast to the facts." Her mother's voice grew strong and adamant. "And the facts are that you are a beautiful young woman. You're talented, you're kind, and anyone would be lucky to be your friend."

Grace sniffed and nodded. It was pointless to keep arguing.

Gentle fingers cupped her cheek, and Grace drank in her mother's smile. "People will see you for the beauty you are. You just have to give them a chance. Look for the good in everyone, *papillon*."

10

LET'S GET WASTED

Beau stood in the library doorway, his ear pressed against the wood as he listened to Grace's tears. His chest hurt in a way it never had before. He didn't understand it. He'd never spared emotion for anyone, so why did he feel it for Grace? Where was this urge to give her a hug coming from?

It was like earlier when Colette was going off at her, being a right bitch about it. He stood there staring at the drama unfolding and fighting the urge to run across and tell Colette to shut the hell up. The wounded look on Grace's face was a punch to the gut. And then *she* apologized of her own free will while Colette had to be coerced.

He didn't understand Grace at all.

And he didn't understand why he even wanted to.

Her tears were a mournful melody that hurt him. She cried. The beast actually cried. She wasn't always strong and stoic like nothing could hurt her. She was human— soft, vulnerable.

Rubbing his chest with a confused frown, he backed away, retreating to his room. He wasn't this guy. He didn't care about people's feelings! And he didn't want to get all soft and mushy over some girl.

What kind of bullshit was that?

Pacing from one end of his bed to the other, he plowed his fingers through his hair until it stood on end. He caught a glimpse of himself in the mirror and quickly straightened it. Gazing at his appearance, he leaned his head from side to side to capture his chiseled features from multiple angles. He'd always liked the way he looked. Ever since he could remember, his mother had been telling him how handsome he was. People checked him out when he walked by. He'd been aware of that for years.

The right side of his mouth curved up in a confident smirk, but then he caught a glimpse of his cool blue eyes and the confidence drained right out of him. It was an open wound he couldn't fix. A knife blade slashing across his abdomen.

With a hard sniff, he glared at his reflection, then turned and snatched his phone off his nightstand.

Three texts later and he'd arranged an impromptu party at Etan's house. The guy's parents were never around, or if they were, they were so checked out that it didn't seem to matter what Beau and his friends got up to.

He left without telling anyone, texting his mother when he reached the grocery store.

. . .

Beau: Out for the evening. Don't need dinner. See you tomorrow.

She replied a few minutes later.

Mom: Have fun, darling.

He rolled his eyes.

Grabbing as much beer as he could carry in two hands, he walked to the counter and flashed his fake ID. The clerk obviously recognized him and nodded at his card, scanning the drinks and barely raising a smile when Beau muttered his thanks.

By the time he reached Etan's place, he'd already finished a can of beer and was feeling a little lighter. He swanned into the kitchen with a dopey grin and was greeted with cheers. His friends loved him, and that was all that mattered. He didn't care what anyone else thought. These people were his family, and they'd get him through anything.

"Let's get wasted!" He held up his empty beer can with a whoop, crushing it before throwing it over his shoulder and grabbing a fresh one.

Cheers rose into a chorus, music thumped in a heady beat, and things became more and more blurry as the night wore on.

Beau was too trashed to drive home, and although he argued as best he could, Julius wouldn't let him get behind the wheel. If Beau had been sober, he would have refused to give up his keys. No one drove his precious baby but him. Unfortunately, Julius was running on one can of beer and completely in control. He drove Beau home and then ran down the driveway to catch a ride with Zari and Amell, who'd been nice enough to wait for him.

With shaking fingers, Beau struggled to unlock the door. He had no idea what time it was but figured it was late. The house was like a crypt—quiet, with only the echo of his shoes on the shiny floors. Gripping the railing, he stumbled up the stairs, desperate for his soft bed and oblivion.

But then he noticed a light on in the library. It shone through the cracks of the doorway, and although he told himself he didn't care, he turned right at the top of the stairs and went to investigate.

The thought that it might be his father didn't even occur to him until he opened the door and blinked into the brightness.

Relief washed through him when he saw Grace curled up on the window seat, a book gripped in her hands. She was wearing pale blue pajamas with glittering silver sparkles, and for some reason, they suited her. Her rich brown hair was loose and free around her shoulders, and those brown eyes were drinking him in—round with surprise.

"Are you okay?" she whispered.

Her genuine concern made his chest tighten, and when she moved to check on him, he held up his hand, swaying on his feet with a stupid grin. "I'm fine."

She stopped, her eyes narrowing as understanding quickly dawned. "You're drunk."

He wished for a witty comeback, but all he seemed to be able to produce was that damn smile. It was his favored weapon of choice, but it didn't seem to be working right now.

Grace's expression was anything but impressed.

He frowned back.

Words like "Who are you to judge?" and "You're no better than me!" coursed through him, but he couldn't say any of it.

Especially the last part.

Because somehow, he knew it wasn't true.

Grace—Beast—was better than him, and at that moment, he didn't know why.

Stumbling out of the room, he groped his way around the stairs and across the hall to his bedroom. When he turned to shut his door, Grace was standing in the library entrance, backlit by the lamps. All he could see was her silhouette. He was grateful for it. He couldn't look into those brown eyes again.

Flicking the door shut, he turned his back and made a beeline for his bed. Crashing onto it like a felled tree, he lay on his stomach and begged for oblivion to take him.

Anything to eradicate this tension in his chest and block out visions of kind brown eyes and pale blue pajamas.

11

NO IS NOT AN OPTION

A soft hum vibrated in her throat. Grace couldn't help a little smile as she listened to her music and helped her mother clean the house. It was Saturday morning, and she offered to pitch in so that her mother could have the afternoon off. She hadn't outright said it, but Grace knew her mom was hankering for some time with Millie. Grace loved how much her mother lit up around her best friend, and if any woman deserved some happiness, it was Leola Bellamy.

Grace frowned, wondering how long her mother would keep her married name. Selfishly, she wanted her to have it forever. She was a Bellamy, and the idea of her mother not having the same last name hurt. But it wasn't just about her.

Thoughts of her father scattered through her, killing the song in her chest and blocking out the pop music that had been keeping her company while she dusted, then folded laundry.

She didn't want to remember the final fight or the bear hug her father had given her before they drove away.

They'd been texting back and forth a little. It made her miss him, but she was used to the distance. He was often away for long stretches at a time, working on different film sets around the country and the world.

But this time felt different.

"Grace, can you restock the upstairs bathrooms once you've finished folding the towels?" her mom called from the hallway.

"Sure, Mom. How many?"

Her mother appeared in the laundry room doorway and gave her clear instructions before bustling off to clean the downstairs bathrooms.

Clearing her throat, Grace paused her music and gathered up the towels, her tension rising as she ascended the stairs. Watching Beau sway drunkenly in the library doorway the night before had been a bit of a turn-off. In some ways that was a good thing. He kept on helping her out. Giving her reasons not to like him.

She didn't want to be judgmental, but it was a little hard to be impressed by a teenager drinking illegally and still thinking he was God's gift to man. That arrogant smirk of his. It was infuriating and completely unfair that he could still look so gorgeous when he was doing it.

Grace felt betrayed by her hormones. Why couldn't logic be the winner at the end of every day?

Reaching the top step, she turned left and jolted still, her breath catching as Beau came out of the bathroom wearing nothing but a towel wrapped around his waist. Droplets clung to the bottom of his hair, one of them breaking free and hitting his shoulder before sliding down his perfectly muscular chest and torso.

He was a model, a Viking god, a poster boy for perfection.

Grace struggled to look away. The heady rush of desire was a powerful force she couldn't counter. The blood in her veins pulsed a thick beat while her heart did some kind of tribal dance that Grace was pretty sure the whole world could hear.

And then Beau looked up, the grumpy scowl on his face morphing to a smirk. His blue eyes glinted, and Grace's eyebrows dipped together.

Why was he—

Oh my gosh, I'm blushing! He knows I'm checking him out!

Panic sliced through her and she swallowed, desperate to resurrect her dignity, which seemed to be lying in tatters on the floor.

Crossing his arms, Beau continued to smirk like an arrogant prince, and it was enough to goad her into straightening her shoulders and walking away from him.

He's a jerk. You don't like him! she reminded herself.

She went to move past, but of course he tacked to the right, blocking her way. She frowned up at him and moved to the other side. He shifted again, seeming to like this game of cat and mouse.

Grace drew in a calming breath and tried one more time, but Beau—who should technically be too hungover to do anything more than groan into a cup of coffee— seemed to be enjoying himself.

With an angry little huff, Grace hugged the towels like a protective shield, squeezed her eyes shut, and spit out the truth. "Yes, you're hot. You know it. I know it. Can we move on with our lives now, please?"

There was a brief, awkward pause, and then he snickered. Not a mean snicker but a playful one that made her eyes pop open. For once, his smirk was gone, and Grace was gazing up at a genuine smile.

It was the most beautiful thing she'd ever seen.

She paused, enjoying it for a moment before pulling herself together and slipping past him. Her hands trembled as she restocked the bathroom with fresh towels and tried to avoid looking in the mirror.

That was so bizarre. What was up with Beau Griffin? Was he still kind of drunk from the night before? Why would he even care that she thought he was hot?

Closing her eyes, she gripped the edge of the vanity and whispered her mother's instructions under her breath so she wouldn't forget them.

But the noise in the back of her brain was a big distraction.

He's so beautiful, and you're not.

You could never compete with his godlike beauty.

You shouldn't want to compete with it!

You're enough! You're enough!

She forced herself to look in the mirror and repeat the words. "You're enough."

Her voice trembled and she couldn't hold her own gaze, quickly spinning out of the bathroom and bumping straight into Mr. Griffin.

"Oh, I'm sorry."

"No problem." He smiled.

She returned his friendly gesture. "Good morning, sir."

"How are you today, Grace?"

"Good, thank you."

"It's such a beautiful, sunny day. Why aren't you out enjoying it?" He pointed to the window at the end of the hall. Light poured through it, drenching the walls and floor like it was reaching in and offering its hand. *Come play with me*, it seemed to say.

Grace smiled at the impish personification in her head and wondered how weird Mr. Griffin would think she was if he knew she gave voices to the inanimate objects around her.

Swallowing, she forced her gaze back to his. "I'm just helping Mom finish up so she can take the afternoon off."

His blue eyes softened with admiration. "You're a very kind girl. Your mother is lucky to have you."

She nodded, pleased with the compliment and wondering why she wished for a different one. Being called beautiful was no better than being called kind. If anything, kindness was better than beauty. She knew this! So why couldn't she feel it as well?

Beau stalked out of his room, adjusting his watch strap before throwing a dark glare at the back of his father's head.

Grace blinked, taken back by the intensity of emotion pouring out of Beau. It was almost as though he hated his father, but she couldn't think why. The man was nothing but nice—sweet, gentle...

The man spun as if sensing his son's death glare.

"Oh, you're finally up, I see. Where were you last night, son?" His voice was clipped and abrupt, as if he were talking to an employee who was out of line.

Grace tensed, wondering how much the man knew.

For reasons she couldn't fathom, she started coming up with excuses for Beau. A sentence or two that would save him for an impending lecture.

Why was she trying to stand up for him?

Beau paused at the top of the stairs. He gripped the railing and peered up at his father, his blue gaze cool and guarded. "Hanging out with my friends."

"You got in rather late."

Beau scoffed and muttered something under his breath. Grace couldn't quite hear it, but she felt the tension in Mr. Griffin immediately.

Swallowing, she wondered how she might quickly slip away, but she didn't want to draw attention to herself by moving, so instead she held still and hoped that not breathing might make her invisible.

"I do care," Mr. Griffin gritted out, "and I like to know that you're home safe. I see the Aston Martin's in one piece, so I guess I can be grateful for that."

Beau's gaze darkened by a couple shades. The silent standoff was beyond awkward, and Grace was contemplating escaping back into the bathroom when Mr. Griffin slapped the railing and stood tall.

"Well, what are you up to today, then?"

Beau sighed and shrugged. "Hanging out."

"Not with your friends." His father shook his head.

Grace could sense Beau bristling.

"I'm sure they're all too hungover to be of any decent company, and I'm sure you have better things to do with your time."

A muscle in Beau's jaw worked, and Grace darted her eyes to the floor. She could feel a rant brewing.

"You can't tell me how to live my life." She wouldn't be surprised if those words popped out of him at any moment.

"Why don't you work on your lines? The play is only weeks away—you could use the extra practice." Mr. Griffin's voice picked up a cheerful edge as he spun and grinned at Grace. "I'm sure this lovely lady can help you with that. She's a Shakespeare afficionado."

Her insides went cold as an arctic breeze shot through her. Laced with panic and dread, she shook her head and murmured, "Oh, no, really, I'm not."

She tried to argue, but Mr. Griffin wasn't listening. "Why don't you two go and grab a milkshake or something, and then you can work on your lines out in the sunshine somewhere." Pulling a wallet from his jacket pocket, he fished out some bills and handed them to Grace. "Go on."

"No." Beau shook his head in protest. "I'm not... working on my lines."

"You need the practice, son."

"I don't think he really wants to," Grace tried again, but Mr. Griffin just grinned at her, pressing the money into her hand.

"I insist." The playful edge dropped out of his voice, and Grace got a taste of Mr. No-Nonsense Griffin. His expression said one thing—*do as I say*—and Grace was powerless to refuse him.

Beau glared at his father as the man trotted down the stairs and called over his shoulder, "Have fun, you two!"

Biting her lip, Grace played with the bills in her hand and shuffled from one foot to the next. "You don't have to," she finally whispered.

"Looks like I do. Führer Griffin had his no-bullshit voice on, and if I want to have a life outside his freaking castle, then I have to toe the line sometimes." Beau spat out the words, shaking his head. "It's his weird-ass way of punishing me for coming home drunk. If I play by the rules today, I'll get my freedom back tomorrow. If I act like a rebel, he'll make my life hell for the next month. You know how it is." He huffed and ran a hand through his hair before realizing what he'd done and straightening it out again.

Grace didn't respond.

She was too hurt by the idea that spending time with her was a punishment.

But she didn't want to let that show.

As much as she wanted to find Mr. Griffin and refuse his request, she didn't think she could, especially when Beau gazed up at her. His blue eyes were guarded and sad, just like his painting in the drawing room.

"I'll go grab my script. Meet you at my car in ten." His voice was soft with defeat.

Grace nodded and waited until he was in his room before racing downstairs to talk to her mom.

"Oh, you are too kind. My sweet girl." Her mother touched her cheek with a grin once she'd finished explaining what she'd be doing.

"But Mr. Griffin's making me go. I mean, I probably wouldn't if he wasn't being so insistent. I told you I'd help you this morning."

"We're nearly done, and I'm happy to finish up. You go. Have fun."

Grace shot her mother an incredulous look, but the woman just laughed. "Oh, baby. It'll be fine. You're just running over lines and helping him out. I know he's not the nicest guy on the block, but this could be a stepping stone, you know? Never underestimate the power of kindness."

Grace tried to smile, but her lips felt too heavy to lift.

"It'll be fine. You're doing Mr. Griffin a favor, and he's such a lovely man. You really can't refuse him." Her mother skimmed her thumb across Grace's cheek. "But make sure Beau buys you a really *big* milkshake." She winked and then laughed as she gently pushed Grace toward her room. "Better hurry. You don't want to keep him waiting."

She didn't know how to feel about the rest of her day. Part of her was hoping her mother would say she couldn't go. But of course she didn't. Of course Grace had to be the bigger person, the kind one. The one to sacrifice her day for the sake of an arrogant, gorgeous, rich boy.

Dread—it filled her stomach, but it was mingled with an overwhelming curiosity, and that was what helped her up the stairs and out the front door.

Beau, on his own without the pressure from his parents or the judgmental eye of his friend group.

"I wonder what that will be like."

ICE CREAMS, MILKSHAKES, AND MONOLOGUES

Beau didn't understand what he was doing. He never usually gave in to his father's demands so easily. The normal drill was starting up a long-winded argument, which he'd inevitably lose, so he'd then huff out of the house and go off to do his own thing anyway. It didn't take long to learn to just agree without a fuss and then ignore the demand as soon as he left the house.

But he wasn't doing that this time.

In fact, he had every intention of taking Grace to buy a milkshake and then work on his lines.

So weird.

He stole a quick glance at the girl beside him. She was sitting in the passenger seat, tucking a lock of hair behind her ear. Her shades covered the brunt of the scars around her right eye, but the ones on her cheek were still prominent. They looked nasty, and it only just occurred to Beau how much they would have hurt when she got them.

How did she get them?

Everyone at school had been speculating, the stories

growing wilder and more hilarious with each iteration. But Beau's curiosity was piqued for the truth.

It shouldn't have been.

He shouldn't even care.

Just get this over with and get home.

Grace drummed out a beat on her knee, and it made him edgy. Cranking up the music, he tore through town, hoping not to be spotted. His favorite place to buy milkshakes was a '50s-vibe soda shop that had everything from the shiny red stools and booths to the Elvis Presley tunes. But he didn't want to take Grace there. It was Saturday and would be way too busy. If he walked in there with Grace beside him, the speculation and whispers flooding the place would be too much. Ugh. They'd follow him to school, and Monday would be torture.

Instead, he headed south along the coastline. There was a family park about a forty-minute drive away. Right next to the ocean, it had an ambling walkway, shady trees among the massive green space, and nobody he knew. He'd discovered the place with his mother a few years ago, and whenever she insisted they spend time together, he always asked for an ice cream at their park. It was a guarantee that they wouldn't bump into any of her socialite friends or any of his either. Sure, his mother struggled with the noisy families and panting dogs that ran past with runners, but she could just get over herself. Beau quietly loved playing pretend, like he and his mother were part of a happy, cohesive family. Being at that park made the daydream possible.

They reached the small town just before the turn-off to the park, and Beau spotted an ice cream parlor. He pulled up to the curb as "Ghost" by Justin Bieber was pumping through the speakers. Grace was singing along—the only words she'd uttered the entire trip. The sound was surprisingly pleasant, and Beau was hesitant to cut the engine; instead, he left it running and murmured, "Back in a second."

Shooting out of the car, he ran into the parlor and ordered two milkshakes—a chocolate and a vanilla. As he was going to pay, he realized he didn't know if Grace liked either of those flavors, so he also ordered a small tub of the strawberry ripple ice cream and threw in his favorite—buttered pecan—for good measure. Hopefully he'd covered enough bases with that.

"Have a great day." The server with blonde hair and cute dimples gave him a flirty smile, and for some reason… he didn't return it.

Again—weird.

All he could think about was getting the ice cream back to Grace, and which song she'd be softly singing along to.

"Fingers Crossed" by Lauren Spencer-Smith.

Her voice was a little louder than before. He could hear it through the window, which was down enough to let the breeze in. He kind of didn't want her seeing him, because he knew she'd stop singing. That sweet sound would be replaced with polite manners and forced smiles.

Gritting his teeth, he slipped into the car. "Here we go."

"Wow." Grace grinned. "Did you get enough?"

Her teasing tone was sweet, and he couldn't stop his smile. Handing her the milkshakes and placing the ice cream in her lap, he then buckled up and checked the road.

"I didn't know what you liked. I wanted to cover the bases."

"You could have just asked," she murmured quietly.

His shoulders pinged tight as he eased into the traffic and prepared for a snippy argument over why he didn't.

But then she smiled at him.

"Let's see what we've got here." She sucked each of the straws. "Vanilla. Yum. Chocolate. So good." She tipped her head back, and Beau couldn't help running his gaze down the line of her throat. She had a pretty neck. Peeking in the tubs, she gave them a sniff and nodded. "Buttered pecan is my favorite, so yep… you've covered the bases."

"Buttered pecan is my favorite too."

"So good, right? Although, I did have a Ben & Jerry's Chubby Hubby recently, and that was a very close rival."

"No way." Beau shook his head.

"I'm serious." She turned to him. "Have you tasted it."

"Nope." He accentuated the *p*. "And it can't possibly be better than buttered pecan."

"Don't judge it 'til you've tried it, dude." She laughed. "Peanut fudge-covered pretzels with fudge and peanut butter swirls in vanilla ice cream. You *have* to taste it."

Her enthusiasm was cute, and he conceded with a grin. "Okay, maybe I will."

"You won't regret it." She nodded like she'd won some argument, and Beau suddenly noticed how the nervous tension they'd been stewing in since they'd left the house had been sliced in half by ice cream.

He couldn't help a quiet snicker.

"What?" Grace took another sip of milkshake, and Beau noticed the soft pink color of her lips. He bet they felt soft too.

He blinked and swallowed, keeping his eyes firmly on the road ahead. "Uh, just... I thought this whole thing might be awkward, but ice cream is saving the day."

She giggled. "I'm sorry if I've been quiet. I'm not sure what to say or how to start a conversation with you. The music's been nice, though. You have good taste."

"It's just the radio."

"Well." She shrugged. "The radio has good taste."

He grinned. "And so do you."

She smiled back, and he wished she wasn't wearing her shades so he could see those brown eyes glow.

His eyebrows puckered with confusion as an odd sensation tickled his chest. He tried not to think about it and let Grace talk music for a few minutes. He found himself entering into her discussion without meaning to, and by the time they reached the park, it had been decided by both of them who the top ten artists of the year were. They'd varied in a few places but generally liked the same stuff.

It shouldn't have been a shock to Beau—Grace was a sixteen-year-old, just like him—but he somehow still found it surprising. She wasn't like any girl he'd ever met, and he was struggling to compute how normal her tastes were.

He parked in the back corner of the lot, liking the privacy of it. Walking around to her side of the car, he helped her with the drinks and ice cream.

"Oh, can you grab my script? It's on the back seat."

"Sure." She leaned in, and he couldn't help admiring the shape of her legs and butt.

Damn, the body's not bad.

Taking his time to study her, he enjoyed following the shape of those curves until she stood tall and looked right at him. Thankfully, his shades were hiding his perusal, but they wouldn't mask the heat in his cheeks.

He turned and started walking before she could notice.

He heard her feet scuffling to catch up, and he slowed his pace as they entered the shaded greenery.

"This is pretty," she murmured as they wove through the first patch of trees. "Kind of like Oberon's kingdom, yeah?"

He grinned before sucking on one of the milkshakes. Her lips had been on this straw, and he shouldn't care.

I don't! I shouldn't even be sharing the milkshake anyway. Germs are gross.

But he sucked on the straw for a little longer before holding both cups out.

"Which one do you want?" he blurted.

"Huh?"

"Chocolate or vanilla?"

"Oh. I don't mind. You choose." Her smile turned slightly awkward, and she winced. "Sorry, it's only just occurred to me that I took a sip from both of them. I should have asked you. I don't know if you're... you know, a sharer... or a germaphobe. Some people have a real problem with that kind of thing, and I should have asked first."

"That's okay." He quickly shook his head, not wanting to make her feel bad. "I'll take the chocolate, if that's cool."

"Awesome." She took the vanilla from his hand and happily sucked away while they ambled through the park.

Kids were climbing all over the playground nearby, their shouts and happy squeals racing across the space.

"There's a quiet patch around the corner." Beau pointed ahead, and Grace nodded, shifting a little closer to him as they walked past a few playful dogs and a puppy that was obviously discovering the wonders of barking.

He steered her down the path and around the corner to a patch of green that looked out over the ocean.

The sun lit the quiet spot, like it was showing them exactly where to sit, and Grace beamed. "So pretty."

Picking up her pace, she plopped down onto the grass, crossing her legs and lifting her face up to the sun. She was the picture of contentment, and Beau wondered what that must feel like.

His breath evaporated, his heart hammering as he watched her lips curl into a smile. Her body was so relaxed, coated in sunlight. She licked her lips and let out a soft sigh, and it caught him off guard.

This sensation in his chest was... something else. He couldn't even identify it, but it was unnerving.

Snap the hell out of it, man! Just sit down already.

Perching down in the grass, he rested his elbows on his knees and studied her until she sat up straight and looked at him.

Damn those shades. He wanted to see her brown eyes.

Would it be too forward if he reached out and slipped them off her?

Uh... yes! Don't go sending the wrong signals, dude. Keep your hands to yourself!

He curled his fingers and gave her a closed-mouth smile, still reeling over the fact that he even thought of taking off her shades. That was like an intimate gesture. The kind of shit you saw in romance movies.

That wasn't him.

"All right." Grace took another pull off her milkshake, then opened the script, oblivious to his torment.

Beau gritted his teeth and stared out at the ocean while she flicked through the pages.

He was finding this whole experience a little too trippy, but he didn't want to leave either.

There was just something about her.

"Which scene do you want to work on?"

A wave of embarrassment coursed through him as he realized he'd have to act in front of Grace. It was so different to being up on a stage, separated from the audience. This was close, almost intimate (there was that word again!), and she'd spot all his flaws.

So, he chose a scene he already knew pretty well. "I probably need to go over that last part where he talks about the couples ending up with the right people."

"Now until the break of day." Grace nodded, flipping to the end of the book. "I actually know a song that includes half this speech." She sang it, and he nodded along, once again liking the sound of her voice. It was soft and sweet, and she seemed oblivious to the fact that she was singing in public.

The tune floated through his head as he worked on the lines.

"Now, until the break of day. Through this house each fairy stray. To the best bride-bed will we. Which by us shall blessed be... Uh..." He scratched his head. "And the issue there create. Ever shall be fortunate."

Grace nodded her approval, her teeth scraping her bottom lip and momentarily distracting him.

"So shall all," she whispered, softly prompting him.

He swallowed, forcing his gaze out to the ocean and quickly rattling off the next part. "So shall all the couples three. Ever true in loving be. And the blots of Nature's hand. Shall not in their issue stand. Never mole, hare lip, nor scar... Nor mark prodigious, such as are..." Clearing his throat, he continued on to the end of the monologue, needing no more prompts as he finished with relish, "Trip away; make no stay... Meet me all by break of day."

"Yay." Grace clapped. "That was so good!"

Her grin made him feel triumphant, and he shuffled on the grass, not knowing what to do with that.

"Are there any scenes you need to practice more? You seemed to know this one really well."

His lips twitched. She didn't miss a beat. Giving in with a small sigh, he admitted, "Some of the scenes with Oberon and Puck in Act Three. I'm tripping up on those ones."

"Okay." Grace flicked through the script and guided him through some practice. He was super self-conscious at first, but she threw herself into the role of Puck, and he couldn't help but be spurred on by her enthusiasm. He was soon acting out Oberon as if he were in fact a king.

Grace giggled. "I love that scene. Puck is so funny."

"Yeah, he is." Beau studied her, wondering why he felt

so light. With the monster headache he woke up with, he'd thought this day would be a write-off, but he was actually having fun.

What? No, I'm not. I'm only doing this because Dad is making me.

The argument fell flat in his brain. What was going on right now?

Why was Grace having any kind of effect on him? What was it about her?

It made him want to work her out, try to understand this subtle magic she wielded. But it also made him want to push her away, because he couldn't be under the spell of this beast.

"Will you be doing my makeup?" The question came out of nowhere, his tone sharp and snappy. For reasons he couldn't understand, he was frowning at her.

Wait, yes, he could. It was time for him to take control of this thing, try to rebalance the weird stuff that was going on in his chest. Couldn't go letting his guard down around this chick, right?

Grace sat back, obviously thrown by the sudden mood swing. Weren't they smiling and laughing together only moments ago while she captured Puck perfectly?

He cleared his throat and felt bad, which was another sensation he didn't like. He wasn't one to feel guilt. That was a wasted emotion. He couldn't be responsible for other people's feelings. That was their problem.

But... she didn't deserve this sudden whiplash. It wasn't her fault he was feeling uncomfortable. Except that it was... even though she wasn't doing anything more than being nice to him.

You are such a dick sometimes, he berated himself... which was a slap to the face, because he didn't do that kind of thing either. He got enough of that shit from his father.

This girl was tripping him out!

"Um..." He licked his lips and softened his voice. "Yeah, I was just curious if you knew which characters you were working on."

Grace was gazing out at the diamond sparkles of light on the water while she softly answered, "I'm not sure. I'll wait and see what Essie wants me to do. I'm just following her lead."

"I've heard you're pretty good."

She glanced at him, her forehead wrinkling like he was confusing her. One minute he was laughing, then snapping, and now he was trying to draw out this conversation instead of using his head and suggesting they go back to the house. Of course she was confused!

The poor girl probably didn't know where she stood... or what was going to come out of his mouth next.

With a sigh, he scratched his head and kept talking. "Your dad's a makeup guy for Hollywood or something, right?" He was trying to keep his tone light and friendly as he dug around in her life.

"Um, yep. He's working on a sci-fi movie at the moment. Lots of prosthetics and stuff. He really loves it. I think he even helped design the look of one of the aliens, so that's pretty cool."

"It must take him hours."

"Oh yeah, those guys work so hard."

"Do you want to get into it one day?"

She shrugged. "Maybe? I don't know. I haven't figured out what I want to do yet. I mean, I know I want to do something artistic, but I'm just not sure exactly what. Dad said I can come and train with him if I want, but..." She bit her bottom lip.

"But what?"

Her nose wrinkled. "It's a very unsettled life. When I was a kid, we used to go with him, and we were constantly traveling around. Mom homeschooled me so we could be totally flexible."

"Was that because of your face?" As soon as the words were out of his mouth, he regretted them.

She just said it was so they could be flexible, you moron!

Grace paused, biting her lips together and not saying anything.

Beau wanted to fill that space but couldn't speak either. His throat had a boulder-sized lump wedged in there, and speaking seemed impossible. It was probably his foot, which he'd just shoved into his mouth like an idiot.

"Um...," Grace eventually murmured, the word trembling out of her mouth. "No, uh... Mom homeschooled me so that we could go with Dad and be together as a family." She nodded, her swallow thick as she was so obviously trying to be stoic and dignified.

Apologize! Now!

Beau wasn't great with apologies. They didn't come naturally, and his mouth was already drying up as he opened it to speak.

But he didn't get a chance to say anything, because a

dog came bounding around the corner and right up to them.

Grace flinched and recoiled, her skin going deathly white as she scrambled back. She looked like she was facing down a ferocious lion, and when the dog barked and jumped toward her, no doubt trying to lick her face, she let out a terrified scream.

13

TRAUMA

Grace couldn't control herself. Her heart was racing so hard and fast it was going to explode. The dog came at her, and she was shot back nine years to the moment that changed her life. The terror returned with a surprising starkness. Despite the therapy her mother had made her go to, she couldn't control the fear riding over her. That dog was going to lunge, and his teeth would sink into her flesh—ripping and tugging.

"Get away!" someone shouted.

The dog lurched back, pulled by its collar.

"Get away!"

And then a body was in front of her, blocking her sight of the dog, forming a barrier—a protective wall.

Beau.

His broad back shielded her as he commanded the dog to get back.

"Sorry! Oh my gosh, I'm so sorry." Footsteps came racing along with a woman's voice. "He got away from me."

"He scared the shit out of her!" Beau growled.

"I'm so sorry. He's still in training, and he just bolted. He's so fast. Super friendly, though. He wouldn't hurt a fly."

With Beau in front of her, Grace found her heart start to regulate… a little. The ability to breathe evenly again was returning, and she wiped a trembling hand over her mouth while Beau continued to tell the lady off.

She apologized profusely, obviously trying to check on Grace, but Beau wouldn't let her. He blocked the woman's view by shifting his body. Grace could picture the scowl on his face and actually felt a little sorry for the woman.

Footsteps hurried away along with the panting of an excited dog. Beau stayed where he was until they were well gone, then finally turned to face her.

She didn't know what to say. How to explain.

Wrapping her arms around her stomach, she stared down at the grass and felt a swift wave of humiliation. Her reaction had been over the top, but…

He crouched down in front of her, his voice featherlight. "Are you okay?"

She nodded but didn't want to look at him. Her lips were trembling too much to smile. All she felt like doing was having a good cry. She hadn't encountered a dog in a long time. She usually avoided parks like this for that very reason, but they were in a sheltered little spot, and she'd felt safe.

Until she wasn't.

Until she was seven again, and a snarling, snapping dog lunged at her, knocking her off her feet and trying to tear her face off.

She ran her fingers down her cheek and struggled to swallow.

"It was a dog attack, wasn't it?" Beau's voice had a tender edge that Grace had never heard before. She glanced up and watched him sit down beside her.

His penetrating gaze made her feel naked, and she looked away from it, staring out at the ocean instead.

"How old were you?"

She sniffed and pulled her knees to her chest. "Seven."

"It must have been terrifying," Beau whispered. "Painful."

Grace squeezed her eyes shut, then forced them open and started cleaning up the remnants of their sugar high. "Can you take me home, please?"

Beau hesitated, like he wanted to talk about this for longer, wanted to unpack her ugly nightmare next to this beautiful ocean view.

Grace worked in a frenzy, gathering everything into her hands and not caring that ice cream dripped onto her shirt.

She stood and Beau followed suit.

"Okay, let's go." He grabbed the script she was about to drop, and they headed back to the parking lot.

They walked in silence, which Grace was grateful for. As they neared the playground again, she felt her insides coil, and she couldn't help flinching when a child let out a scream, then started giggling.

Beau shifted closer, resting his hand on her lower back and steering her away from the man approaching with his dog. Without meaning to, she leaned into him as they walked, and before she knew it, his arm was wrapped around her shoulders. She flinched again when two rambunctious pups started barking.

"They're just having a friendly play," Beau assured her before directing her away from the green.

He took her down a path through a wooded area, and they popped out farther from the car. Grace didn't care; she was grateful for his help and knew she should say so, but she couldn't find the words.

She didn't feel truly safe until she was shut inside Beau's car and knew that no dog could reach her.

They're not capable of punching through the glass.

She tried to be logical and hoped it would override the debilitating emotions. She hated how weak and vulnerable she felt.

"Do you want to talk about it?" Beau started the car. The engine roared to life, but that was not why Grace jerked in her seat.

The question surprised her. Beau sounded like he genuinely cared. She had expected mocking laughter and a quick dismissal, not a protective arm around her and an offer to chat. It seemed out of character for him, and she didn't know how to process his reaction.

She swallowed, and as they pulled out of the parking lot, she shrugged and murmured, "I used to love dogs. I so badly wanted one but couldn't because we traveled around too much. For my dad's work."

Beau nodded, his eyes trained on the road ahead.

She licked her lips and forced herself to keep going. "One day, I was playing in my backyard, and this stray dog was on the street. It looked so lonely, and I wanted to pet him. I thought I might be able to convince my dad to keep him. Mom was out, and Dad was easier to convince." Her smile was soft and a little brittle, memories flooding her.

Why was she doing this? Why was she telling him?

Tears scorched her eyes, and her voice grew tight and small. "I ran toward it, calling out hello, and maybe I scared it, I don't know, but... it... it snarled and growled, and then it was on me." She sniffed. "I don't remember much, just pain and fear, really." She sucked in a shaky breath and crossed her arms, staring out the window so Beau couldn't see her tears.

"That must have been really traumatic."

She nodded. "The multiple surgeries and hospital stays were pretty horrific too. I got an infection, and..." She shook her head. "People always ask me why I didn't bother with plastic surgery, but after what I went through... the thought of going under again, of waking up and having to deal with the pain again..." Her lips pursed, then dipped into a sad frown. "I just can't do it."

A heavy silence fell between them, and Grace shifted in her seat, feeling that familiar flush of embarrassment as she waited for him to respond.

"I'm sorry that happened to you," he finally croaked. "Life's not fair. You didn't deserve that."

She glanced at him then, studying his profile. He shot her a look she'd never seen before. It was soft, tender almost, and her heart pulsed in a new way. A dangerous way.

She swallowed and turned back to look out the window. "Don't be," she whispered her mother's words for her. "It's made me who I am... and I like me."

She flashed him a smile, although it felt weak and tumultuous.

He murmured a response that was so soft she could barely hear it. For a second, she thought he said, "I like you too," but that couldn't be right.

She shook her head and kept her eyes trained on the scenery flashing past them.

No, that definitely wasn't what he said.

Beau would never like her. Sure, he was kind and sweet about the dog attack, but he wasn't about to walk the school halls with her or sit with her at lunchtime.

He'd never want to touch her face or kiss her.

As much as she liked who she was, she was smart enough to know that girls with her kinds of scars didn't end up with guys like Beau Griffin.

14

SOMETHING WAS VERY WRONG

Beau couldn't stop thinking about his day.

Darkness smothered his room, but he'd been awake long enough to make out all the shadowy shapes. He should really turn on his light and read a book, play on his phone, do something to distract himself, but it was the early hours of the morning, and he needed some sleep.

Every time he closed his eyes, images flooded him. Grace sucking on a milkshake straw, Grace playing the part of Puck, her giggle before she dug her spoon into the buttered pecan and popped it into her mouth. He'd had fun with her.

He tucked a hand behind his head and stared up at the ceiling.

That stark fear on her face. The way he'd jumped in front of her. It'd been instinctual. He'd just wanted to keep her safe, protect her, take away the fear. She'd leaned into him as they'd walked back to the car. Putting his arm around her had been automatic. He almost regretted getting to the car, because it'd meant he'd had to let her go.

What the hell is wrong with you, man?

He rubbed a hand over his wrinkled forehead. The lines of tension were causing a band of pain around his head. This wasn't cool. He needed sleep!

I wonder if Grace is asleep.

Is she okay?

Is she having nightmares?

The thought hurt his chest. She was two floors below him in her little room that looked out over the pool. Was she curled on her side, fighting off images of snarling dogs? Or was she awake like him, staring wide-eyed at the ceiling?

He hoped she was okay. The urge to get up and check on her was overwhelming. He nearly gave in to it a couple times but managed to bunch the sheets in his fist and stay put. He didn't want to be some stalker creeping through the house at night. What if she was asleep and he was staring at her? What if she woke up? He'd scare the crap out of her, and he didn't want to add any more stress to what had already been a rough day.

He closed his eyes and whispered, "I hope you're okay. I hope you're sleeping peacefully."

He pictured that scenario, that soft contented look she got on her face sometimes, like she was outside her body in a place of pure safety and peacefulness.

That look on her was beautiful. So were many looks.

In his mind, he trailed his fingers across her face, brushing away scared tears, gently exploring her scars. He wanted to feel the softness of her lips. What would it be like to kiss her?

He imagined it, then sat up with a jolt.

"What is happening?" he whispered, flopping back down and shaking his head. "You need sleep, man. Just go the hell to sleep!"

He rolled onto his side and fought for oblivion.

It eventually took him, but he woke feeling groggy and unsettled.

Shooting out of bed, he threw some clothes on and tried to make himself presentable in the bathroom without making it look like he tried too hard. Pushing up his sweater sleeves, he trotted down to the kitchen with a set smile, ready to greet Grace and see if she was doing okay.

But the kitchen was empty.

With a frown, he spun and wandered into the dining room.

His mother was sipping coffee while reading something off her phone.

"Where is everyone?" he asked.

She seemed surprised by his question. "It's Sunday. Your father's playing golf."

"Oh, yeah, of course." Beau tried to pull his expression into line and act casual as he leaned against the door-frame. "Anyone else around?"

"Just me, although I'm leaving for Manhattan in half an hour. I'd like to get a little shopping done before catching an exhibit at the MOMA. I'm going with Avril Garnier." She looked smug, like Beau should know who the woman was. He didn't, but he could tell by his mother's expression that she must be someone rich and important.

"Cool." He shoved his hands into his pockets. "Anyone else around?"

His mother blinked. "Who else would be around?"

"Well… the other people who live in this house." Geez, being subtle was hard! He cleared his throat and tried to sell it. "I guess I'm trying to figure out if I have this place to myself today."

"Oh." His mother grinned. "You're in luck. Leola and Grace are out for the day, and Chapman is driving me to New York."

"The gardener is driving you to New York?"

She smiled. "He doesn't mind being my chauffeur sometimes too. Besides, he can catch up with his cousin while I'm at the museum. It's a win-win." She set her phone down and finished her coffee. "You have fun today, darling. Don't do anything too naughty. Your father will not want to come home to some chaotic party. Whatever you want to get up to with your friends, try to be a little bit sensible about it, okay?" She winked at him and sashayed past.

He watched her go and slumped with a sigh.

Grace was out for the day.

The disappointment was heavy and confusing. He shouldn't feel this way. He had the freaking house to himself! He should be sending out a text bomb and inviting everyone over. Instead, he slumped back to his room, flopping onto the mattress and trying to figure out what the hell was wrong with him.

15

DREAMING OR REALITY?

Monday rolled around quickly enough. Grace had spent Sunday with her mother and Millie, baking up a storm in Millie's little bungalow. The woman was on a mission to make the perfect brownie, and not one to ever think inside the box, she came up with a variety of recipes, from milk chocolate and raspberry to salted white chocolate with a caramel swirl and bacon bits (of all things) to a dark chocolate and marshmallow concoction, which kind of worked but wasn't Grace's favorite. To her utter shock, her favorite was actually the white chocolate and bacon. There was something about that combination of salty and sweet that was delicious.

She came back to the Griffin house on a sugar high, which quickly turned into an exhausting sugar crash, and she ended up in bed before dinner and fell asleep while reading.

With a groggy moan, she stumbled out of bed, reality sinking in quickly when she reached the bathroom and realized it was Monday, which meant school.

The weekend had been such a nice reprieve, especially with Saturday having that bizarre twist. Hanging out with Beau had actually been kind of fun... until the dog scare, but then he'd been really sweet about it, protecting her all the way back to the car. She still wasn't sure if that was some kind of dream.

"Gracie? Are you awake yet, baby? You're gonna be late," her mother called down the stairs.

Grace checked the time on her phone and gasped. How had she overslept? Why hadn't her alarm gone off?

She checked her settings and made sure it was on for tomorrow before picking up her pace and rushing to get ready. The week ahead was kind of huge. *Midsummer Night's Dream* had its first official performance on Thursday, and the next few days would be busy with makeup trials, plus technical and dress rehearsals. Nerves jittered through her as she wondered whose makeup Essie would ask her to do. She prayed it wasn't Colette's.

Brushing her hair, Grace arranged it into a braid over her shoulder, then finished getting dressed. Her mom had ironed her school uniform, and she felt pristine and out of her comfort zone as she ran upstairs for a flying breakfast. She'd probably have to eat in the car.

Maybe I should just skip it. I can fast for a meal. It won't kill me.

The smell of coffee hit her as soon as she walked in. It almost made her stomach turn until someone passed her a travel cup of her favorite herbal tea and then a bagel.

She gaped at the last person she expected to find smiling at her in the kitchen. And definitely the last person she ever expected to hand her breakfast.

"Come on, we're gonna be late." Beau's friendly grin had her blinking several times.

She couldn't find words as she took the food and drink from his hands.

What is happening right now?

He popped the last piece of toast into his mouth and brushed his fingers over the plate. "Thanks for breakfast, Leola."

"You're welcome." Grace's mother smiled and handed him a coffee to go. "Good luck today. Have fun with all you've got going on." She winked at him, and Grace blinked again.

Seriously, what is happening?

"Thanks." Beau picked up his bag and then Grace's. "See ya."

"Take care, Beau." She smiled and waved, and Grace was sure she still hadn't woken up yet.

That was why she'd missed her alarm, because it hadn't even gone off.

She was in a dream, and she'd wake up any second and not be running late. She'd get ready without rushing, then have a leisurely breakfast with her mom before a surly Beau stormed past the kitchen and barked that he'd be waiting in the car.

She stayed rooted to the spot. Her eyes would open properly any second now.

"Grace, are you okay?" Her mother rubbed her arm.

"Huh?"

"Baby, you're gonna be late. Go on, Beau's already taken your bag out to the car." She kissed her cheek. "Go have fun today, okay?"

"But…" Grace pointed in the direction Beau had gone.

"I know. It surprised me too. He seems very happy this morning, but just go with it. Butterfly wings, remember?" She winked.

Grace frowned and, thanks to a push from her mother, shuffled after him. Caution wrapped around her, and she tried to break free of its bonds with some logic.

They'd had a nice time together on Saturday; maybe this was just the aftermath of that.

Still, when she slipped into the car, she kept her smile small and in control. "Thanks for helping out this morning. I'm sorry I'm late. My alarm never went off."

"That's cool. I was up early for some bizarre reason. I don't always question the universe. It likes to do its thing, you know?" He started up the engine and got some music playing before he sped down the driveway.

Grace sipped her tea, then grinned. "I love this song."

"Really?" Beau slowed to make his way through the gate, then turned left toward school. "I love this band. They're one of my favorites."

"Me too." She took a bite of bagel, glad it was cream cheese and not something sweet. She was pretty sure the sugar from the brownie experiment would tide her over for a month.

Beau didn't race to school like he was competing in the Indy 500. It was a nice change, and Grace wondered if it was a conscious thing or whether he wasn't in his usual hurry.

She wondered why, then decided the universe was just playing a bizarre game today and maybe, just maybe, he was enjoying her company for a change.

Was there a catch?

She still wasn't sure.

Just go with it. Butterfly wings.

It was a concept her mother came up with, and Grace had always loved the idea of transformation. The hope that anyone could change.

Although, glancing at Beau, she still wasn't sure if she could trust it.

In spite of the fact that she felt like she'd entered a parallel universe, she decided to heed her mother's advice. The woman was so often right about things. Maybe Saturday had been a turning point for them. Was it really that transformative?

As the questions swirled in her mind, she realized she'd never thanked him for what he did. So, just before they reached school, she turned down the music and angled her body toward him. "Hey, um... I wanted to thank you for looking after me on Saturday." Dipping her gaze, she played with the rim of her travel mug. "You were really nice about it, and I was so grateful to have you there."

He slowed the car a little more and slipped off his shades. His eyes were brilliant in the morning sunlight, his smile the most genuine she'd ever seen. "That's okay. I'm glad I was there."

Her lips curled at the edges, and she could feel a blush rising from her neck to her cheeks. She swiveled back to face the front, and Beau slipped his shades back on. As they turned into school, the mood in the car kind of shifted and became oh so familiar when they pulled into a parking space and Colette waltzed up to the car with her arrogant smirk firmly in place.

Grace's insides twisted at the pretty girl's derisive smile.

Biting her lips together, she placed her mug in the cupholder next to Beau's unfinished coffee and wiped bagel crumbs off her jacket.

The second Colette opened Beau's door, his entire demeanor changed. Gone was the sweet smile, and in its place was a haughty, unaffected look that turned him into a cover model. Or maybe one of those mannequins with blank eyes and no personality.

Slipping out of the car, Grace grabbed her bag and hugged it to her chest, walking into school and realizing that her morning—and even Saturday—had just been some weird blip in the matrix.

Beau wasn't about to sprout a set of butterfly wings anytime soon.

For once, her mother was wrong.

Beau was who he was. He had friends who were obviously important to him, and he didn't need some girl who was afraid of dogs messing up his life.

Pulling in a long breath, she repeated her mother's mantra in her head. She was beautiful and enough. She didn't need Beau, and even though it'd been pretty cool hanging out with him on Saturday, he wasn't the source of her happiness.

She wished that he didn't have to be someone else around his friends, but they had history, and she was just some new girl who he probably didn't want disrupting his life.

"That's okay," she whispered to herself. "You're okay."

She willed her mind to make Saturday a sweet memory and move on.

Beau Griffin was not going to own her day.

Determination set her chin, and she walked to homeroom with her head held high. It was going to be a good day, because she would make it so.

16

BECOMING OBERON

Today was turning out to be the worst. Beau couldn't even figure out why, but he was in a foul mood. Maybe it was the fact that Grace walked away from the car this morning without so much as a goodbye. Or maybe it was the cold look of disdain on Colette's face. Maybe it was because he didn't do anything about it and just *let* Grace walk away.

He was torn over what to do. He'd love to bring Grace into his circle somehow, but it was impossible. His friends would never accept her. If anything, they'd annihilate her, and he didn't want to put her in the position.

Yet his friends had always meant everything to him. They understood him more than his family ever would. They'd stuck with him, and they looked out for each other. They were tight.

He felt more loyalty from them than he did from his own parents. He couldn't just ditch all that because he'd enjoyed a few laughs with Grace. So what if they shared the same taste in music and she had the sweetest voice?

Who cared if she made the most adorable Puck in the world? It didn't matter that she'd fit perfectly against him as he guided her trembling body back to his car. The fact that it felt so good to protect her that way didn't really mean anything. At all.

Grace wasn't his type.

Colette was. She was stunningly beautiful, and confident, with a quick wit and sharp tongue. She knew her mind and wasn't afraid to speak it.

Neither is Grace. She just does it with a gentle kindness.

His insides deflated as he wove around human traffic and walked to his table on the outskirts of the cafeteria. Colette had already gotten him a tray of food. See? She could be nice.

Sitting down, he murmured his thanks and began picking at the pasta and salad. The food at Lincoln was pretty damn good, and he would usually devour his plate in minutes, but he was in a nibbling mood. Picking up a cherry tomato, he popped it into his mouth and frowned at the way Zari and Amell were eating each other for lunch instead of their food.

Seriously. Those guys were handsy in all the wrong places.

"Get a room," he muttered under his breath.

No one heard him, so he tuned in to listen to Ella and Colette giggling over Maisy Swanson's new hair.

"She looks like a freaking porcupine!"

"I can't believe she just chopped it all off like that. What was she thinking?"

"Her body's still hot." Etan glanced across the cafeteria

with an arrogant smirk. "I'd still do her. Who gives a shit about her hair?"

The girls rolled their eyes while the guys cracked up laughing. Beau just stared, wondering what Grace would have to say about that.

Who cares what she'd have to say! She's not your friend.

The thought sat ugly in his stomach, and he dropped his fork, giving up on his pasta and slumping back in his seat for the rest of the lunch break. His friends continued to laugh and mock those around him, oblivious to his silence while he drank from his water bottle and slumped into a sullen mood. They'd seen him like this before, so if any of them did notice, they'd probably roll their eyes and figure he was in a mood.

Fine by him.

He *was* in a freaking mood.

A freaking bad one, and he wished he understood why.

The day finally came to an end, but he still had rehearsals to get through. Fisting his bag strap, he tried not to think about the fact that he might see Grace. Part of him was elated by this, but he shouldn't feel that way, so he set his scowl in place and walked into the drama theater only to face down a beaming Mr. Lassater.

"Afternoon, Beau." His smile was broad and totally contagious.

Beau gave in to a small half grin. "Hey."

"Did you manage to work on those lines over the weekend?"

"Yes, sir." He nodded, not wanting to admit who he'd practiced with.

He caught a flash of movement from the corner of his eye, and his chest hitched.

Grace.

She glided past with a serene smile, her eyes focused on Essie, who was animatedly telling her about something.

"Essie, Grace," Mr. Lassater called them over.

Beau stopped breathing. Colette appeared on his right. She crossed her arms, her eyes narrowing in on Grace like she was a bug that needed exterminating. He shifted, trying to block Colette's view, but she just moved around him so poor Grace was facing down everyone as she approached the group.

She kept her eyes on the drama teacher.

"I was hoping to do some test runs with makeup today. I know you ladies have been working on ideas, and I'd love to see them so I can do a critique before the real thing."

"Sounds great," Essie bubbled. "Why don't I take Colette, as we've already had a chat about what she wants. Grace, are you happy to do Beau?"

She swallowed, her gaze darting across his face before dropping to the floor. "Uh… yeah, I guess so."

Ouch. That hurt. Could she be more unenthusiastic?

Beau clenched his jaw, annoyed that he was stung by her reluctance. Why should he even care? They weren't friends or anything.

No, you just live in the same house, and you can't stop dreaming about her. No biggie.

Beau rolled his eyes, slumping into the makeup chair and gripping the arms.

"Are you okay?" Grace asked as she tucked tissues into his collar.

Her fingers brushed the skin of his neck and he swallowed, gritting out a quick "I'm fine."

She gave him a knowing look, and he rolled his eyes again, averting his gaze so he couldn't look into her beautiful brown eyes.

Beautiful eyes? Man, shut up!

Grace turned to inspect a sheet of paper, and he couldn't help noticing the way it trembled in the air. Was she nervous?

He swallowed, shifting in his seat and convincing himself that *he* definitely wasn't. But then she turned back to him, moving into his space with a pad of foundation. Her touch was gentle and controlled, her look of concentration kind of endearing.

She smelled good.

He didn't know what the scent was except sweetness. It suited her. She was sweet. The sweetest person he'd ever met.

Closing his eyes, he tried to ward off the gooey thoughts. This wasn't him. He wasn't gooey; he didn't care about sweet.

He liked hot, sassy, doable—as Etan would so eloquently put it.

His insides writhed. Doable. The idea of Grace being doable, like she was some slab of meat, made him grip the chair even tighter. Why did Etan think that way?

You *think that way!*

He swiftly countered the thought in his head.

Not with Grace. She's not that kind of girl. You don't just do someone like Grace.

Oh really? You wouldn't?

He thought about her body and how she'd looked on Saturday, reaching into the car to get his script. The way the fabric had pulled over her toned butt.

She *was* hot. Doable.

But no…

She was Grace.

She was more than just a quick screw at some party or a steamy make-out session in his car, because she was kind and she listened and she made him feel…

"Okay, I'm getting there," she murmured near his ear. "Do you like that? Around the eye?"

He opened his eyes and blinked, his mouth dropping open. She really was an artist. Turning his head to look in the mirror, he couldn't stop staring at the way she'd made his left eye pop. With blues, greens, and a heavy dose of eyeliner, she was making him look like the king of a forest. The leaf she'd crafted from his left temple down to the top of his cheekbone had a 3D quality to it.

"Wow, how do you do that?"

She grinned. "Do you like it?"

"Yeah. It's amazing. Keep going."

Her smile in the mirror made his heart warm, and he sat back, closing his eyes again, so she could finish off the rest of his face.

By the time she was done, he'd been transformed. Beau didn't exist in this makeup. He was Oberon, and he felt it all the way to his core.

"This is…" He shook his head, standing tall and leaning closer to the mirror. "You're incredible."

"Whatever." Colette stood from her chair, ripping tissues out of her collar and throwing them on the floor. "If she's so damn good, why doesn't she use it on herself?"

Grace's beaming smile disintegrated. Essie flushed, obviously embarrassed but not willing to say anything.

Beau turned to Colette with a frown. She ignored it, snatching his hand and trying to pull him toward the stage.

She looked amazing, all Titania-like, but he pulled his hand free and stood his ground, letting her walk out by herself. She could have her grand freaking entrance solo style.

Turning back to Grace, he reached for her, but she shuffled back, giving him a dignified nod before starting to pack up the makeup.

"Are you okay?" he asked.

She glanced up like the question surprised her, then put on a smile. "Yeah." Pulling the tissues out of his collar, she balled them in her fist and crossed her arms. "Don't worry about it. I've been living with this for a long time. It's nothing new."

His frown was pained, he could feel it, and memories of her tears in the library swamped him. "I—"

"It's okay," she quickly interrupted. "Go rehearse. You look amazing, Oberon. Have fun with it." She winked, just like her mother always did, and pushed him toward the stage.

He stopped and turned back… and she grinned at him, her brown eyes sparkling.

Beautiful.

His heart whispered the word before his brain could catch up with it, and he walked into the rehearsal, once again trying to figure out what was going on.

"Oberon!" Mr. Lassater clapped. "You look amazing!" He let out a hearty laugh, then got down to business, arranging everyone into their positions and shouting, "Action!"

Beau slipped into the role of the fairy king and put on the performance of his life.

Maybe it was the makeup. Maybe it was Grace's wink.

He didn't know, but he felt alive on that stage in a way he never had before.

17

SWEET ENTHUSIASM AND PUTRID WORDS

Grace watched from the sidelines, admiring Beau as he worked. He was on fire, his performance dynamic and mesmerizing.

"Wow," Essie murmured. "Imagine what they'll look like with their costumes on as well. It's going to be the most beautiful show this school has ever seen!" She grabbed Grace's hand in excitement.

Grace squeezed back with a grin, her gaze quickly tracking to the stage again.

Her fingers still tingled from applying makeup to Beau. She loved the shape of his face. He was refined, like a marble sculpture, his angles striking. And he smelled good. Whatever cologne he wore tickled her senses, giving her a heady rush. Being that close to him had been...

She bit her lips together, trying to hide her grin.

And then he'd asked if she was okay. He'd loved her work. She'd... she'd winked at him!

He was softening. She could sense it. That was why

she was finding the courage to be a little more open and fun-loving.

But what if it isn't true?

What if this is all just a dream?

He's under a spell, just like the characters in this play.

He'd snap out of it at any moment and go back to being that cold-faced guy who showed up the second they pulled into the school.

But he wasn't cold faced just now. He was nice to you.

She wasn't used to it. People didn't make a habit of being kind to her. She didn't realize how vulnerable it would make her feel. Letting someone in, lowering her guard... the chances of getting hurt were so high. Did she really want to take that risk?

Beau was the type of gorgeous, enigmatic guy who could destroy her. The way Dad tried to destroy Mom. Not intentionally, just... because he was him. He broke her heart, and Beau had the power to do that to Grace. Even if he never loved her back, he could ruin her.

Backing away, she returned to the makeup station and did some extra, unnecessary tidying. She then made sure everything was set up for removing the makeup after rehearsal. Essie joined her and they spent the rest of the rehearsal sorting out costumes and going over last-minute details. Grace was hand sewing some extra sequins to Titania's gown when the troupe returned.

Flopping back down in his seat, Beau seemed electrified, and Grace couldn't help grinning at him while she wet a makeup pad with the clear solution.

"You did good," she murmured.

"It felt amazing! My best performance yet." The

sparkle in his voice matched the dancing in his bright blue eyes. He was pumped… and he'd never looked more gorgeous.

She giggled, loving his enthusiasm. "Better save some up for the real deal."

"I think the makeup helped pull me into character more, you know?"

She paused and arched her brow. "Want me to leave it on?"

He laughed, the carefree sound capturing the attention of everyone in the room. Essie bulged her eyes at Grace, who gave her an awkward smile and ducked her head, focusing on Beau's makeup removal. Her hands trembled just a little, and her heart skipped a beat when she caught Beau's gaze in the mirror. He was watching her with a softness she'd glimpsed after the dog incident. It was a beautiful look, and it made her feel—

"Well, that was amazing. Did you guys see me? I was on fire!" Colette waltzed in, and Grace quickly looked away from the mirror, but not fast enough.

She caught Colette's sharp gaze and felt the talons coming out to play. They'd scratch and nip, chipping away at Grace's dignified veneer until she felt raw and wounded.

Grace steeled herself for the inevitable, smoothing out her expression and getting down to work.

"You were dynamic, Beau. So freaking good." Colette's saccharine smile turned Grace's stomach into a ball of knots.

"Yeah." Beau nodded. "I think the makeup really helped, right? I just felt more in character."

"Absolutely. Too bad yours wasn't perfect, but..." She shrugged. "Hopefully you'll get Essie on the actual night. She is in charge for a reason." Colette sat in her chair, smiling at Essie. "I expect you'll be doing all the important roles for the performances, right?"

"Uh..." Essie glanced over her shoulder, catching Grace's eye. "Well, no. Grace is really good, so we'll divide and conquer."

"Oh really?" Colette's voice took on a faux innocence that set Grace's teeth on edge. "You have a lot of other parts. I think Grace is better suited for the simpler stuff, don't you?"

"Uh, hello!" Beau pointed at himself. "You saw my makeup today. It kicked ass."

Colette gave a nonplussed shrug, and Beau dropped it, much to Grace's relief.

Unfortunately, Colette didn't.

In a sugar-coated voice that reeked of mockery, she said, "I just don't understand how you can be such a wonderful artist." Her piercing gaze hit Grace like a bullet, and she momentarily froze up.

The room went silent, the stillness thick and debilitating. Grace forced herself to keep moving, keep working within this awkward tension, but her movements felt stiff, her heart racing at the speed of light.

"I mean, according to Beau, you create a masterpiece on his face, but every day... you walk these halls totally exposed. We have to look at your face *every day*. How can you create something amazing on him, yet we have to suffer your scars? Can't you just cover them up?"

Grace stayed silent, her skin rippling with hot

146

pinpricks, her throat swelling to the point of painful. She saw Beau's grip tighten on the seat, his nostrils flaring.

"Don't," she whispered in his ear.

His body stayed tense while Colette continued.

"Hello! I'm talking to you! You don't think it's worth getting up a little earlier each morning to cover up? Or would it just take too long? Is that the problem?"

Ella tittered before covering her mouth, then dropping her hand to add, "Maybe it's an impossible task."

"You guys, stop," Essie murmured, then chickened out when Colette's sharp gaze hit her like a wrecking ball.

"She could at least try," the blonde bombshell snapped. "Instead, we have to be exposed to Scar Face every day. Thank God you don't eat in the cafeteria, Grace, because if anything's going to put me off my food..." Colette's eyebrows rose with a pointed look, and Grace could feel the tears forming in the back of her eyes.

But she would not give in.

Colette was cruel, but she was doing it to get a reaction, and Grace refused to give her one.

"Aren't you going to say anything?" Beau muttered. "Tell them to shut the hell up."

"That just stokes the flames even hotter." She rested her hand on his shoulder and smiled. She could do this. His anger was actually helping. It gave her the calm she needed to hold on to her dignity. "They're only words, and they can only hurt if I let them. Believe me, I've learned this the hard way."

"How can you smile right now?" He turned to her with a confused whisper. "And don't tell me you're not affected, because I know that's a lie."

She paused, her eyebrows dipping together. How did he know it was a lie? Had her guard slipped while he was watching? She was trying so hard to keep it together.

And besides, she didn't want it to be a lie! She didn't want to be affected by anything these cruel girls said to her. It'd been happening most of her life, and she'd been fighting every step of the way to be numb to every taunt, every repulsed frown and dry-retching heave she walked past.

She fought to keep her composure. "What do you want me to do?" She leaned so close to his ear, her lips were practically touching him. "Bite back? Run and hide? Start crying?"

"I don't know," Beau softly growled. "But *something*. I don't know how you just stand there and take it all the time."

"What are you two whispering about?" Ella tipped back on her heels, a playful, wicked gleam in her eyes.

Beau turned with a thunderous glare. "We're talking about how bitchy you guys are being."

Colette gasped. Obviously Beau had never insulted her before, and the look of indignant rage was so pronounced it was almost comical.

Grace rested her hand on Beau's shoulder and gave it a light squeeze. "That's not true," she rushed to defuse the situation. "We were talking about how I respond when people speak to me the way you guys do."

"Oh really?" Colette spat. "Miss High-and-mighty. Always above us with your angelic smile."

Grace closed her eyes with a soft sigh.

Ugh! I seriously give up. She's impossible.

"You can't ignore me forever, Scar Face." Colette's tone was soft and lilting.

"I'm not ignoring you." Grace kept her tone mild. "I hear every word you say."

"Yet you're so unaffected?"

"Do you want me to be hurt?" Grace stopped and looked directly at Colette. "Do you want to make me cry? Is that your goal right now?"

Colette clamped her lips together, shuffling in her seat and facing the mirror. "Such a cardboard cutout. You're like an ugly cartoon character, and I don't appreciate having to see your face every time I walk into my school."

"That's enough!" Beau barked, slapping the arm of the chair.

Everyone jumped, including Grace, who nearly dropped the bottle of makeup remover.

Beau rose from his seat, pointing at Colette with a scowl so deep it contorted his entire face. "Shut your mouth!"

She gasped again, leaning away from him as he stalked toward her chair.

"The garbage spewing out of you smells putrid, and I don't want to be around it for one second longer!" Swinging around, he took Grace by the arm and pulled her away from her workstation. "Come on. Let's go. You can finish taking off my makeup at home."

Slipping his arm around her waist, he guided her out of the room, stopping only long enough to snatch their bags. She was so stunned by his behavior that she didn't have a chance to protest.

No one had ever stood up for her that way before, and

she wasn't sure what to do with the emotions charging through her.

The electric air didn't dissipate either. It seemed to follow them through the corridors as Beau stormed to the car, his pace so fast that Grace had to run to keep up with him. He didn't say anything, and Grace felt sure that trying to clear the air would be the wrong move, so she silently slipped into the car beside him, gazing at the Oberon side of his face yet knowing she was driving home with a raging beast.

18

BUTTERFLY WINGS

Beau couldn't control the volcano in his chest. His head was spinning with Colette's nasty diatribe and the way Grace just took it with such dignity. She didn't deserve to be spoken to like that, and he'd never hated anyone as much as he despised Colette right now.

His foot was heavy on the accelerator, and he didn't even notice until Grace's breath hitched when he took a corner too fast. He slowed down, muttering under his breath.

Grace wasn't saying anything, and it only occurred to him that maybe she was a little afraid of his reaction. Did she think he was mad with her or something?

He decided to make it perfectly clear where his anger lay.

"Those bitches!"

Grace sighed, her voice soft and smooth. "Would you stop calling them that?"

"Why?"

"Because they're your friends, and insulting them isn't going to make you feel better."

He took a sharp turn into his driveway and didn't slow down until he reached the house, slamming on the brake and jolting them both. He felt instantly bad but couldn't find the words, his anger making any kind of pleasantries impossible.

"I don't get you," he spat. "At all! How do you put up with that shit?"

She licked her bottom lip and turned to him with a calm smile. "Years of practice, I guess."

He huffed, slamming out of the car and nearly ripping his bag strap when it caught in the door. He had to open it again and take it out, his jerky movements not helping. It only fueled his wrath as he continued to spit and complain. "They deserved to be brought down!"

"And they will be..." She walked around the car, gently untangling the strap and closing the door for him. Her nutmeg gaze was calm when she looked up at him, and the storm inside began to settle. "Or maybe they'll be redeemed. I don't need to do that for them. Life has a way of teaching people lessons."

He didn't know how to respond to that.

"Come on." She grinned, taking his hand and pulling him toward the house. "I'll finish taking your makeup off in the bathroom."

He let her guide him through the house, grateful they didn't bump into anyone along the way. Her fingers were strong, her skin smooth. He liked her touch, the way her small hand fit inside his so perfectly.

He drew in a shaky breath, Grace's mellow demeanor

working on him like some kind of balm. She sat him on the edge of the bathtub and started humming as she extracted wipes and cleaner from beneath the sink. He'd never been into the downstairs bathroom. It was simple with only a few essentials lining the vanity. It was a far cry from his mother's en suite, which was overrun with expensive products. He didn't even know what half of them did.

Tipping his head with her light touch, she started wiping away the makeup, humming softly under her breath. Her nearness, the light melody oozing out of her, was a weird kind of comfort, and finally he was in control enough to carry on the conversation.

"I don't get how you do it," he whispered. "How do you stay so calm and in control?"

She stopped working to gaze down at him. "I don't always feel like it, but…" She shrugged. "Butterfly wings."

"What?" he snickered.

"I have to believe in butterfly wings."

"O-kay, crazy lady."

She giggled, wiping the last of the makeup free. Throwing the dirty wipes away, she washed her hands, then stood in front of him. Without thinking, he took her wrist, exploring the shape of her delicate hand before gently rubbing his thumb across her palm.

She went still, her breath catching before she slipped her hand free and turned to walk away. "You're all done."

"Don't leave."

She paused, resting her hand on the doorframe.

"Explain it to me. What's *butterfly wings*?"

She turned back, her smile soft as she sat on the edge

of the tub beside him. Her hand rested right next to his thigh, and it took everything in him not to thread his fingers between hers. But he didn't want to scare her off. He needed to know what she meant. He needed to unravel the butterfly mystery.

Her pink tongue licked her bottom lip before she captured him with those eyes again. "It's the idea that transformation is possible for anyone. If a caterpillar can change from a bug that crawls around on its belly to a beautiful butterfly, then anything is possible. Nasty people don't have to stay nasty forever. Anyone can learn to be something new." She leaned forward, resting her elbows on her knees. "After the accident... once all the swelling had gone down and the infection had healed, I could see properly again." She swallowed. "That first time I looked in the mirror, I was horrified. I crawled into bed, threw the covers over my head, and refused to leave the house." She let out a self-deprecating laugh, like it wasn't a big deal, but he could hear the trembling in her voice. "Mom and Dad tried everything, but I was one stubborn... *heart-broken* little girl."

Beau pictured the scene and felt like his chest was being crushed in a vise.

Grace stood, facing the mirror and staring at her reflection. "It took a really long time, but Mom wouldn't give up. She found every book on butterflies that she could, the ugly duckling—any books on transformation. She read them until my ears bled." She snickered and shook her head. "And then she got me looking in the mirror and telling myself that I was a beautiful person—inside and out. I had to look at my reflection and say, 'I am beautiful.'" Grace's voice pitched, and for a moment, Beau thought she was going to cry. But she lifted her chin and stared her reflection like it was a challenge she could conquer. "I cried the first hundred or so times, but eventually I started to look right into my eyes and see it."

Glancing back at Beau, she touched his arm, fiddling with the sleeve of his T-shirt and smiling like she knew a secret he didn't. Her voice dropped to a lilting whisper, and he leaned forward, wanting to savor every word out of her mouth.

"I don't always feel it, but I know I'm worthy. I'm beautiful. I'm enough just the way I am." She bit her lips together, her fingers shaking as she brushed them over his shoulder. "Some girl who doesn't even know who she is is not going to change my mind about that. All I can do is pray for her. Pray that Colette the Caterpillar will one day go into her cocoon and come out the other side a beautiful-hearted, kind, compassionate person."

Beau couldn't breathe as he gazed up at her, seeing the beauty she spoke of. "You're amazing," he whispered.

She blinked, dropping her hand like she only just realized that she'd been touching him.

Her smile was soft and tentative, her blush enough to crack his heart wide open.

He was pretty sure that was exactly what happened, because when she walked out of the bathroom, he sat there, gripping the edge of the tub and having to admit that he was feeling something for this girl. Something he'd never felt before in his life.

19

BEAU, THE FAIRY KING

Opening night.

Grace knew it wouldn't be a relaxing affair, but she didn't expect to be this stressed either. She was trying to keep it all locked in as she helped the cast into their costumes and applied makeup. Essie had gotten a few extra helpers, but Grace felt run off her feet as she dashed from one end of backstage to the other, collecting forgotten, last-minute things, pinning stray curls into hairdos, and reapplying foundation to shiny noses.

"You're done." She smiled at the extra whose name she didn't know, feeling slightly bad that she hadn't learned it, but he was one of so many and her brain was frazzled.

It had been a challenging, exhausting week.

Beau was changing. His icy veneer was dropping away to something warm and enticing. It made her nervous. He was looking at her differently, and she was so used to derision that his kind smiles made her vulnerable. She'd been keeping busy and trying to avoid him at school, but then worried that her slightly distant behavior might hurt his feelings as well.

When it was just the two of them, driving to and from school while listening to music, she started to relax and feel better. She could smile, laugh, sing along. After school, he'd sit with her in the kitchen, and they'd talk about anything and everything, like the world outside his home didn't exist.

But it did.

She knew it every morning when they drove through the academy gates and reality kicked back in. Colette and Ella would be waiting by the big tree on the edge of the parking lot with Etan and various friends. Their stare-downs were enough to turn her blood to concrete. Beau had actually gotten into the habit of pausing by the pathway so she could get out before he parked the car. He didn't like it, but they both innately knew that it was easier.

Colette had forgiven Beau for his thoughtless outburst, and as much as he wanted to tear her to shreds over it, Grace had persuaded him not to. Making enemies of his friends was not her goal. They'd argued about it the entire way to school, but she'd noticed when she spied him later in the day that Colette was laughing at something he was saying.

She figured he'd listened to her advice, and that felt really good.

What didn't feel good was seeing Colette laughing beside Beau when that was where Grace wanted to be.

Every day she shuffled off to either the library or the art room, reminding herself that although Beau's friends didn't really bring out the best in him, he needed them. She couldn't imagine a guy like Beau content with a lonesome life like hers. Sure, she'd made friends with Essie, but the flamboyant costume designer already had a close circle she hung out with at lunchtimes. They were all seniors, and Grace didn't want to muscle in on what they had. They probably wouldn't mind her presence, but books and artwork were so much safer.

Friends were hard to make... and keep.

Which was why she didn't want to destroy Beau's friendship group. Not only because he thought of them as family, but also because they were the type who could turn on him, and she didn't want him putting up with everything she did. She would spare anyone that kind of torture.

The drama queens had iced her out completely, treating her like a contagious virus. They'd gotten most of their friends on board, to the point where some of the actors wouldn't even let her do their makeup.

Mr. Lassater was fuming, but all Grace could worry about was Beau and the awkward situation it put him in. It was like he had to choose sides, and she never wanted that for him.

Instead, he was trying to stay on his friends' good side *and* hers. He'd covered hanging out with Grace by saying his father was making him and kind of acting like it was a pain in the ass. That hurt, but she understood why he was doing it, trying to put herself in his shoes. When they were alone together, his friends ceased to exist, and it was all good again.

It irritated Beau a little that she was so understanding,

and deep down, he probably wanted her to tell him off for being such a doormat, but she just knew that getting on the wrong side of his friends was a really bad idea.

"Can you fix my hair?" Beau appeared behind her, making her jump and blush.

Busted!

Did he know she'd been obsessing about him?

She glanced up and noticed the part of his hair that was drooping. She'd tried to style it with a little flair before starting his makeup, but it wasn't holding properly.

She frowned, pursing her lips and pointing at the chair.

"Sit," she murmured.

He sat and watched her as she fluffed around with various bits of greenery she and Essie had been collecting over the past few weeks. They'd wound wires through them to create different crowns and leafy jewels that could be attached to costumes.

"Let's try this." She stuck some bobby pins in her mouth and began arranging an earthy tiara for him. It wasn't part of the original design, but it would work with his makeup and hide the hair problem.

He watched her work. She could feel his gaze on her, and it made her fingers tremble.

"What's she screwing up now?" Colette sauntered past, looking stunning. Too bad her icy blue glare ruined the entire ensemble.

Or maybe it doesn't. Titania is a strong, powerful character. Colette is perfectly cast.

Grace forced a smile. "I'm just adding a crown. I think it'll look good."

Colette ignored her comment and focused on Beau. "Whatever she's doing, don't stress. You're hot no matter what."

She brushed her hand down his arm, then left a big lipstick kiss on his cheek.

Grace tutted, sighing at the mark that she would now have to wipe off and re-makeup.

With a giggle, Colette sauntered away while Beau gripped the chair, clenching his jaw. Grace watched the taut muscles strain his face and had to bite her lips together.

"You sure pretending like her bitchiness doesn't matter is the right move?" he gritted out while she finished his crown, then reached for a wipe.

Grace turned back, focusing on the lipstick mark and wondering how much of the area she'd have to redo. Working gently, she wiped the mark away and tried to avoid Beau's gaze. This close, it felt like his eyes were practically touching her.

"She's your friend."

"Why?" he quipped. "She treats you like crap."

"She's the center of your circle." Grace reverted back to the conversation they'd been having all week. "You cross her and half the student body will turn against you. Do you honestly want that? You love your friends. You like being popular."

He opened his mouth to say something, then sealed his lips.

"I can handle it," she reassured him. "They're just words, nasty taunts. They can't affect me if I don't let them." She grabbed the foundation and started her patch-up job.

"I hate the way she treats you."

"You didn't use to."

His brows deepened into a deep scowl. "Maybe I did."

"Well, you never let it show. And as flattered as I am that you're doing it now, I don't need you to. Just… be nice to me, and that's all that matters. I don't care what anyone else says."

She hoped the words would soften him. She basically just admitted that his opinion was important to her. That was huge.

But he continued to glare into the mirror, and she began to wonder if he even heard what she'd said. By the time she was done, her shoulders were as tense as his, and she couldn't wait for this freaking play to start so she could get some space from this confusing guy.

"I think that's blended okay." She dropped the brush onto the counter and turned back to face him.

He nodded, ripping the tissues out of his collar and standing tall.

"Fairy people, get ready!" Mr. Lassater walked through backstage, organizing everyone. "Act Two's about to begin."

There was a fierce buzz of activity and excitement as the actors prepared themselves.

Beau turned to leave, and Grace impulsively snatched his wrist. "Wait."

"What?" he spun back with a bark.

She gave him a soft smile and whispered, "Break a leg.

Do it for me." She added in a wink, and a small grin curled his lips.

His beautiful gaze softened with a look that made her heart warm before he walked for the curtain, lining up beside Colette and looking so gorgeous that Grace could barely breathe.

When he disappeared and walked onto the stage, Grace snuck up to the curtain to watch him. He was amazing—commanding, confident, the perfect Oberon.

The crowd lapped it up. Their laughter and cheers filled Grace's heart with pride. Beau was killing it, and she'd never enjoyed her favorite Shakespeare comedy more.

THE BOYFRIEND CARD

.

The show was a huge success, with three nights of performances plus two matinees. Everyone was exhausted but on a high after the final Saturday night performance. The after-party carried on to the early hours of the morning, and Beau let out a soft groan as he woke to daylight streaming through his windows. He'd forgotten to shut the drapes when he got home. Squinting against the brightness, he checked his watch and was pleasantly surprised to see it was already ten o'clock. Nothing like a slow start to a Sunday morning. He'd earned the lie-in.

Acting more like a tortoise than a hare, he crawled out of bed and slowly got himself dressed and ready. He didn't know what the day held, but he hoped to catch a few moments with Grace. After their tense week and then a few days drowned in *Midsummer Night's Dream* mania, he felt he'd hardly seen her and couldn't shake the yearning within him.

It was crazy.

How had he gone from wanting to steer clear of this girl to finding every excuse to be around her?

How had he gone from insulting her behind her back to bristling every time one of his friends put her down? He didn't know if he agreed with her whole stance on letting them insult her like that. He wanted to tell them all to shut the hell up, although she did have a point about staying on Colette's good side. But did he really want to be dominated by his friends this way?

Ugh. He didn't know.

Running a hand through his hair, he winced at the remains of hairspray still clinging to the locks and decided to have a quick shower.

His mind ran through the weekend as he relived the applause and praise lavished on him after every performance. It'd been pretty damn awesome, but he owed some of that success to Grace. She'd turned him into Oberon. She'd helped him with his lines. She'd inspired him.

He needed to do something to show her how much he appreciated her.

Cutting his shower short, he rushed to get dressed and head downstairs. Even though it was Leola's day off, he crossed his fingers that he'd find them in the kitchen. And he was in luck. Grace sat at the counter, nibbling on a piece of buttered toast and nursing a steaming mug of something that smelled freaking amazing.

"I'll have what she's having." Beau slid onto a stool with a broad smile.

Leola turned with a little laugh. "It's my day off, so the bread is over there. I'm assuming you know how to work a toaster." The woman grinned and winked at him while Grace covered her mouth to hide her giggle. "However, since you worked so hard the last few nights, I will make you a latte."

"Thank you, Leola." Beau gave her a chagrined smile and walked to the toaster. As he opened the bread bag and put two slices in, he glanced over his shoulder at Grace. She was grinning at him over her mug, her hair all mussed up and wild, her brown gaze softly telling him he was the only guy in the room.

He wondered if she knew she was doing it or not.

While his bread cooked, he turned and studied her, mirroring her expression. She jolted, her eyes growing wide with vulnerability before her cheeks flushed pink.

His smile grew a little wider, and he was struck with an overwhelming desire to kiss those lips of hers. If her mother hadn't been standing right there, clearing her throat and giving him a pointed look, maybe he would have.

He spun back to butter his toast and made sure his smile was extra grateful when Leola handed him his coffee.

"So, Oberon. I know you've already heard this from your rampant fans, but you should know I thought you did a wonderful job." Leola patted his hand and nodded. "My Gracie made you look the part, and your acting was *very* good."

"Thank you." He sipped the coffee and nearly moaned at how good it tasted. "I had so much fun. And Grace was amazing." He turned to her. "That crown thing you made was incredible."

She grinned. "I like that we changed it up just a little with each performance."

"My favorite one was the last one you did. That was cool."

"Yeah, me too. I really loved that one."

"You have your father's talent," Leola murmured. Beau couldn't decide if it was a reluctant confession or not. Grace's mother bit into her toast and kept her eyes on the breakfast island they were sitting at.

He glanced at Grace, who was gazing at him with a dopey grin. As soon as their eyes connected, she flinched like she'd been busted, and he enjoyed that sweet blush again. He winked at her and gave her a dopey grin of his own, then started chatting about his favorite parts of the Shakespearean experience. They laughed over Puck's blunder at the first matinee, which he turned into a comical routine that made the middle school students giggle. They rolled their eyes at Hermia's hysterics, but they ended up laughing at that too. She calmed down by the third performance and ended up being a hit.

The morning passed by while they dissected the show, and Beau couldn't believe how content he felt hanging out with Grace and her mother. He had no idea where his parents were, and he almost hoped they didn't appear. His father would only create a cool wind to ice down the kitchen. He'd given him a gruff "Good job" after the one performance he came to, whereas his mother had been to every single one, and her over-the-top gushing to anyone within a ten-foot radius had become painful.

It was too much, and he seriously was not in the mood for it.

There was something so natural and genuine about Leola and Grace. It made him feel like a better human being just hanging out with them.

A knock sounded at the door, and an instant disappointment rushed through Beau. He hoped it wasn't one of his friends showing up unannounced to disrupt the fun he was having. He crossed his fingers that it wasn't one of his mother's friends that he'd have to say hello to either. He just wanted the world to leave them all alone and not pop this happy bubble he was floating in.

"I'll get it." Leola rose with a grin and walked out of the kitchen.

Grace traced a pattern on her plate through the toast crumbs, then licked the tip of her finger. He watched her every move, wondering what that would have tasted like, imagining the feel of her tongue touching his. He swallowed, surprised by just how strong his desire really was.

He wanted to reach for her. Just one touch.

Resting his hand on the counter, he inched his fingers across the marble but was suddenly stopped when Leola returned with a tight smile. Her expression was anything but happy, and her voice was small and strained.

"Grace, your father's here."

She jolted upright, blinked a couple times, then shot out of her chair and ran into the entrance. "Dad!"

"Hey, kidlet," a deep voice boomed.

Beau watched Leola frown, her jaw tensing as she cleared plates off the counter and started wiping it clean with a ferocity he'd never seen before. Her black eyebrows dipped into a sharp V as the conversation carried into the kitchen.

"What are you doing here?" Grace asked.

"I came to watch the performance last night. Had to check out the makeup and costumes."

"Aw. That's so nice. Why didn't you tell me you were coming?"

"Well, I wanted to wait around after the show, but Scarlett wasn't feeling that well, so…"

Leola winced, her skin paling, and Beau nearly asked her if she was okay, but he wanted to hear the rest of Grace's conversation with her dad.

Actually, he wanted to get up and sneak a peek into the entranceway at the Hollywood makeup man with the booming voice.

"Scarlett's here?"

Beau nearly missed Grace's question. Her voice was soft and so obviously trying to be kind.

"Yeah, she wanted to come too."

There was a pause, and Beau couldn't help leaning a little closer to the entrance. Leola had started drying dishes with hurried movements, working like it wasn't her day off. Her ponytail swung when she spun around to start putting pots into the drawer beneath the gas cooktop.

Beau didn't know what to say or if he should leave. Something uneasy stirred in his stomach and he stayed put, not wanting to leave Leola when she was obviously so upset.

"Anyway, I thought I might take you out for the afternoon before I have to fly back to LA tonight."

"Uh… yeah, that'd be fun. I can show you a few places

I've found. Or we could check out the Darien Historical Society. I've been wanting to go to it."

Beau raised his eyebrows. He didn't know she was interested in that place. He could have taken her.

Really? You would have taken her?

He frowned, annoyed that his answer used to be a resounding no. A scoffing no. An "Are you kidding me?" no.

Why had he been such a prick when she first arrived?

"Okay," Grace's father said. "Yeah, sounds good, sweets. Why don't you go get ready?"

"Well, I've just finished breakfast, so we can get going right now. I'll just tame my hair and put some shoes on."

Beau could hear the smile in Grace's voice and couldn't help a grin of his own. She was cute.

"You… um… don't want to…" Mr. Bellamy's deep voice faltered.

"Want to what?" Grace asked.

Beau tensed when he noticed Leola's nostrils flare.

Straining not to miss one word, he listened in and heard a sigh. "Sweetie, why don't you go put some makeup on? Scarlett hasn't met you yet, and maybe it'd be easier if we… you know, ease her in. Plus, if we're going all over town, wouldn't you prefer to be covered up?"

Leola slammed the plastic container she was drying onto the counter, muttering something under her breath.

"I'm happy to wait." Grace's father sounded like he was doing her a favor.

More mutterings gushed out of Leola's mouth. They were in a foreign language, and Beau could tell they weren't pretty. He was beginning to understand the frenetic kitchen cleaning since Mr. Bellamy had arrived.

"Oh, I guess I can..." Grace's voice was growing smaller by the syllable. "I... I don't want anyone to be uncomfortable."

Leola let out a soft scream and noticed Beau watching her. Stormy eyes stared back at him, but the anger quickly morphed to a look of sad desperation.

"Even her father can't accept her the way she is," she whispered, tears lining her lashes.

Beau jumped out of his seat before he could think better of it. He didn't know what he was doing, but he strolled into the entrance with a confident smile plastered on his face.

"Hey." He walked up to the broad man towering in the doorway and extended his hand. "Mr. Bellamy, right? I'm Beau Griffin."

The man nodded like he didn't really care but extended his hand anyway. "Hi, Beau."

After they shook, Beau glanced at Grace. She gave him a tentative smile, then murmured, "I'll go get ready."

Before she could retreat, Beau swung his arm around her waist and pulled her close. Ignoring her surprise, he looked up at her father and asked, "So, where are you whisking my girlfriend off to today?"

Every eye in the room bulged with surprise, but he kept his grin in place and decided he was going with the lie for as long as he possibly could. Grace needed someone in her corner today, and even though he probably could have called himself her friend, there was something way more powerful about playing the boyfriend card.

ALL FOR SHOW

What was Beau doing?

Did he just say he was my boyfriend?

She wanted to correct that mistake immediately, but she was too surprised to say anything.

You can't lie to your father!

She opened her mouth, but when she looked up at her dad, she noticed his expression had changed. He looked impressed, his eyebrows rising when he caught Grace's eye. His silent message seemed to say, *"Wow. He's a catch."*

Why would he think that? Grace wondered. Her father didn't know Beau at all.

But he's beautiful, and appearance matters, remember?

She dipped her gaze to the floor, struggling to control her erratic heartbeat and find the courage to end this charade. Beau would never be her boyfriend, and she didn't even know why he wanted to pretend. What was he playing at?

He couldn't just spring this on her. Why was he even doing it?

For a second, she wondered if this was some kind of sick prank, but when she glanced up to frown at Beau, he was gazing at her with such sweetness, she couldn't help but sink into it.

His subtle wink made her feel like they were in on this together, and when he turned to her father and asked, "Mind if I tag along too?" she couldn't deny him.

"Not at all." Her father grinned, throwing in another eyebrow wiggle.

Grace internally cringed but forced a smile. "I'll... go get ready."

"Your shoes are right here." Beau pointed at the cupboard by the front door where everyone kept their shoes. Grabbing out the pair she seemed to wear the most, he plopped them in front of her feet, then started putting on his own shoes.

He then snatched his wallet out of the top drawer and slipped his phone into his back pocket.

"Right, let's go." He threaded his fingers through hers and started walking for the door.

Grace tensed, waiting for her father to say, "Hold up. Grace isn't ready yet."

But he didn't.

For some bizarre reason, he seemed to have forgotten about his earlier request... or maybe he just wasn't willing to say anything in front of Beau, who was acting like she was the most beautiful thing on the planet.

If anything, he was putting it on a little strong. Was any boyfriend ever that doting?

When her father turned to walk out the door, she

frowned at Beau, but he just winked again and whispered in her ear, "Just go with it. Do it for me."

Her gaze was withering, but his adorable grin was too cute to deny. In the end, she snickered and shook her head. "You're crazy."

His smile grew, and he called over his shoulder, "See ya, Leola. We're heading out for the afternoon."

She popped her head out of the kitchen with a grateful smile. Her mother's glistening gaze landed on her, and Grace suddenly understood.

Her mother would have heard that conversation and been furious at her father's request to ease Scarlett in. Beau must have stepped up to help her out. He was doing this to get Grace out the door just as she was.

He was doing this for her mother.

Grace had no idea why he was pretending to be her boyfriend in order to do that, but he'd just asked her to go with it, so she lightly squeezed his hand and let him pull her out the door.

"See ya, Mom."

"Have fun." Her voice had lost its strain, and her smile was relaxed as Grace shut the door and followed her father to his rental car.

It felt weird having such a handsome guy holding her hand… or any guy for that matter. As they drove into town to meet up with Scarlett, who was waiting for them at a café, she was sure they'd be getting stared at all afternoon. But would they be staring at him or her?

It felt weird to know that they were a total contrast. He got looked at because he was so hot and gorgeous. She got looked at because of her hideous scars.

Maybe she should have covered up?

Ugh. Why was Beau doing this to her?

His thumb lightly rubbed the back of her hand as they drove into town together.

Her father chatted happily with Beau, finding out about him and raving over his performance in the school play. He'd only just realized that Beau had played Oberon.

Grace sat there quietly analyzing it all and feeling worse by the minute. Why had her father brushed off the makeup request? Was it only because of Beau?

So, as long as she wasn't an outcast and had a hot boyfriend, the scars were acceptable, but without those things, they weren't?

If felt wrong somehow, but why was she complaining?

Beau was holding her hand!

He was giving her sweet smiles and talking to her dad like he was trying to impress him. Like it mattered, because he needed to win the big guy over in order to date his daughter.

You have got to put a stop to this charade!

But it was too late. If she came clean now, she'd make Beau look like an idiot. She'd just have to call her father in a few days and casually say they had broken up or something.

The idea killed her. Beau was being a sweet, attentive boyfriend, putting on the best show.

She could get used to this!

It was kind of heartbreaking to know it was all pretend.

WHICH DRESS IS YOUR FAVORITE?

Beau liked holding Grace's hand. Her skin was soft, and her elegant fingers curved around his knuckles perfectly. Sure, her palm was a little sweaty, but he put that down to nerves. She'd basically been vibrating with them since his spontaneous "you're my girlfriend" announcement, and he'd do anything to calm her down.

He wanted her to enjoy the afternoon with her father.

He wanted her to feel protected.

That's all it is. You're just doing her a favor. This is your way of thanking her for the Oberon-makeup thing.

He thought it like he meant it, but as he closed the car door after Grace and took her hand again, he couldn't help feeling like he could get used to this very quickly.

Smiling at her, his insides turned to goo when she shared a secret grin with him before slipping on her shades. He missed that brown gaze immediately, but at least they still had a physical connection.

He lifted their joined hands to his mouth and lightly

kissed her knuckles. Her cheeks flared red, and she bit her bottom lip.

Yeah, he did want to kiss her.

The thought surprised him yet again, but in spite of himself, he started wondering if he could use the boyfriend charade to steal a kiss before the afternoon was done.

"Scarlett." Mr. Bellamy raised his hand and caught his girlfriend's attention.

She was a petite blonde with a strong Marilyn Monroe vibe. So much so that Beau wondered if she was actually *trying* to look like the iconic actress. Jumping up from her spot with a bright smile, she kissed Grace's father on the mouth before turning to say hi.

"This is my daughter… Grace." His voice trailed off at the end. He'd obviously just remembered that Grace had left the house makeup free, and it was hitting him that his request hadn't been followed through with.

Grace extended her hand and even took it one step further, taking off her shades to reveal her slightly drooping eye.

Scarlett swallowed and forced a bright smile, shaking Grace's hand and so obviously trying not to study her scars.

"You can look," Grace said boldly. "Everyone else does."

"Grace," her father softly reprimanded. "Don't be rude."

"I'm not. I just… I don't want her to feel uncomfortable."

"Which is why you should have gotten ready like I

177

asked you to," her father murmured, but everyone heard it anyway.

Beau's hackles went up, and he squeezed Grace's hand, saying probably a little too loudly, "I think she's beautiful just the way she is."

With a pointed look at the couple across the table, Beau pulled out a chair for Grace to sit down.

She caught his eye, and he wondered if she was thinking, *You sound just like my mother!*

Well, good! He hoped he did.

Leola was right. Grace shouldn't have to hide. Those scars were part of who she was, but they didn't make her ugly. Nothing could. She was a beautiful person, and Beau wished he hadn't taken so long to see it.

Her father squirmed and then attempted to make awkward small talk, but Grace saved him easily, turning the conversation to focus on Scarlett. Like most people, the woman liked to talk about herself, and Grace's questions seemed to relax her father's girlfriend and get her talking about how amazing Hollywood was and how much she loved acting.

Grace then drew Beau into the conversation, and they talked Shakespeare while they drank coffee and nibbled on cake. By the time they were done, everyone seemed to have found a happy groove, and they went to the museum together. Beau had always thought the Darien Historical Society was lame, but Grace saw things differently, and before he knew it, he was admiring the intricate crafts-manship of the historic dresses on display and agreeing with Grace's comments about how so much care was put into the finer details back then.

"I think it's sad that we've lost that... although I understand it, of course. Society values different things now. Not that it's a bad thing, but..." She shook her head, her smile a little dreamy as she gazed at the dressed mannequins. "Wow. Those really are stunning." She turned to him. "Which one's your favorite?"

"Uh..." He shrugged, then cast his eye along the line of dresses. "Maybe that one?" He pointed to the red one with the intricate flower pattern sewn into the skirt.

"Nice choice. Although, I wonder what it was like to wear a corset. If it made women feel pretty or imprisoned."

"I'm guessing it depended on the woman."

"True. I still think that today." Grace giggled. "Some people wear clothes that look so uncomfortable. You know, like those red-carpet events where the dresses have to be taped to the skin just to keep them in place and the shoes are so high. I don't know how ankles don't get snapped." She shook her head. "That is just so not me."

Beau grinned. "What makes you feel pretty?" He ran his hand down her back and shifted a little closer to her. She struggled to answer, and he lightly squeezed her waist. "Come on. What would make you feel like a million bucks if you walked out the door wearing it?"

"Um..." She let out an awkward laugh, tucking her hair behind her ear. "I don't really..."

"Come on, Grace. Indulge me."

Her eyes darted to his, so big and beautiful, the hint of a smile lighting those brown orbs. "I guess I'm most comfortable in—"

"No, I'm not talking comfort. I'm talking *I'm the queen of the ball* pretty."

Her smile grew wide, but her forehead wrinkled into a frown. "I'll never be queen of the ball."

The soft statement hurt him right in the center of his chest, and he gently spun her to face him. "You'd be the queen of my ball. Every time."

She studied him like she was trying to figure out if he was serious or not.

He was.

Oh man, he was.

A smile tugged at his lips, and he whispered, "I'm serious."

A soft pink hue filled her cheeks, and she looked to the floor, like she wasn't sure if she could believe him.

He wanted to tell her that she could. That he was sorry to ever make her doubt it. That he shouldn't have been so rude to her when they first met. That he hated the way he'd treated her.

But then she started mumbling something about a ball gown she'd once seen that was covered in butterflies.

"They were blue and purple, and it was the most beautiful dress I'd ever seen." She pulled out her phone and searched for the image.

Beau used the excuse to lean over her shoulder and get as close to her as possible.

"Wow. That is gorgeous." He stared at the phone, softly inhaling the scent of Grace's shampoo.

"Right?" She enlarged the image. "The entire bodice is butterflies."

"You should wear it to prom."

She bulged her eyes at his suggestion.

"It's coming up… in about a month or so."

After a breathy laugh, she shook her head. "I won't be going to prom."

"Why not? It's a junior/senior event. You're invited."

"By who?"

"Uh… the school."

"No." She closed her eyes, her closed-mouth smile kind of sad and resigned. "Who would take me? No one at Lincoln Academy is going to ask me to be their date."

He stared at her, wishing he could but sensing how impossible that would be. Walk in the door with Grace on his arm? His friends would completely flip out.

"You don't have to have a date to go," he offered. "You could be like Cinderella."

She giggled. "And would you be the prince I dance with?"

"Yeah." He nodded. "If you came to prom, I'd totally dance with you."

"No, you wouldn't." She shook her head with another giggle. "Your friends would be horrified. It seriously wouldn't be worth it."

He hated to think she might be right. His friends would hassle him, be confused, get mad… and then probably punish Grace. He didn't want that to happen to her.

Beau gave her a sad frown but couldn't help following it up with a smile. He did like the idea of dancing with her.

"What are you two talking about?" Mr. Bellamy approached, and Beau took a small step back but kept his hand around Grace's waist.

She showed him the picture, and then Scarlett came over and started oohing and aahing over the image before launching into a story about her favorite gown. It went on for a while, but Grace stayed attentive and kind like she always did.

Scarlett seemed young and a little flighty, which was a weird thing for Beau to think considering he was only sixteen, but he felt like he was hanging out with a high school student, and that was a massive contrast to Leola.

He studied the side of Mr. Bellamy's face and was still trying to decide what he thought of the guy. Appearance obviously mattered to him, and Beau understood that. He'd grown up around it and was aware of every stare and double glance they got from people.

Usually they were looks of admiration, but today they were a mix. It made his insides burn, and he wanted to cover Grace just so she didn't have to put up with it.

Maybe that was where Mr. Bellamy was coming from.

Beau couldn't get the thought out of his mind as they drove back to the house. Leola wanted to display Grace to the world to make the point that her daughter was enough the way she was. Mr. Bellamy wanted Grace to cover up so she didn't have to put up with people's reactions.

Did they both have a point?

Which one of them was right?

"Thanks, Dad. I had a really good time." Grace hugged her father and was engulfed by his big arms. He kissed the top of her head and stood back.

"It was fun. Thanks for being so nice to Scarlett. You've got a heart of gold, you know that?" He lightly pinched her chin, his smile a little sad before he let her go and stepped back to shake Beau's hand. "Thanks for looking after my girl."

"My pleasure, sir."

Mr. Bellamy's grip tightened, and Beau could see the warning in his eyes. *"Don't you hurt her."*

Beau nodded and stepped back, the silent threat making him feel raw and exposed. They waved goodbye to the departing vehicle, then slowly wandered into the house. No one seemed to be around, and they paused in the front entrance.

"Well…" Grace lost her words, her mouth opening and closing before she gave up and shook her head.

"Did you have a good time?"

She shrugged. "Yeah. I mean, it was fun hanging out with you and playing pretend, but… it also felt weird being around my dad and this new woman." Her nose wrinkled. "She's so different from Mom."

"Yeah, totally." Beau ran his hand down her arm. "I like your mom better."

She grinned. "Me too." Blinking, she looked to the floor. "I really wish it hadn't fallen apart for them. I wish they were still together." With a heavy sigh, she slipped off her shoes and put them away. "I just wish I'd never been attacked by that dog. It didn't just change my life, it… changed theirs too. It was the beginning of the end, you know? They just couldn't agree over what to do with me after that, and… and logically, I know this doesn't make sense, but it's hard not to blame myself for their marriage failing."

Her voice wobbled, and Beau pulled her into a hug. "It's not your fault."

"I know. But emotions and logic don't always match, and sometimes it's hard to believe the right thing."

He stepped back so he could look at her face. Tears had escaped, and he caught the trails with his thumbs. Those brown eyes gazed up at him, so vulnerable and bright with emotion.

You're beautiful.

He wanted to tell her, but his throat was too clogged to speak.

So he showed her instead.

Resting his hand lightly on her neck, he leaned forward and drew her toward him. Their lips met for the briefest moment before she pulled back with a gasp.

"What are you doing?" She touched her mouth with trembling fingers.

"Sorry." He winced, his heart thrumming out of time. He'd never had a girl react to him like this before, and he felt his skin heat with embarrassment. "I just... I wanted to kiss you."

Her eyes bulged. "But why? I mean, Dad's gone now. You don't have to keep pretending."

His heart kicked out of rhythm. No, he didn't.

But maybe he wanted to.

With a smile that felt kind of shy and foreign, he watched her carefully before reaching for her soft brown hair and rubbing it between his fingers. "Grace." He whispered her name like it was sacred.

She blinked up at him, and he wondered if her heart was beating as fast as his was.

"Do you, uh... do you want to kiss me?"

Her swallow was thick and audible, and for a second, he thought she was going to shake her head. But then her lips twitched and she gave him a nod, her voice wobbling when she croaked, "Yeah. I do."

Relief flooded him, and he slowly stepped back into her space. Running his finger down the side of her cheek, he leaned forward and whispered, "Then you know why."

Her gaze started to glisten with a smile, like she couldn't quite believe this was happening.

"I'm scared," she rushed out just before their lips connected.

He paused. "Of a kiss?"

"Of falling in love with you."

Wow. Step back. She's falling in love with me?

Instinct told him to turn and run, bolt through that door so fast he'd leave a Beau-shaped space in that stained glass window.

But for some reason, he stayed.

For some reason, he kept holding her cheeks.

For some reason, he admitted, "I'm scared too."

Was he? Should he be saying that to her?

Yes, because it's true.

Holy shit, it's true!

Resting his hand on her hip, he pulled her a little closer and waited for her reaction. He felt like he was playing with an open flame, daring himself to be burned to a crisp.

Her soft breath hit his chin, her brown eyes still trying to work it out. Trying to decide if this was actually real.

It is. He wanted to reassure her, but he couldn't speak.

He couldn't do anything but gaze at her and hope.

Hope.

Hope.

Resting her hand on his chest, she glided her fingers up and over his shoulder before curling them around his neck and beckoning him forward.

It seemed to take an age to reach her, but then those sweet lips were touching his, and he sank into the kiss like he was experiencing the sensation for the very first time. She was sweet and pure, her lips tentative, yet he could sense an eagerness too.

Taking a risk, he deepened the kiss, his insides lighting like fireworks when her breath caught, and then she touched her tongue to his.

23

KISSING BEAU

It was the best feeling she'd ever had.

Grace sank into the kiss like she was born to do it. To kiss Beau.

How is this happening?

He's kissing me!

Curling her arm around his neck, she pulled herself against him even more. As their bodies pressed together, her heart went into overdrive.

People talked about the wonders of kissing, but she'd never really understood it… until now.

Until Beau opened her heart to a whole new dimension. The feel of his tongue sweeping against her was heady and addictive. A soft moan grew in her throat. She couldn't stop it if she wanted to.

Beau drew back, and her heart froze, fear sizzling through her as she waited for the inevitable.

It was a prank. He didn't mean it.

Or… she wasn't a good kisser. He didn't like it.

Or…

Beau tipped his head the other way before diving in for another taste of her.

Of her!

He wanted her.

It didn't seem believable, and Grace's brain jarred her with that reality, beating her over the head with it. Her body wasn't done with this kiss, but her brain was doing everything in its power to ruin the moment for her.

Easing back, she rested her hands on his shoulders and pushed herself away. Just a little. Enough to be able to breathe and maybe attempt thinking straight.

Shaking her head, she let out a soft laugh. "You kissing me is so not going to help on the 'not falling in love with you' thing. You have no idea."

His eyes lit with a tender smile that she was pretty sure she could drown in. Her gasping heart was barely functioning as it was.

"I'm starting to get an idea," he murmured, then leaned in to continue their make-out session.

She pulled back.

He was getting an idea?

What?

No. That wasn't possible.

He was Beau… beautiful, popular Beau. He had no idea. How could he possibly fall for her?

Studying her face, he went quiet for a moment, like he was searching for the right words to say. She gripped his shirt and waited, needing to move away yet unable to do it.

Beau licked his bottom lip and blushed. "You know… that terror of liking someone that…" He shook his head.

He liked her?

This didn't seem real somehow.

How could it be?

He could have any girl he wanted. How could he possibly understand the terror of falling for someone?

She stepped so far back, she bumped into the side table. Embarrassed, she wrapped her arms around herself and walked into the dining room.

Distance. The ability to inhale a full breath. That was what she needed.

Surely those things would help calm her thundering heart.

He followed her, and she nearly let out a whining whimper.

"Grace? Are you okay?"

She bit her lips together and spoke her fear before she could stop herself. "You don't have to be nice to me out of guilt or anything. I really appreciate what you did for me today, with Dad and everything, but you don't have to keep pretending. I don't need your pity."

His beautiful face scrunched into a frown. "Uh… what?"

She bit her bottom lip, feeling bad for insulting him. "I'm sorry, I just—"

"I'd *never* kiss you out of pity." His frown was still in place as he walked toward her, so she turned her back to him. Making him angry was not helping with her erratic heartbeat. But then his hands gently touched her arms, sliding down to her elbows and around her waist. His voice turned soft and light when he rested his chin on her shoulder and whispered, "I kissed you because I wanted to. Because I couldn't do anything else."

"And what does that mean?" She turned within his embrace so she could see him.

She had to know the truth, to study his face, hunting for the smallest hint that he might be lying.

He smiled down at her, brushing a lock of her hair behind her ear. "It means I like you. And you like me. And we should probably kiss again."

She narrowed her eyes, hunting... still hunting... but all she could find was a sweet honesty.

Her skin heated instantly, her body crying out a hallelujah.

He means it! He likes me!

She fought a grin, her nose wrinkling as she once again strove for reality. "Your friends will hate it."

"They don't have to know."

Grace's brow wrinkled, and he let out a soft laugh.

Ducking down a little so they were eye to eye, he winked at her, his gaze glinting with delight. "A secret relationship would be so fun, don't you think?"

She bit her lip.

"We could sneak out of class, meet up in quiet corners, steal kisses in the library. And none of my people would suspect a thing."

He made it sound so daring... so thrilling.

"It's just a way of keeping you safe. I like looking after you." He pulled her against him, kissing the side of her head. "Those narrow-minded jerks will never get it. And I don't want you in their line of fire." He leaned back so she could see his face. "We'll be like spies, sharing secret looks when we pass each other." He started wiggling his eyebrows at her.

She giggled, and he kissed her smile.

He kissed her like it was the most natural thing in the world.

And she liked it.

No, she loved it.

Rising to her tiptoes, she tentatively kissed him back, then found her arms wrapping around him once more. She wanted to believe in everything he was saying.

A secret relationship with Beau.

The gorgeous guy who liked her.

It seemed surreal.

Too good to be true.

Grace shut her eyes against the idea that maybe it was. That someday soon this would all fall apart, and she'd be left a tattered mess.

Don't go there. Just be in this moment with him.

Be Beau's girl and relish every second of it.

24

BEAU'S GIRL

Secret dating.

Beau had never done it before, but the idea kind of thrilled him.

As they drove to school together the next morning, Beau couldn't wipe the grin off his face. Kissing Grace had been freaking magical, and he couldn't quite believe it. They'd spent the rest of the day making out, then snuggling on the couch in the movie room watching *Stardust*. When Grace's mom got home and came to find them, Grace jumped off him like she'd been electrocuted. They'd scrambled to opposite ends of the couch, the picture of innocence when her head popped around the corner. After a breezy conversation, she'd finally left them to it, and they'd erupted into a fit of laughter, crawling back toward each other and kissing all over again.

The day had been perfect. The evening had been just as good, spent in the library where he taught her how to play chess. She got the gist of the game but wasn't the most natural player. But he loved every second of her smiling face and sweet titter as she lost spectacularly three times in a row.

He was pretty sure he floated to bed after a secret kiss at the top of the stairs.

He'd never expected to fall for someone like her. In fact, he kind of didn't know what had come over him, but man, it felt good.

Taking her hand, he drew it to his lips and kissed her knuckles.

"You good?" he asked.

"Yeah." Her smile was sweet, and he saw the beauty in it.

She looked different to the way she used to be, and he couldn't understand how he was once disgusted by her.

Shame scorched him and he clenched his jaw, determined to never make her feel that way again.

Slowing the car, he pulled into the academy. Grace reclaimed her hand and tucked it under her leg, her body tensing like it always did.

"It's okay. Now that the production's over, you don't have to deal with Colette anymore."

"*You* still have to." She frowned.

"Yeah." He shrugged. "But I've got a secret weapon now."

"What's that?" Her confusion was cute, and he grinned at her.

"I've got this amazing girlfriend with the sweetest lips and the most beautiful eyes… and just knowing she's mine will get me through the day unscathed."

Her blush made his heart warm, and he wished she'd say something reassuring back, like "Secretly dating you is the best thing that's ever happened to me." But she bit her lips together, looking around the school as they drove in.

He parked and wanted to kiss her goodbye, but she slipped out of the car before he could even touch her. Probably a good thing since Colette, Ella, and Etan were heading his way.

Shutting his car door, he sauntered over to them, checking once on Grace as she hustled to her locker. His friends gathered around him and started talking about how awesome they all were in the play. Colette pouted that she hadn't seen Beau yesterday and he hadn't even bothered replying to her texts.

"I crashed out." He shrugged. "Barely got out of bed. Weren't you exhausted after last week?"

"I obviously have more stamina than you," she giggled, wiggling her eyebrows at him.

He returned her seductive grin with a tight smile and glanced away from it. Grace had disappeared from sight now, and he felt the loss. He wished she could be standing right beside him, but he knew that was a no-go. His friends wouldn't understand how the beast (ugh! Had he seriously thought of her that way?) had grown on him, how her sweetness and purity had gotten under his skin... made him want to be good enough for her.

They would never understand that she was the best of them all. That *she* was the one they should be striving to be like. That she was the most beautiful girl in the school.

They'd probably fall all over each laughing and then be on the warpath with only one target: Grace Bellamy.

If you can change, maybe they will too.

The idea was tempting, but he decided to play it safe and keep his mouth shut.

He couldn't just ditch his friend group; the backlash wouldn't be worth it. He had to play this right. A time would come when they'd soften up to Grace. Surely it would, right?

She'd work her way into their hearts, just like she worked her way into his.

The thought settled him, and he followed his friends into school, trying to concentrate on what Julius was saying and not search the hallways for a pair of sweet brown eyes.

He didn't see Grace for the rest of the morning, and by lunchtime, he couldn't help himself. Sneaking into the library, he wove through the shelving and found her in a back corner. There was a small seating area, cast in light, with two couches. She was on her own, pencil in hand and completely absorbed in a sketch. Her frown of concentration was adorable as she chewed on the edge of her pencil, then switched to a cashew nut. She had a small bag of trail mix that she was nibbling on, and he watched her with a smile as he quietly approached.

"Hey," he whispered just before he reached her.

She jumped, slapping the sketchbook against her chest. "What are you doing here?"

"Just had to see ya." He crouched down to peck her lips, and she drew back with a soft laugh, her face filled with wonder. "I told you secret dating would be the best." He winked, and she rested her hand on his cheek. "What are you drawing?"

Her smile morphed into a wince, her nose wrinkling. "I don't know if I want to show you."

"Why not?"

"It's embarrassing."

"Oh, come on. Be brave."

She hissed and spun the book in her hands, revealing a pencil sketch of his face.

His lips parted, the air in his lungs evaporating as he stared at himself. He was smiling, his eyes tender with affection... and he'd never seen himself like that before.

"I still have to work on the shading around your chin, but..."

"This is how you see me?" he whispered.

"Yeah. I mean... you looked at me like that when we were playing chess last night, and I think my heart kind of melted a little bit." Her voice caught, and she let out a shaky laugh. "I hope you don't mind that I drew you."

"I love it." He couldn't get his voice past soft or wispy. He was awestruck by her talent, by the care she'd taken with him. She really did like him, and it made him feel...

He blinked and swallowed, rasping out a compliment that didn't seem enough. "You are... incredible."

Her cheeks flushed pink, her smile kind and gentle. "No, I'm just me."

"Incredible you." He handed back the book with a pointed gaze.

She shook her head and giggled, quickly changing the topic. "You having a good day?"

"Yeah, it's going okay. You?"

She bobbed her head, her smile growing. "I spent my free period in the art room, so I'm a happy girl." She wiggled her paint-stained fingers, and he grabbed them, kissing the tips.

His phone dinged and he ignored it, leaning in to kiss her smile.

She giggled into his mouth. "Aren't you worried we'll get caught?"

"That's all part of the thrill," he murmured against her lips before deepening the kiss.

His phone dinged again.

And he cupped the back of her head, sweeping his tongue into her mouth.

His phone dinged once more.

And he relished her delicate moan, gently sucking her bottom lip before changing angles and stealing another taste of her.

His phone dinged yet again.

Pulling back with a sigh, he checked the screen and rolled his eyes. "They're looking for me. I better go."

"Okay." Grace smiled. "Thanks for the lunchtime kiss. I've never had one of those before."

"Well, I have plenty to spare, so get used to it." He winked and stood tall when his phoned dinged for the fifth time in two minutes. Leaning back down, he kissed her one more time and let out a soft moan of approval when she swiped her tongue across his bottom lip.

He teased her mouth open and melted against the thrilling taste of her. She didn't seem to mind, gripping his collar and pulling him in close.

He kissed her until his phone had sent him two more alerts.

She giggled. "Go."

He stood, then bent down to peck her lips again. She let him but then pushed him away with a laugh.

"Go."

With a sigh, he walked away... backward, so he could still keep looking at her.

"You're going to walk into—"

He hit the shelving, and she winced.

It hurt a little, but it was worth it. Her smile was adorable.

"See you after school."

"Bye." She waved at him, and he took a mental snapshot of her adoring grin, tucking it into his heart for the rest of the day and wishing he was talented enough to sketch it. He wouldn't mind a picture of her in his pocket that he could sneak out and gaze at.

"Hey! I'm talking to you."

A carrot stick hit his nose, and his friends all laughed when he jolted.

"What is your problem?" Colette asked.

"Nothing, I'm just tired."

"Seriously. Stop acting like such an old man."

He grinned at her, stealing a carrot stick off her plate and munching it. She gave him a simpering grin, but he couldn't get Grace's sweet gaze out of his head.

"Now, tell us what you think we should do for the prom after-party. It has to be something parent-free and epic." Colette drilled him with a look, but all he could do was shrug and think about the conversation he'd had with Grace.

Her not going to prom in a butterfly dress seemed like a sin against humanity.

"I say we leave right after the king and queen have been announced so we can get the real party started." Etan wiggled his eyebrows. "We can take over my pool house. I'll stock the fridge and get my brother to load up the liquor cabinet."

Zari let out a pleasant giggle, and Beau glanced down the table in time to see Amell kiss her shoulder and whisper something in her ear. He could only guess what he was suggesting with that look on her face.

He shifted his gaze back to Colette, who was grinning at Etan and making jokes about her crown. She was pretty confident about getting prom queen, but Zari was a strong contender, too, and she definitely didn't piss off as many people as Colette did.

Beau wished he could take Grace, but when he tried to imagine it, he couldn't get past his friends' confusion and contempt. They wouldn't want her at the after-party. She wouldn't want to go either. A booze-fest? That was so not her thing.

Was it his?

Well, yeah, partying it up had always been his thing, but... the idea of a romantic night with Grace suddenly seemed more appealing.

What the hell was happening to him?

He kinda loved it... although he found it confusing.

The rest of the afternoon was spent in an internal tennis match. He swung between loyalty to his friends and just wanting to be with Grace. He wished he could make the two worlds blend, but how?

It wouldn't work. This secret was keeping Grace safe, and he decided to focus on that. Protecting her made him feel like a man. Like he was doing the right thing. He'd just go to prom flying solo, then make up some excuse about his father *forcing* him to dance with Grace for at least one song. Yeah, that would work.

By the time the final bell rang, he was feeling settled about his decision, though he still couldn't wait to get out of there and spend a little private quality time with his girl.

He had to sit there waiting for Grace, much to Ella's confusion.

"Don't you just make the beast walk home?"

He gritted his teeth, resisting the urge to snap Ella's head off. He had to play it cool or word would spread like wildfire that he was standing up for her. Then Grace would no doubt be the one to get burned.

Determined to protect her, he forced himself to shrug and mutter, "My old man's being an ass about it. I have to take her to school and drive her home or he'll take the car away from me."

"Ugh. Parents suck."

He nodded, relieved when he saw Grace walking to the car with a serene look on her face. He'd come to recognize it as her armor. And it was beautiful. Hell, it was one of the first things that made him start to see her differently, the way she was able to stand up against the worst behavior with a look of such peaceful dignity. He knew she didn't always feel that way. Her tears in the library that night still haunted him. She was vulnerable, and that sent his protective instincts into overdrive.

Grace slipped into the car, obviously aware that Ella was watching her every move. She didn't say anything to either of them, buckling her seat belt and staring straight ahead.

Beau looked at Ella, rolling his eyes like this was such a drag.

Apparently his acting skills weren't just for the stage.

Ella giggled, throwing Grace a derisive smirk before sauntering off. Beau shot her a glare behind her back, then reversed out of the parking lot and drove home.

As soon as they pulled away from the school, they both relaxed and Beau cranked up the music, smiling when Grace sang the lyrics with gusto. Slipping his hand into hers, he gave it a light squeeze and took the long route home.

And that was the way he kept driving every day.

They fell into an easy routine filled with stolen kisses in the library at school and make-out sessions in his library at home—under the guise of studying, of course. They did study, but probably not as hard as their parents thought they were. Long drives filled their weekends and afternoons. They shared milkshakes, laughed together over their favorite sitcoms, and the days seemed to pass in a whirl.

If this was falling in love... it was the easiest thing in the world.

Life was great.

In fact, he couldn't see how it could be any better.

Well, other than the slightly icy treatment he was

getting from Leola. He didn't understand it. They'd been getting on pretty great, and he knew she appreciated the way he'd stuck up for Grace when her father came to visit, but something had shifted in the last week or so.

He wondered if she'd figured out that he and Grace were together. They'd managed to hide it so far, but secrets like this couldn't last forever.

Was she not happy about Grace dating him?

But why?

He knew he should probably ask, but he didn't want to know the truth, and so he made a concerted effort to stay polite and charming when Leola was around and then avoid her as much as he possibly could.

25

POISONOUS WORDS

Grace hummed the song "Heather on the Hill" in her head. It was such an earworm, but it was a good one, so she didn't mind. The Celtic vibe was playful and fun, and she'd been listening to Nathan Evans's album nonstop since it'd released. A smile curled her lips as she got swept up in the romantic lyrics, thinking of Beau and kissing in the moonlight as she ironed sheets and pillowcases to help her mother out.

Beau was hanging with the guys this afternoon, playing basketball. She missed him, but he needed to be with his friends, too, and it wasn't like she could go and watch. They'd want to know why she was there, and she didn't want to make things awkward for Beau.

Their secret romance was in place for a reason, and although it was challenging at times, it was also fun. Beau's kisses were the best, and she loved the way he made her feel. The way he watched her when they studied upstairs in the library, the way he smiled at her when she sang, the way he talked to her about everything from his hatred of quadratic equations and complex numbers to his passion for nice cars and every country in the world he wanted to visit.

More and more, Grace had let her guard down and they'd dreamed together, making plans to visit Stratford-upon-Avon where Shakespeare lived and seeing one of his plays performed outdoors in some English country garden. They talked about touring Italy and walking the streets of Paris.

Her smile grew as she remembered that afternoon, lying side by side and dreaming the hours away together. It was like they were the only two people on the planet... until Beau's phone started dinging and reality kicked back in.

She focused on the iron, running out the wrinkles in the bedsheets and glancing up when Leola stormed in. She'd been in a mood for the last few days, and she couldn't figure out why. Part of her wanted to ignore it, but it was the weekend, and she had time. Her mother would never let her stay grumpy for so long; wasn't she deserving of the same courtesy and care?

"Hey, um..." She set the iron upright and watched her mother shoving the laundry from the washing machine into the dryer. "You seem a little... not yourself. Is everything okay?"

She huffed and slammed the dryer door shut, poking at the buttons with force. They beeped urgently before the dryer started to whirr, and her mother finally spun to face her. Folding her arms, she stared at Grace, her look morphing from irritation to unrest. "Are you? Are you okay?"

Grace blinked in surprise. "Yes. Why wouldn't I be?"

Her mother gave her a pointed look, and Grace frowned in confusion. She wanted to say, "I can't read your mind," but Leola turned her back and started folding the basket of clean towels before she could. Her sigh was almost grating, and Grace wished she didn't have to work so hard for this.

But her mother was always patient with her, so she could extend the same consideration.

"Has something happened with Dad?"

Her mother swallowed, her voice a little croaky. "It's not that."

"Then what is it? Why are you struggling to tell me?"

Her mother spun back, fisting a towel in her hand and looking like she was about to cry. "I need to talk to you about Beau."

A tight knot instantly formed in Grace's chest. What about him? Had something happened? Was he okay?

Panic tore through her, and Grace had to stop ironing. She flicked off the switch and rested the iron upright again. Staring at her mother, she managed to rasp, "What do you mean? Has something happened?"

Leola nodded, her nostrils flaring. "I know you two are together."

A cold flush tore through Grace's body, but it was followed swiftly by relief. Beau was okay. This was just about them…

But wait. Why was her mother so upset? And how did she even know they were together?

Grace rubbed her forehead and was about to ask when her mother started speaking.

"I saw you two kissing in the library a few nights ago. It looked way too familiar to be a first-time thing." Her eyebrows rose. "I wanted to say something, but I've been trying to figure out how. I knew you liked him. The way you look at him sometimes..." She tutted and slapped down the towel. "I should have known. You've been different ever since your father's visit and Beau pulled that crazy fake-boyfriend move. I thought it was just for the afternoon!" She huffed and shook her head. "I didn't realize he was..." She trailed off with another sigh.

Grace took her time responding. She was trying to figure out why her mother was so upset about all this. Was she mad that Grace hadn't told her? Or was it something worse?

She chose her words carefully, fidgeting with the edge of the sheet as she decided to start with the worst. "Do you not want me dating Beau or something? I thought you liked him."

"I do! I mean, he's okay. I just..." Her shoulders slumped. "Why didn't you tell me?"

Grace bit her lips together, feeling bad. She usually told her mother everything. "Well, we... we thought it'd be best to keep the relationship a secret."

"Why?" Leola's gaze turned steely, and Grace flushed.

So this was it.

This was the problem.

She cleared her throat. "Well. It's... it's romantic."

"No, it's not. Tell me the truth." Her mother's tone was precise, to the point, in a way that left no room for BS.

Grace sighed, her insides writhing as she fought to

keep her tone light and unbothered. "It's… it's just easier that way. His friends don't like me, and—"

"Why don't they like you? Huh?" Another towel was snatched out of the basket and folded with such rapid, forceful movements that Grace almost felt sorry for the fabric. If Turkish cotton could bruise, that poor white towel would be black and blue.

Grace's jaw worked to the side, and she failed to respond quickly enough.

"Were you mean to them?" Her mother's tone was morphing from precise to sharp. Like little needles, the words poked at her, demanding the truth. Demanding that she start to see things for what they really were.

Grace wondered if she should lie, but her mother would never buy it, so she shook her head and admitted in a small voice, "No."

"So, they don't actually know you at all, but they don't like you because…" Leola spun her finger in the air, obviously expecting Grace to finish the sentence for her.

With a heavy sigh, she obeyed. "Because of the way I look."

"Exactly." Her mother slapped the counter. "And you're dating a boy who is hanging out with these people. Someone who wants to keep you a secret because he doesn't have the guts to admit to his friends how wonderful you are. That is *not* romantic."

"It is!" Grace argued, her voice suddenly rising. "He's trying to protect me."

Leola shook her head. "He's trying to hide you! Don't you see?"

Grace's heart started to thunder, and tears came out of

nowhere. She blinked at them, trying to deny the burning in her throat.

Her mother was wrong! Beau was *protecting* her!

"You don't get it," Grace whispered, then sniffed, willing the tears not to fall.

"Oh, I get it," her mother snapped. "I've seen it! Don't you think I know how much it hurts to have you rejected when you are the sweetest, most beautiful person I know?" Tears glassed her eyes as she shot a look at Grace, her face crumpling with sadness. "I don't want you dating some boy who is ashamed of you. I want you to be with someone who is proud to have you by his side. Who'll shout his love from the rooftops. Who will hold your hand in public and introduce you as his girlfriend. I want someone to take you to prom and dance with you in front of everybody!"

Grace looked to the floor. She was losing the tear battle. Her eyes were flooding, making it impossible to see clearly. Why was her mother saying this stuff? She was ruining the best thing that had ever happened to her!

Anger flared, but she couldn't let it show.

Instead, she tried to reason. "I care about him. We like each other. I'm falling in l—"

"Don't say it!" Leola held up her finger, her eyes blazing.

Grace's chin bunched, and she couldn't stop her tears for a moment longer.

They slid down her cheeks as her mother's shoulders deflated. The high tension in the room shifted to one of gentle sorrow as she reached out and took Grace's hands. "Don't say it unless you truly know it."

"I do."

Her mother's eyes glistened with tears of her own. "*Papillon,*" she whispered, caressing her face. "You deserve to be more than someone's secret."

The words were said with such compassion, but they still felt like a punch to the face.

Grace wriggled out of her mother's grasp and walked out the door. Her heart was pounding as she slashed tears off her cheeks. Racing to her room, she shouldered open the door leading out to the pool. All she could think about was getting away. She didn't want to hear her mother's reasoning. She didn't want to be filled with doubts.

Beau liked her.

Her cared about her.

He wanted to protect her!

But as hard as she tried, she couldn't get her mother's poison out of her brain. Because maybe it wasn't actually poison.

Maybe it was a truth elixir that Grace wished she didn't need to drink.

26

DON'T HURT MY GIRL

Parking in the garage, Beau shot out of his car and immediately went to look for Grace. He'd had fun hanging with the guys and shooting hoops, but he couldn't get her off his mind. It was a Saturday, his chance to be with her and not worry about his friends, yet he'd said yes to Julius's invitation.

Grace had told him to go. She convinced him that a little guy time would be good for him, and maybe it was. They just played basketball. They didn't talk about anything else, and that part had been awesome. But now he wanted to see his girl.

His girl.

The idea made him grin.

Bounding up the stairs, he walked to the kitchen and grabbed a glass of water before starting a systematic search through the house. He went to the library first, because it was a sunny day and that spot by the window was her favorite. But she wasn't there. In fact, no one was around. He frowned and trotted back downstairs, texting her a quick message while searching the middle floor before heading down to her room.

He was walking past the laundry room when he heard a snap of fabric and ducked his head in to find Leola folding linen.

She glanced up, her expression hard and unfriendly.

"Uh, hey, Leola." He tapped his finger on the doorframe, trying not to let her massive change-up unnerve him. He missed the warm housekeeper with her motherly smiles, and he still didn't know what he'd done to annoy her.

It kind of irritated him, but he kept his expression neutral. "Do you know where Grace is?"

The woman neatly folded a towel and placed it in the basket, refusing to answer him.

He frowned.

She spotted his expression and sighed. "Why do you want to see her?"

"We were gonna hang out when I got back. She hasn't replied to my text, so…"

"So, maybe she wants to be left alone."

"What?" Beau's head shot back. Leola's tone was only getting icier.

What the hell is her problem?

Lifting the basket off the counter, she let out another sigh and murmured, "She went for a walk. I don't know where she is, but she went out by the pool, so I'm guessing she's somewhere along the river."

An uneasy foreboding made his stomach quiver. "Is she okay?"

Leola shrugged.

He huffed, irritated by her evasive behavior. He wanted to ask her why she was being so unhelpful but didn't want to get into some argument with his girlfriend's mother. That would not go over well.

Gritting his teeth, he spun on his heel and stalked toward the pool, but she stopped him with a sharp warning. "Don't hurt my girl."

"What?" He spun to face Leola, the warning sinking into him like wet concrete.

"Don't. *Hurt*. My girl."

"I would never hurt her."

"But you won't claim her," she snapped, resting the basket on her hip. "You'll kiss her. You'll lock her into some secret relationship, but you won't be proud to have her by your side."

The blood drained from his face. He could feel it.

Leola shook her head. "If you could only walk one day in her shoes," she muttered, her voice trembling.

He wasn't sure how to respond, so he just stood there staring at her as she gave him another disapproving frown, then charged up the stairs to deliver the clean laundry to his bathroom.

He stayed where he was, staring out the glass at the deck chairs around the pool.

Leola's words sat ugly inside him, and he didn't know whether to be pissed off, insulted, or sad. Of course he would never hurt Grace! And he wasn't claiming her to keep her safe. Leola didn't know what she was talking about.

Shoving the door open, he stormed past the pool and around to the gate. Pulling out his phone, he sent Grace another text, his irritation only growing as he searched the surrounding area. Why wouldn't she reply? What had Leola said to her? Was she trying to break them up?

The idea made his chest hurt.

Storming down the dirt path with curled fists and a curdling stomach, he was getting ready to unleash a little hellfire on the trees around him when he spotted Grace on the sand. She was hugging her knees and staring out at the water. The breeze was playing with her hair, and he could picture those gentle brown eyes drinking in the view. A couple strolled by with a dog on a lead.

Beau picked up his pace, wanting to reach her in case the puppy gave her a fright, but they passed without incident and Beau relaxed. As he took a seat beside her, his anger had dissipated to a mild simmer. That was the effect she had on him. She could always make him feel better.

"Hey." He tucked a lock of hair behind her ear and smiled at her.

Dammit! She's been crying.

His jaw muscles clenched, and it was taking maximum effort to keep his anger to a simmer. He wouldn't take out his frustration on her.

"Hi." She smiled, leaning in when he put his arm around her and kissed the top of her head.

"You okay?"

She shrugged. "Mom knows about us."

"Yeah," Beau sighed. "I don't think she's too happy about it."

The water was a soothing soundtrack to their quiet conversation, and Beau tried to focus on the calming rhythm as Grace shook her head.

"No, she… um, I don't think she likes it very much." She pulled away from him, creating a distance that felt like a canyon.

It tore at him, but he didn't reach for her. Instead, he grabbed a stick off the ground and snapped it in half. "You want to break up with me?"

It was logical. She refused to come between him and his friends; how could he not extend her the same to her? Grace and Leola were tight. He couldn't do anything to ruin that relationship.

Grace's breath hitched, and she shot him a wide-eyed look before quickly turning back to look at the water.

It made him nervous.

Was that little gasp because he'd guessed right or wrong?

"Grace?" The word came out small and barely audible.

"No," she whispered. "I love being your girlfriend. I just want this to be easier."

Biting the inside of his cheek, he reached for her fingers, needing the connection. He traced the shape of her digits, then threaded their fingers together. She let him, giving his hand a soft squeeze. The relief flooding him was intense.

How had she gotten such a hold on him? It was like he'd drunk Oberon's elixir and woken up to see Grace first.

"What'd your mom say? I mean, I thought she liked me."

"It's not that. It's just…" Grace shook her head, and when she bit her lips together, Beau wondered if she was going to keep him in the dark, but she eventually let out a soft sigh and murmured, "I haven't done anything wrong, yet your friends despise me. *You* didn't like me at first, and it all comes down to the way I look. It makes my mom furious that people won't give me a chance. These scars are surface features that don't even matter, but to so many they do."

"But they don't." He squeezed her hand, trying to reassure her.

She turned to him, her soft gaze trying to strip the flesh off his bones.

It was a look he couldn't counter. It seemed to say *"I know you"* with such depth that he couldn't respond. He looked to the sand, wishing he had the right words, but he was coming up empty.

If they didn't matter, why was he hiding her? Was that what she was thinking?

"You don't really know what it's like being me. Looking like this," she whispered. "I know you try to understand, but you don't really know…"

He worked his jaw to the side, then huffed. "Well, show me. Explain it to me. Help me to understand."

She snickered. It was a sad, hopeless sound. "The only way you'd truly get it is if you looked just like me. If you had to walk around with scars all over your face."

He brushed the back of his finger down the side of her cheek. He usually tried to avoid touching her scars. He didn't know why. He told himself it was out of respect for her, but…

Resting his finger on the bottom of her chin, he turned her to face him. And he looked. He studied each scar, lightly running his fingers along the jagged lines across her cheek and up to where her eye drooped.

"Let's do it, then," he whispered, then had to swallow.

She took his hand off her face and frowned. "What?"

"You're amazing with makeup, right? Dress me up. Give me some scars, and I'll walk around for a day and see how it really feels."

She shook her head, her smile pitiful. "No."

"Come on. It'd be a great experience for both of us. Do you have the stuff you need?"

She chewed her lip.

"Or maybe we can go and buy what we need. Give me a list." He was surprised by his own enthusiasm over this, but he was compelled to do it. To walk a mile in her shoes. To understand.

Besides, it would prove to Grace how much she meant to him, right?

"Grace, what do you need?"

She let out a reluctant sigh. "Dad gave me a box of his old stuff for me to mess around with. There might be something in there I can use."

"It's settled, then." Beau stood with a grin. Brushing the sand off his shorts, he reached down to help her up.

"Are you sure about this?" She winced.

He studied her face and nodded. "Definitely."

27

THE MELTED MAN

Grace talked Beau into waiting until the next day. She needed time to prepare and figure out if she could actually pull it off. She needed to make it convincing, and she wanted to do the best job she could.

Going through her father's leftover makeup box, she figured she had enough to pull off something. She then sat up late researching and watching YouTube clips to brush up on the techniques her father had taught her. By the time she finally went to bed, she had a design for Beau's face and ended up dreaming about it most of the night.

The next morning, she waited for her mother to go out for breakfast with Millie before heading upstairs to find Beau. She bumped into Mr. Griffin on the way to Beau's bathroom and gave him an embarrassed smile when he asked her about the suitcase she was carrying.

"Oh, just some stuff for an experiment."

He gave her a confused frown.

"For school," she lied.

"Wow." His eyebrows rose. "Homework on a Sunday

too. You are one dedicated girl." His grin was infectious. "I'm off. I'll see what you've been up to when I return."

She let out an awkward laugh and waited until he'd reached the bottom of the stairs before sneaking into Beau's bathroom.

He was waiting there for her, his knee bobbing as he sat on the edge of the tub.

She studied him for a moment before asking, "Are you sure about this?"

He nodded, looking completely unsure.

Touching his beautiful face, she ran her fingers over his smooth skin, and he smiled at her. Her heart bloomed with affection, and she gave him a quick kiss before getting to work.

It took hours, but she slowly, meticulously worked on his face, adding a couple of prosthetics and blending around them to make it look as natural as possible. By the time she was done, Beau was unrecognizable. She didn't want the effect to look like he was a tough guy who'd gotten into a bar fight, so instead she'd gone for burn scars, changing his nose to make it look as though one nostril had melted out of shape. The side of his mouth drooped to the right, along with his eye. The skin was mangled, and she took that effect down to his neck. She didn't have enough stuff to work over his ear and make it look good, so she placed a beanie on his head, which gave the impression that he'd lost half his hair and was trying to cover it up.

Beau was very patient and didn't even ask to look in the mirror as she worked. He sat for hours, and she tried to fill the space with chatter and soft music. She wanted to keep him calm, yet his knee still bobbed and his fists clenched. He was nervous, and she understood why.

He was going from a flawless, model complexion to a scarred man.

In his mind, he'd be going from beautiful to ugly. That would be his first thought, she just knew it.

"Okay, I'm done." She stepped back. "Want to take a look?"

He nodded and stood, flinching when he caught his reflection in the mirror. He leaned forward, lightly touching his scars. "Wow. This is amazing. It looks so real."

She nodded. "It's not as good as what my dad would do, but I think the effect will pass as long as people don't study you too closely."

"You've done a great job." His eyes looked a little tortured as he gazed at himself. He opened his mouth to speak, then obviously changed his mind.

"Um…" Grace ran her finger over the shiny bathroom vanity and cautiously asked, "Do you… did you want to go out somewhere? You're really sure?"

"Yes." He turned and took her hand. "I have to know what it's like for you, and even though staring at a bathroom mirror gives me some idea, I won't truly get it until I'm around other people."

She nodded and turned back to the extensive makeup kit. "Well, let me just get ready, then."

"What do you mean?" He frowned in confusion, and Grace was happy to see that the prosthetics were moving quite nicely with his expressions. Her father would be proud.

"If you truly want to know what it's like, I can't look this way." She pointed at her face and quickly got her things ready.

She'd done this a few times before. Her father had walked her through the process step by step every time he was going to take her out. Her mother would fume and pace, then would press her lips together when her father asked, "Doesn't she look great?"

The tension in the air had always been so thick and horrible. Grace hated it. If she hid her scars the way her father wanted her to, her mother would be upset. If she let them show, her father would be embarrassed. She could never win.

It was a miracle her father even let her meet Scarlett the way she looked, and she put that down to Beau stepping up and protecting her.

See, he did want to claim her!

But not around his friends. There's a difference!

She winced and continued to apply the makeup that hid her scars so well. Beau had gone to change into jeans and put on his jacket. When he returned, he looked pretty amazing, and Grace admired his figure as he walked up and stood beside her.

He leaned against the counter and watched her work. "I understand why you don't want to go through this before you leave the house every day."

"Yeah, it's pretty time-consuming." She blinked at her reflection. "Plus, Mom's told me to own who I am... and she's right, even though it's hard sometimes."

Beau nodded and crossed his arms. She was aware that

he'd been avoiding the mirror since returning to the bathroom.

"Did you want anything to eat or drink before we go?" She gave him an out, and he jumped at it.

"I'll go make some coffee."

"Actually, pick something you can drink through a straw. I don't want anything on your face getting damaged."

"Oh, yeah. Okay." He nodded and left the room.

Grace tried to speed up a little. Beau probably wanted to be out of his makeup as soon as possible. One quick trip through town and he'd get a decent idea of what it was like.

Attaching a set of false eyelashes, she stood back and gazed at her reflection. She'd gone a little more over the top than usual, and she looked stunning. She admired herself, feeling pretty but knowing it wasn't her true appearance. It was fun to dress up, though, even if the makeup itched a little.

Tucking her hair back, she took a mental picture of her face. This was what she would look like if that dog hadn't attacked her. How different her life would be.

Maybe her parents would still be together.

Maybe her father wouldn't have buried himself in work to avoid the guilt of allowing Grace to get so badly hurt.

It wasn't really his fault. Yes, he was the one watching her that afternoon, but it wasn't like he ordered that dog to pounce on her. Maybe if he'd been outside watching her and not caught up on the TV... but what-ifs were a waste of time.

Grace shook her head. She couldn't go there.

Besides, if her life had taken a different path, she never would have met Beau.

And how could she ever regret that?

Beau walked in just as she finished packing everything away. He jerked to a stop in the doorway and stared at her.

She could tell by the look in his eyes that he thought she was beautiful, and it made her nervous.

Gripping the edge of her skirt, she shook her head. "I can't do this for you every day. I need you to like me just the way I am. I need—"

"Grace." He shut her up with a soft whisper. His smile was kind, his eyes warm with affection as he held out his hand.

She took it, her stomach jittering with a mixture of anxiety and giddy butterflies. This afternoon was going to be a huge challenge for both of them, and she didn't know what would come from it as they snuck down the stairs and drove into town to walk in each other's shoes.

28

UNDERSTANDING

Beau's heart was racing. As he parked the car along the street, he could barely hear above the pounding in his ears. He hadn't been able to enjoy the music—probably because Grace didn't sing this time around. Was she as nervous as he was?

He glanced at her, and she gave him a little smile.

"I think you're really... brave." Her smile grew. "What you're doing is..." She blinked and sucked in a breath. "It means a lot."

Taking her hand, he drew it to his lips and lightly brushed her smooth skin.

She looked stunning. It took his breath away when he first walked into the bathroom and spotted her. If she'd first arrived at his house like that, he would have flirted from the outset, turned up the charm, and not cared about her personality. He would have tried to win her over and... and probably missed all the good stuff. All he would have cared about was the physical, and he never would have gotten to know her.

223

The thought irritated him. What kind of person was he? Some shallow asshole?

Yep. Pretty much.

He internally growled but managed to keep his voice even. "Come on, let's do this."

"Okay." Grace got out of the car, and it took Beau three full breaths and sheer willpower to open the door. He walked around the car and took her hand. Threading their fingers together, he gazed around him and immediately spotted the little boy who looked at his face and gasped. Burying his nose into his mother's skirt, he hurried past, and Beau tried not to let it sting.

It's only makeup. It's just—

The woman in front of them winced, then gave him a sympathetic smile. The guy trailing behind her didn't even notice Beau. He was too busy checking out Grace.

Beau frowned.

That lust-filled look in the guy's eye made Beau want to punch him.

He pulled Grace a little closer to his side.

"You doing okay?"

"Uh-huh." He nodded but couldn't say more.

They walked into his favorite café and took a seat by the window. Grace ordered for them. Beau was having trouble speaking. His throat was thick, and he couldn't swallow past the lump. It hurt.

He kept his eyes on the table, only glancing up to notice Grace smile at a stranger. It was another guy, a slightly older man this time, drinking her in. She looked beautiful, and it irritated Beau. Not the fact that she looked so gorgeous but the plethora of guys checking her out. She was probably unaware of it, but he was counting, and he'd just spotted number five.

He understood that lingering gaze all too well. He'd spent all of his teenage years using it, and his threat barometer was on overdrive.

When she returned to the table, the first thing he did was reach for Grace's hand. He played with her fingers while they waited for their order to arrive. It was hard to speak, so they just sat there in silence, him tracing the shape of her nails while she gazed around the café and smiled at various people. He kept his eyes on the table, feeling the curious glances and hushed whispers around them. It made his skin crawl.

The waitress returned to the table, delivering their food, then ducking down to look at him. Her eyes were filled with pity, and she spoke to him like he was disabled or something. "Can I get you anything else?"

"No," he barked.

She flinched a little at his tone but forced a friendly smile before cringing at Grace and walking away.

Grace watched her leave, picking up the long-handled teaspoon and unwrapping it from the paper napkin. "Which is worse, the curious stares or the sympathy?"

Beau's eyes darted to Grace, and his stomach clenched. He didn't want to answer. It'd make her realize just how much he was struggling with this.

He eventually muttered, "Both suck," before diving into the caramel sundae they were sharing.

Grace took little nibbles, and he watched her lips curve around the spoon before her tongue darted out to lick the back of it. Yearning shot through him, and he wanted to lean across the table and kiss her mouth, but he didn't want to ruin his makeup.

At least that was what he told himself.

But was it really the truth?

Did he care about his makeup, or was it more the fact that he didn't think he deserved to kiss her beautiful face when he looked so freaking ugly?

A cold sensation washed through him. Was that how Grace felt sometimes? Like she wasn't good enough because of the way she looked?

His appetite fled and he laid down his spoon, resting back in his chair and watching Grace eat. She seemed tense and soon gave up on the treat as well.

Setting her spoon down, she leaned her arms on the table and gazed at him. Her brown eyes were soft with affection. "Are you done?"

Did she mean the dessert or the masquerade?

He wanted to shout, "Both!" He wanted to beg her to take him home and get this stuff off his face, but what right did he have to ask that? She lived with it every day.

He gritted his teeth and shook his head.

Pursing her lips, Grace fidgeted with her teaspoon before taking a sip of water. Conversation was not flowing today, and Beau wondered if it was his fault. But he felt debilitated by the stares and double glances. Some were curious, others were revolted, and then there was the pity. Okay, that did suck.

Did Grace get that all the time too?

He was on the cusp of saying, "Let's go," when the shop door opened and in swanned his friends. He froze, cold dread rushing through him as he wiped sweaty palms on his jeans. Colette and Ella were standing close, whispering to each other, while Etan and Julius stared up at the main board behind the counter.

Colette began to turn, and Beau shuffled in his seat.

Don't look at me!

Don't recognize me!

She gave him a cursory glance, and her nose wrinkled like she was repulsed. And then she whispered something to Ella, who spun around to look at him. She stuck her tongue out and shuddered before turning back to giggle and whisper something else.

"Let's go. I'm done." Beau shot out of his seat, grabbing Grace's hand and making a beeline for the door.

Grace could barely keep up with him, but neither of them was fast enough to miss the cutting comments.

"...should introduce him to Grace. They'd make the perfect pair. Ugly One and Ugly Two." Colette snickered.

"I don't know how the hell he ended up with her. She's—"

Beau tugged Grace outside before he could hear the rest of that sentence, but he didn't miss Etan's lingering gaze. He was checking out Grace's ass. Beau growled, wrapping his arm around his girlfriend's waist and pulling her so close that she nearly tripped over his feet.

"Are you okay?" Her face wrinkled with concern.

"I just wanna keep you close," he murmured, rushing her to the car.

She slipped into her seat, calmly buckling her seat belt while he fought his and had to swear a couple times before winning over the buckle.

"Maybe we should go home." Grace's voice was soft

and lilting, like she was trying to deal with a toddler on the verge of a meltdown.

"No. I said I wanted to do this, and I have to see it through! Let's just drive up the coast a little and go someplace else."

"Okay." She nodded. "Whatever you want to do."

He internally scoffed and shook his head.

What I want to do is get off this ugly train and go back to life as normal!

The thought made him feel bad. He wasn't coping with this, and it just made him realize how freaking weak and pathetic he was. Grace lived with it daily, and he couldn't even put up with one hour?

As he started the engine, he noticed another guy smiling at Grace through the window, and he couldn't help a growl. He sounded like a freaking tiger, but he couldn't stop himself.

"What's the matter?" Grace asked as he tore out of the parking spot.

He bit his lips together, not wanting to rant and rave. What right did he have to do that?

"Beau, it's okay to talk about it. You're obviously struggling with this, and it's only natural. It took me years to come to terms with my new appearance. You can't expect to adjust in one afternoon. You just wanted a taste, and seriously, if it's too much... I won't judge you at all. I—"

"That's not why I'm growling," he snapped. "Every guy we walked past is checking you out. It's like you're a piece of meat and we're living in a land of hungry lions!"

Grace blinked at him like that was the last thing she expected him to say. And then she snickered.

He frowned at her.

She slapped a hand over her mouth but couldn't keep the laughter at bay.

"What! What's so funny?"

"I'm sorry." She giggled out the words. "It's just... I didn't even think about that side of things. Your jealousy is adorable."

"I'm not adorable," he moaned.

"You are... and I'm so flattered. This never happens to me. It's always the other way around. Girls are checking you out all the time. Even some guys do. You are the most beautiful human being I've ever met. I'm serious!" She countered his incredulous look. "The first time I saw you, I could barely breathe. You were so freaking hot, and I felt like I was meeting a supermodel or something."

He shook his head.

"You have no idea how gorgeous you are, Beau."

"Not today I'm not," he grumbled.

Grace went quiet, her speech cut off at the knees. The flash of hurt that flew across her face made his insides clench.

They drove up the coast in silence, Grace keeping her eyes out the window and Beau trying to figure out what he'd said. It took him nearly half an hour as they meandered the back streets to Compo Beach, but finally it hit him.

He wasn't gorgeous today, and he'd made it sound like a really bad thing. Like the worst thing in the world. He'd made it sound like someone with scars couldn't possibly be beautiful.

His stomach sank like a warship that had just been hit with a torpedo.

How the hell must Grace be feeling after he said that?

He parked the car and gripped the wheel, not sure how to fix his faux pas and make it better.

"The sky is so blue today. Come on, let's walk out to the point." Grace got out of the car before he could say anything.

The breeze played with her hair and caught the hem of her skirt. She grabbed it with a laugh, holding it down so she didn't flash her underwear to the world.

Beau watched her, his insides hitching.

He didn't deserve her.

The realization hit him like a wrecking ball, tearing through his insides. Never in his life had he felt he didn't deserve something. He was used to getting exactly what he wanted. Whatever he asked for, his mother would make happen. Whatever he suggested at school, his friends would capitulate. Everyone always wanted to be in his good books. They loved being attached to him, associated with him.

He'd even won Grace over pretty easily.

But did he even have a right to do that?

His insides were heavy as he followed her out to the point. She took his hand and chatted away, marveling at their surroundings. He tried to engage, but his insides were filled with tar. A dull ache had formed in the back of his head, and all he wanted to do was close his eyes and block out the world.

With a contented sigh, Grace leaned back against him. He wrapped his arms around her, feeling unworthy of such a moment. She felt so perfect against him, and he nestled his cheek on her head. They gazed at the ocean together while she gently caressed his forearm with her soft fingers.

"I know this afternoon has been hard on you," she said. "But this moment right here... perfection." She grinned up at him, and he wished he could smile at her, but his lips weren't working properly. His eyes burned like they wanted to cry, and he didn't know if he could add that humiliation to everything he was already feeling.

"Mind if we head home?" he rasped.

The request made her sad—he could tell by her eyes—but she still managed a smile and a nod. "Sure."

Grace reached for his hand as they walked back to the car. He felt obliged to take it, even though he wanted to hunch his shoulders, bury his fists in his pockets, and stalk back to the car. His mood was gray, foul, tortured.

How did Grace do this every day? How did she smile and laugh and—

He shook his head. Those questions made him feel weak, shallow.

They drove home with music playing, but neither of them sang or seemed to enjoy it. This day had been a write-off, and Beau hated himself for not coping better.

As soon as they reached the house, he dove out of the car and made a beeline for his bathroom.

He didn't make it to the second staircase before bumping into Leola.

She jerked to a stop, blinking in surprise... and then gazing at him with a soft smile.

"Now you understand," she murmured, leaning forward to kiss his cheek.

He flinched but stood his ground, not wanting to offend her.

The urge to cry rounded over him again, and he shot up the stairs before Grace could see him. He didn't want her pity, her sympathy... her kindness. He didn't deserve anything from her.

29

BEAUTY AND THE BEAST

Grace gave her mother a worried frown.

Leola shrugged and then let out a soft laugh. "Now he knows, *papillon*."

"He hasn't coped that well. I've never seen him so quiet and morose before."

"It's good for him." Leola rested her hand on her cheek, giving her a proud smile. "You did good. Your father would be very impressed."

"Thanks." Grace flushed and smiled, but then she thought of Beau's distress and her face crumpled into a frown again. "I better go." She pointed up the stairs, and her mother let nodded.

She ran into the bathroom and found Beau standing in front of the mirror, desperately trying to rip the prosthetics off.

"Wait, I'll help you."

He shook his head. "Take yours off first." He spun to face her, his eyes bright with desperation. "I want to see *you*."

The request kind of confused her, but she complied, removing her makeup as fast as she could. Gazing back at her usual self, she felt that catch of sadness. It'd been fun being pretty for a day.

You are pretty!

Forcing herself to look in the mirror, she repeated her mantra in her head.

I am beautiful.

I am enough.

She said it five more times before turning to face Beau. His eyes were glistening, and he took her face in his hands. Tracing the lines of her scars with the tips of his fingers, he seemed to marvel at her. It quickly became off-putting, and she stepped back, ducking her chin.

"Sit," she softly ordered, pointing to the edge of the tub.

He perched, gripping the sides as she got to work, carefully removing the makeup and washing away the glue. It took a while, but finally his face was back to normal.

"There you go." She smiled, hoping it would revive his mood.

He stood and gazed at his reflection.

Resting her arm around his waist, she leaned her cheek against his shoulder and smiled. "Everything's okay now."

To her surprise, he didn't grin or saying anything. Instead, his eyes flooded, and he sniffed, ducking his head and covering his face with one hand.

"Beau? What's the matter?" Worry coursed through her as she guided him back to the edge of the bath and sat him down. Kneeling between his legs, she rubbed his thighs and tried to persuade him to look at her, but he stayed hidden, a hand clamped firmly over his eyes.

"Beau," she whispered. "Talk to me."

Finally, after a sniff, he looked up. His eyes were a vibrant blue, and tears trailed down his cheeks as he looked at her. He started to trace her scars again, and she let him, not backing away even though instinct was telling her too.

"You are the beauty," he rasped. "And I… I am the beast." His voice broke over the words, and a fresh wave of tears followed.

Grace's heart felt like it was breaking in half. She didn't realize Beau was capable of crying, but his tortured gaze was so endearing. And those words… his sincerity…

Her insides flooded with affection as she shook her head. "You're not a beast."

"I am. I don't even know what you see in me! Grace, you're so far out of my league."

The idea surprised her so much that she couldn't help a soft giggle. "I don't think you understand that phrase."

"Don't you get it?" His expression crumpled, like he was tormented by this truth. "I don't deserve you. I had a taste of your world today, and I hated every second of it. You have to live with this every single day, and you're so kind and good and dignified… and… and I don't deserve you! What do you see in an asshole like me? Why do you even want to be with me?"

He squeezed his eyes shut. His anguish held a certain beauty. She'd never seen him so vulnerable, and it only made her heart open that much wider.

Cupping his cheek, she gently forced his head up so he would look at her.

She smiled and whispered, "I see butterfly wings."

He went still, searching her face.

She loved him.

She loved him more in this moment than she ever had.

"And I feel…" Her voice caught with emotion. "I feel…"

Nope. She couldn't do it.

She couldn't speak past the swelling in her throat.

Rising up, she pulled him against her and kissed him. Everything she couldn't say was poured into the kiss, and he responded in kind. Wrapping his arms around her, he drew their bodies together, splaying his fingers over her back. She melted against him, owning his mouth, his tongue, his breath.

He held her like he never wanted to let her go, and when he pulled out of the kiss, she felt the loss keenly.

Resting his forehead against hers, he let out a shaky sigh, then whispered, "I don't want to secretly date you anymore."

Her heart plummeted, riding the roller coaster straight down to her knees. "What?"

"You're my girl, and I want the world to know it."

She leaned back, searching his face to really make sure he meant it.

He did.

Oh man, he really did.

She couldn't decide what she was feeling.

Elation?

Affection?

Sheer terror?

Maybe a little of all three.

They were going public?

That was huge. Terrifying.

He grinned, the light coming back into his eyes. The cloud from earlier had been lifted away, and she barely had time to react before he pulled her back against him.

She was lost to his kiss.

Lost to him.

And for some reason, nothing else seemed to matter.

30

IT'S NO JOKE

Beau rested his hand on Grace's knee, giving it a gentle squeeze before turning into school. She'd been nervous this morning. He could tell by the way she spilled the sugar across the kitchen counter and then managed to whack her hip on the doorframe when she was walking out of the house. She rubbed it with a hiss and swore she was okay, but her tight smile made him second-guess his decision.

"We don't have to tell everyone if you don't want to," he'd mumbled reluctantly.

Yeah, he was nervous, but it just felt like the right thing to do. He was convinced of it, and he didn't want Grace backing out.

But a good boyfriend thought about his girl first, and if she didn't want—

"I do. I'm just nervous," she admitted.

He loved her honesty and spent the car ride to school trying to lighten her mood and distract her. It mostly worked. They sang along to "There's Nothing Holdin' Me Back." Grace nailed the fast-paced chorus, getting all the words and staying in time like it was the easiest thing in the world. He ended up laughing in awe, which gave her the giggles, and they were the only two people on the planet until he turned into school and reality smacked them in the face.

"It's gonna be okay," Beau murmured, parking the car, his own stomach tensing when he spotted his friends congregating under the big oak tree near the parking lot. "Stay in the car."

"Why?"

He slipped out of his seat, shutting the door on Grace's protest. Straightening his jacket, he walked around the vehicle, relieved that his girlfriend had acquiesced to his request. It was time to make a statement.

Opening her door, he held out his hand, shooting her a tender smile and winking at her perplexed expression.

"Come on, *papillon*, I'll walk you to class."

She blushed, her smile adorable as she dipped her head and took his hand.

Threading their fingers together, he clenched his jaw and ambled toward his friends. It was in the direction she needed to go anyway, and he figured they may as well get this over with.

Colette's bright eyes flashed, then narrowed into an intense glare. Zari and Amell shared a dubious glance. Ella's mouth dropped open, and Etan let out a derisive snicker that made Beau want to punch him.

Grace squeezed his hand, though whether she was

reminding him to stay chill, like they'd talked about, or she was drawing strength from him, he wasn't sure. But he squeezed back as he stopped by his friend group with a relaxed smile. At least he tried to keep it relaxed.

"Hey, guys." Julius had a bemused grin on his face and wiggled his eyebrows at Beau. That scored him a swift nudge in the stomach from Ella.

Julius was always slow to pick up on the group's vibe.

His expression morphed to a frown and he crossed his arms, giving in to peer pressure like a putz. Beau shook his head and stole a quick glance at Grace.

She was trying to engage the girls with a smile but getting nowhere.

They were in shock, which was freaking ridiculous.

Beau cleared his throat. "So, I can tell you're all weirded out by this, but the truth is, Grace and I have been secretly dating for weeks, and we thought it was about time you guys knew. We're sick of hiding it for all the wrong reasons, so yeah..." He nodded, hoping his explanation was good enough.

Colette scoffed, then blinked again like she was trying to wake up from a bad dream. "You can't be serious. Is this a joke? Are you pranking us or something?" She started laughing, but it was a forced, hollow sound.

"It's no joke." Beau's voice was deadly serious, but Ella kept shaking her head.

"Beauty doesn't date the beast."

What she thought was a clever comeback actually fell flat, because Beau let out a snicker. "Ella, that's exactly what she does. And I guess I'm just lucky enough that Grace was willing to date me."

Giving her hand a little tug, he pulled Grace away from his disbelieving friends and walked her to class.

They didn't say much. How could they when they spent the entire time dodging surprised gasps and the flurry of whispers that followed in their wake?

His anger was bubbling by the time they reached her homeroom, but then she rested a gentle hand on his chest and smiled up at him.

"We knew it was going to be hard." Her voice was soft and sweet, the look in her eyes daring his heart to melt on the spot. "Thank you for not being ashamed of me."

"Ditto," he whispered, running his fingers lightly over her scars. "I'm proud to have you as my girl. You're better than everyone here."

"No." She shook her head. "I'm just me. I'm nothing special, but I do feel very lucky to have you as my boyfriend." Her smile grew along with her blush, and he had to kiss her.

Taking his time, he slowly cupped her cheek, leaning in and pressing their lips together. She melted against him and he deepened the kiss, just a brief brush of their tongues before the bell pulled them apart.

"I'll see you at break time." He kissed her nose, then walked backward, his smile kind of goofy.

She giggled and slipped into class, completely unaware of just how amazing she was.

Beau slapped a hand across his heart, shaking his head and grinning… until he walked around the corner and came face-to-face with the people he had a sinking feeling would never understand.

"What the hell, Beau?" Colette laughed again, that

hard, hollow sound that made his insides shudder. "Please tell me you're pulling a Josie Grossie on this thing. That can be the only explanation."

His temper spiked at Colette's reference to that old movie *Never Been Kissed*. In that, the coolest guy in the school tricked Josie into thinking he was into her, asking her to the prom only to show up on the night and throw eggs in her face.

The idea of something like that happening to sweet Grace killed him, and he couldn't stop the soft growl in his throat. "This is real, Colette, and I'd never do anything to hurt Grace. She's freaking amazing. You have no idea. Yeah, she looks different, but she's a really cool person. You need to give her a chance."

"Uh... o-kay." Etan's expression was so skeptical, his laughter gruff and mocking.

Ella giggled. "Seriously, Beau. We know you can act, but cut the crap with us. We're your friends. What's your play?"

His nostrils flared as he leaned toward Ella, getting right in her face and spitting out the truth. "My play is to date the nicest girl I've ever met in my life, and to keep dating her for as long as she'll have me! You think I deserve her? You think any of you assholes do?" He shook his head. "We don't know shit. I'm the luckiest guy standing here."

His friends glared at him like he'd lost his mind.

The late bell trilled, and a teacher walked around the corner, barking at them for not already being in class. They dispersed, Beau taking the longer way around so he didn't have to walk with his "friends."

He knew it was going to be challenging, but he didn't expect this level of disbelief.

What the hell was he going to do?

31

A BITTER TASTE IN THE CAFETERIA

Grace was used to people pointing, staring, and whispering about her as she walked past them. She was *not* used to people talking to her, getting in her face and drilling her on why she was dating Beau Griffin.

"I can't believe it!" Felicity, a girl who had never even spoken to Grace before rested her butt on the edge of Grace's desk and grinned down at her. "You're dating Beau Griffin?"

"Uh… yeah." She shrugged.

"How did you do it? I've been trying to get him to notice me since seventh grade!"

"Oh…" Grace forced out a chuckle. "Well, we just clicked, you know. These things sometimes naturally fall into place."

"And you've been having this secret affair for weeks?"

That revelation caused, Chantel, the girl in front of them to spin around with a gasp. "Are you serious?"

"It's not an… affair." Grace tried to laugh it off. "We're dating. Just… you know… boyfriend and girlfriend." Her cheeks flushed and she looked down, embarrassed by this new form of attention.

Were people suddenly willing to talk to her just because she was going out with one of the hottest guys in school? That seemed like a very shallow reason to befriend someone.

Just take the win, Grace! People are talking to you for a change. You're no longer a leper!

But it felt wrong.

Why should Beau suddenly make her acceptable?

She should be that in her own right.

The teacher walked into the room, forcing everyone to their seats, and Grace sank back in her chair, relieved to have the spotlight off her. She didn't know how to respond to these strangers. It made her insides writhe, and she struggled to focus on the lesson.

As she was leaving the room, the two girls flanked her, continuing to pepper her with questions as they walked to their next class.

"Is he a good kisser?" Felicity asked.

Chantel swooned. "I wouldn't mind that guy's hands all over me. Like seriously, I would let him do whatever he wanted." She arched her right brow. "*Whatever* he wanted."

Grace swallowed and leaned away from the girl.

Ugh. They were so… She didn't want to be offensive, but these girls were not her kindred spirits. She picked up her pace, rushing to the art room so she could lose herself in her favorite subject.

Unfortunately, the gossip followed her right through the doors.

Titters, insults, and the odd impressed eyebrow wiggle hounded Grace no matter where she went.

By the time she reached the library at lunchtime, she wanted to weep with relief.

No one was in her corner, and she burrowed into the armchair, too exhausted to even read or draw. Closing her eyes, she leaned her head back and let out a long sigh.

Her body was finally starting to relax when a soft voice made her head jerk up, her eyes pinging open as the tension curled over her again, gripping her muscles like talons.

"Hey." Beau smiled at her, but she couldn't return the gesture. Crouching down in front of her chair, he kissed her knuckles with a grin. "I thought we were doing lunch in the cafeteria today."

"I can't." She shook her head.

"Why?"

"I'm not hungry, and…" With a heavy sigh, she sat forward, taking one of his hands and running her thumb between his knuckles. "I can't do it. I need space."

"What?" The fear in Beau's expression made her insides lurch. "Are you breaking up with me?"

"No." She touched his cheek, smiling to reassure him. "It's not that at all. I just… I can't handle the stares."

"But…" He winced. "You're kind of used to that, aren't you?"

"These stares are different." Her face bunched, her eyes suddenly burning. "Everything about today has been different, and…" Her voice wobbled. "I don't know if I'm cut out for it. Maybe you should just tell everyone that it was a big joke, and then we can go back to secretly dating again."

"Grace." He tipped his head. "I don't want to secretly date you anymore. I want people to know how I feel about you."

"But none of them get it."

"So, we'll make them understand." He leaned forward and kissed her. "Come on. I can't do this without you. I don't want to hide."

Grace closed her eyes.

"Come have lunch with me. Please." His expression was so sweet and endearing, she felt her will bending like a piece of gum. He made her so pliable, and she was helpless to stop it.

With a soft snicker, she shook her head and whispered, "Okay."

"I'll look after you." He helped her stand, threading their fingers together and walking to the cafeteria.

People greeted him as he wove through the school. Some even said hi to Grace.

It bugged her, for reasons she didn't even understand, but she was polite and smiled back the way her mother taught her to.

By the time they reached the cafeteria, she was so tense she thought she might snap, but she tried not to let it show. Beau really wanted them to be together, and she could do this.

He carried her tray for her, and they sat down next to his friends, who all stopped talking the second her butt hit the seat.

"Hi." She gave them a little wave.

They didn't respond.

Beau frowned at them, but none of them took any notice, icing her out as they continued their conversation. Beau kept attempting to include her, but they acted like she wasn't there.

She tried not to let it get to her. Their behavior wasn't surprising, but it bothered her on Beau's behalf. How could they do this to him?

After ten minutes of watching her boyfriend try and fail, she was about to tell him that she might just go back to the library, but then he slapped the table with a growl. "Are you guys my friends or not?"

Their heads snapped around to frown at him... and then Colette simpered, "Of course we're your friends."

"Then stop treating my girlfriend like shit. What the hell is your problem?"

"What is *your* problem?" she shot back. "We're a tight group, and you've been lying to us for weeks. How do you think that makes us feel?"

Beau closed his eyes, and Grace couldn't tell if Colette was being genuine or manipulative.

"Look, I'm sorry," Beau murmured. "I didn't know if you'd get it, and I wanted to protect what Grace and I have."

He reached for her hand. Her fingers were trembling as she slipped them into his.

Ella stared at the connection, shooting daggers at Grace before pasting on a serene smile. "We don't get it. We'll never get it."

"Yeah, man." Etan shrugged. "It's hard to wrap your head around total insanity, you know?" He gave Grace a derisive frown that made her skin crawl. It was taking every ounce of willpower she had not to bolt away from the table.

Beau huffed, shooting out of his chair and tipping his head toward the door. "Come on, let's go."

Grace followed him out, having to run to keep up with his fast pace.

"I can't believe this," he snapped. "I thought they were my friends. A few months ago, I would have sworn that they were my family, the people I ran to when I needed help. Now, I don't know what to think."

"You've thrown them a big curveball. You need to give them time to adjust."

Stopping with a jerk, he rested back against the wall and scuffed his shoe on the ground. "I was stupid to think this would be easy."

"If it's too hard, we don't—"

"Please." Beau snatched her hand, cutting off her sentence. Pressing her fingers against his lips, he held them there for a moment before looking at her with sad desperation. "Don't talk like you don't want to be with me anymore."

"I'm not. Of course I want to be with you." She stepped into his space, pressing their foreheads together. "I just hate coming between you and your friends."

"It's their problem."

"But it becomes yours."

He sighed. "How do I make them see you the way I do?"

She shrugged, wishing she had the answer.

Gently kissing her, he held the side of her face and

made her a promise. "I'm not giving up. We shocked them today, and they're still processing. They'll come around." He nodded, like he was reassuring himself.

Grace forced a smile, wanting to encourage him, but she didn't know if she believed him.

Gazing back toward the cafeteria, she wondered what they were saying. Did they hate her more? Or did they care enough about Beau to accept her?

Her gut told her something she didn't want to hear, so instead she clung to the hope that every human had something decent inside them. Even if it was buried deep, only love and kindness could unearth it.

So, that was what she had to do.

For Beau's sake... for his friends' sake... she had to be loving and kind.

32

GIVE HER A CHANCE

It had been a shitty week. Beau's friends could be stubborn assholes when they wanted to be, but he'd liked to think that they cared enough about him to give Grace a chance. That was the tact he tried just before leaving school, and he was pleased to see that Amell and Zari at least looked a little ashamed. Colette didn't have a comeback either, which was refreshing.

Grace had been nothing but patient and kind with all of them, yet still they pestered and complained. Beau wondered if he should give up on the lot of them, but where would that leave him? Friendless.

He'd have Grace, and she was enough, but they couldn't always be together, and the thought of his friends icing him out sat cold and uncomfortable inside him. He wanted to win them over. Why couldn't they see how amazing Grace was?

He just wanted approval from someone in his court.

He wasn't sure why he needed it, but it'd be nice to know someone thought he was doing the right thing.

Leola did. She was super proud of him, and that felt great, but...

"Hey, Beau." Colette walked up to his locker, her sweet smile in place.

Even so, he tensed.

Ella wasn't around, and it made him wary. Her little cling-on usually followed her wherever she went.

Curiosity made him ask, "Are you all right? Where's Ella?"

"She's coming. I just rushed ahead because I want to ask you something."

Flipping his locker shut, he turned to face her, resisting the urge to check the time on his phone. School was nearly finished for the day, and he didn't want Grace waiting by his car for too long.

"What's up?" He tried to keep his tone amiable, but after the week he'd just put up with, it was a challenge.

Colette tipped her head, reaching for his hand and rubbing her thumb over his knuckles. He wanted to snatch it away but didn't want to stoke the flame, so he gritted his teeth and let her touch him.

Colette's big eyes looked up at him, and for a second, he thought she was about to cry. It was so surprising that he actually drew in a breath.

"Look, I'm sorry we haven't adjusted to Grace more easily." She cringed. "I know you really want us to, but she's just an... unusual fit, you know? I figured you were conducting some kind of experiment."

"She's not an experiment." His voice grew gruff, and he pulled his hand out of hers.

Colette looked perplexed, hurt by his burst of annoyance. "You've changed so much."

He pressed his lips together and nodded.

"Because of her."

His lips twitched with a smile.

"I don't get it. I don't..." She crossed her arms, blinking and seriously fighting tears. Her voice began to wobble. "This isn't you. I'm worried, Beau."

He stood tall, rounding to face her properly and lightly take her shoulders. "Don't be. I'm feeling like a better man. I just..." Bending his head forward, he tried to catch her eye. "Please, Colette. Please just give her a chance."

His friend's expression crumpled with a frown. She stared down at her gold rings, winding them around her fingers. "You know, I was trying to find a way to lead into this, but you're not making it easy on me."

"Lead into what?"

"Prom." She looked up at him, her gaze glassy and bright. "We talked about going together, remember? We'll no doubt be crowned, and it just seems right that you take me."

His insides tensed as he gave her a sad smile. "Colette, you know I can't ask you to go with me. I'm taking Grace. She's my girlfriend."

Her eyebrows dipped together, her sadness dwarfed by a sudden thunder that was venomous. Her pleading, soft voice was nowhere to be seen as she leaned forward with a scathing whisper. "I can't believe you're actually serious about that Frankenstein."

"Don't call her that!" he snapped, rage scorching him. Colette was such a freaking fake! He was pissed off that he bought into her tears, that he tried to play it nice. With a throaty growl, he shot back, "She's more beautiful than you will ever be!"

Colette gasped as if he'd just slapped her across the face. Her fingers trembled as she splayed her hand over her chest and looked like she was about to keel over.

It took everything in him not to roll his eyes and scoff at her. Grace's soft voice whistled through the back of his mind. *"Anger won't win them over."*

He clenched his jaw.

But anger is easier! Colette is being a bitch!

Grace's sweet gaze filled him, those gentle brown eyes softly beseeching him to take the high ground.

With flaring nostrils, he drew in a breath and forced a calm he was far from feeling.

"Look, I'm sorry." He looked to the ground, letting out a sigh. "I didn't mean to be rude or anything, but I just hate it when you put her down like that. You don't know her like I do. She's kind and caring, and she'd make the best friend. You just have to look past the things you think are ugly and realize that she's gorgeous. She's so... *gorgeous.*" His voice took on a dreamy quality, and he grinned down at Colette like the lovesick guy he was.

Colette stared back as if she didn't even know him. "Who are you?" She shook her head and stumbled away. She was making it clear that he was about to join the same leper colony that she'd dumped Grace on.

Closing his eyes, Beau wondered if he'd just lost her for good.

How big of a loss is it really?

Maybe not that bad, but still, they'd been friends for

years, and it felt weird to watch her walk away, knowing he'd probably just destroyed any hope of him remaining in his friendship group.

He'd never felt more alone.

Even though he knew Grace was waiting for him, he couldn't shake this feeling. His friends had become his family. They'd accepted him, loved him through it all. They used to greet him each day like he was important to them. There were no looks of derision or disappointment. He didn't have to prove himself or be anything different.

Until now…

He growled in his throat, stalking to the car and slamming the door so hard that Grace actually flinched.

He wanted to apologize, but all he could do was sit there puffing and raging like a bull about to charge.

Grace watched him quietly, studying his every move and not saying a damn word. He couldn't decide if he was grateful or furious. Why wasn't she saying anything?

Clenching his jaw, he started the car and reversed out of their spot. A light rain had started falling, and it speckled the windshield.

"Do you want to talk about it?" she finally asked as they drove out the school gates.

"No!" he barked, then winced. "Sorry, I just…" His voice faded away, and he couldn't find the words.

"That's okay." She smiled at him. "I'm here if you need me."

He stole a glance at her. Just the sight of her sweet smile seemed to cool his nerves. The pressure in his chest dissipated, dissolving on a soft sigh, and it brought home the realization that Grace was really all he needed. This fight with his friends sucked, but if it came down to them or Grace, she would win.

Because he loved her.

She was the best thing that had ever walked into his life.

She was more precious to him than anything.

Reaching for her hand, he threaded his fingers through hers and felt that familiar contentment curl around him. By the time they reached home, his anger had evaporated, and he walked into the house with a grin.

Grace veered left to go and find her mother. Beau was about to follow her when he spotted his father coming down the stairs.

That familiar tension rolled through him, and he gripped his bag strap, staring up at his father. "What are you doing home?"

His father shrugged. "My meeting finished early, and after such a busy week, I thought I'd come home for the afternoon."

Beau nodded, the air around them getting dry and awkward as they stood there. Conversation never really came easily between them. If Grace were here, it'd be different. She could defuse anything.

She could—

"Can Grace and Leola join us for dinner tonight?" The question popped out before Beau even had time to mull it over.

His father's eyebrows rose with surprise, but he also had a happy twinkle in his eye. He nodded. "I think that's a wonderful idea."

"What is?" Beau's mother appeared on the stairs, adjusting her bracelets and looking between them.

"Beau's asked if Grace and Leola to join us for dinner."

"Really?" His mother looked confused but didn't argue.

Beau wasn't sure why. It seemed out of character for her to just shrug and go along with it. Maybe she was curious.

Beau's request was so unlike him, but he just... he needed to know.

Was everyone but Leola against their relationship? Or would his own family step into his corner for once?

It was a test, in some ways.

Nerves rocketed through him as he went to find Grace and her mother, but he refused to bail. Grace had told him that people can surprise you, and he'd give anything to be pleasantly surprised tonight.

Leola served dinner as she usually would and then slipped into the seat beside her daughter. Grace looked kind of nervous as she fiddled with her cutlery, but he kept trying to catch her eye, and whenever he did, they shared a look that reinforced his decision.

As hard as this was, he was making the right choice.

Grace was worth any fight.

"So, Leola, how are you enjoying your time in Darien?" Mr. Griffin started the conversation with a relatively benign question, but at least it got people talking.

Leola gushed about loving the area and all the places she'd explored with Grace and Millie. This led Beau's mother to join in, waxing eloquent about some of the charities she supported and why certain places in the area were in fact so beautiful because of the part she'd played.

Beau couldn't help rolling his eyes.

His father noticed the gesture, and Beau was waiting for a dark glare, but instead he caught a hidden smile and a little wink.

He relaxed a little, cutting off another bite of steak before answering a question from Leola. They chatted about school, and this led the conversation around to prom.

Beau was surprised to find out his mother was involved. She laughed at his confusion.

"Darling, I'm involved every year. It's my forte. I love being on the committee. We guide the students with decorations and organizing the ticket sales. Don't you remember? I asked you to join last year, and you refused."

He shook his head, not recalling the conversation.

"Well, I didn't even bother mentioning it this year." Her smile grew tight, but she let out a fake laugh and took a sip of wine. "It shall be a night to remember."

Beau raised his eyebrows, trying to show that he was impressed.

"If you're involved, I'm sure it's going to be spectacular." Grace's sweet compliment was met with smiles all around, and Beau figured now was as good a time as any.

"Do you want to go with me?" he asked, then instantly regretted it. He could have been so much more romantic than this. She deserved the world's best promposal, and he'd settled for asking at the dinner table with the parents sitting right there.

But her answering smile erased his disappointment.

"Yes." Her voice caught with emotion, and her eyes were shimmering as she bobbed her head. "If you're sure you want to take me."

"Of course I'm sure." The words came so easily… because they were true. There was no other girl. She was it.

"Oh, Gracie." Leola leaned over and kissed her cheek before grinning at Beau and mouthing, "Thank you."

He grinned back, feeling kind of triumphant. This was actually perfect. He was wondering how he was going to ease their relationship status into the dinner conversation, and he just had.

"But… Beau, sweetheart…" His mother set her glass down and blinked at him. "I assumed you'd be taking Colette. Her mother and I have been discussing it. We know exactly what you should both wear. I was going to talk to you about it this weekend."

Beau shook his head. "Colette's not my girlfriend."

His mother scoffed in surprised. "And Grace is?"

"Yes," he answered softly at first, but then his voice grew with confidence and he reached across the table for her hand. Her fingers were trembling just a little as she laid them in his palm. He gave them a squeeze and smiled at his parents. "We've actually been dating for weeks."

There was a thick, dull beat of silence that got his hackles up. He could feel the tension simmering up his spine.

His mother spluttered on her sip of wine, her eyebrows popping high as she grabbed the napkin off her lap and wiped her mouth. "You're together?"

"Yes." Beau nodded.

"And you didn't think to tell us?"

"I wasn't..." His voice trailed off, but then he caught sight of his father's expression.

The old man was beaming. Raising his glass, he murmured, "Good job, son," then took a sip of wine.

Beau couldn't explain the sensation running through him. His father had never looked at him that way before. Was that pride?

Was this what it felt like? To finally be looked at like he wasn't the world's biggest disappointment?

He wanted to burst, laugh, do something to expel the emotion inside him.

Grace let out a soft giggle. He looked to her, and he could tell she'd read his mind. It was like she could feel everything he was going through, and she was so incredibly happy for him.

I love you.

He wanted to say it right there and then, but he didn't think his mother could cope.

She was still blinking at the tablecloth, trying to process this information.

"Isn't it wonderful, Celine?" His father grinned, then turned his gaze on Beau. "All I've ever wanted for you is your happiness. You've been lost for so long, and now you're finding your way. I've noticed the change in you, son, and I was wondering where it came from. Now I know."

Beau swallowed, unable to speak.

His father had noticed him?

And there was that pride again.

Beau nodded his thanks, then spotted Leola. She was beaming too. It was enough to light the room and ward off any shock from his mother.

He *was* happy.

In spite of his week and the tension at school, he was the happiest he'd ever been, and it was all thanks to the beautiful girl across the table.

33

BUTTERFLIES IN BLUE

It was prom night, and Grace was a ball of nerves.

Beau asking her at dinner had sent her insides into a frenzy, and she'd floated through the last two weeks. Things at school had seemed to calm down a little. People were adjusting to the idea of them as a couple, and even Colette and Ella had been talking to her.

It was weird, but they'd come up and asked her what she was wearing to prom. They'd spent the lunch break discussing fabrics, colors, and designs. It had been a surreal experience, and Grace had struggled a little, wondering if she could trust it. But then she spotted Beau's relieved smile, and she figured it didn't matter.

She had to do this for him.

The next day, Colette had waved to her again and even waited at the lockers so they could walk to class together. Ella flanked her other side, and they chatted in high speed about things Grace wasn't really into. Some show about people getting married at first sight. Grace couldn't imagine doing anything that reckless and wasn't surprised that it hardly ever worked out between the couples.

But Ella and Colette thought it was hilarious. She tried to laugh along with them, but it was hard to do that when her mouth was dry with tension.

After school on Friday, they'd loitered around Beau's car. Grace watched the way Colette laughed and touched his arm but tried not to let it bother her. She trusted him and would not turn into a jealous girlfriend.

"See you guys tomorrow night." Colette wiggled her eyebrows at them.

"Prom night, baby!" Etan whooped and raised his arms in the air.

Ella wiggled her hips with a giggle, and Grace forced out a laugh. She'd been nervous then, and that emotion had morphed into a weird kind of terror.

She hated being the center of attention. What if Beau wanted to dance? She wasn't confident with that. What if they did that thing they do in movies where they form a circle and people dance in the middle with everyone watching?

She felt ill but forced herself to swallow.

She couldn't let Beau down. He was excited for tonight, and she'd do everything in her power to make it a wonderful evening for him.

Adjusting her bra strap, she wriggled her shoulders and made sure the top part of the dress was sitting straight. It was a simple design—fitted bodice with a draping long skirt. The thing that made it so stunning was the outer layer of lace, which had butterflies sewn onto it.

Their dancing wings flew up from the bottom hem, moving and shimmering every time she walked.

It was the perfect dress for her, and Grace knew for a fact that her mother had stayed up late into the night all of last week, sewing the butterflies into place. It was a testament of her love, and Grace cried when she was first presented with the dress.

"It's so beautiful."

Her mother beamed. "A beautiful dress for a beautiful lady."

Grace touched the ends of her dark hair. The wide curls rested against her shoulders. Turning her head, she admired the braid crown Millie had painstakingly done to perfection.

With a light touch of makeup and some mascara to make her eyes pop, Grace had never felt more lovely.

Her mother stepped up behind her, touching her shoulder and looking a little tearful. "I'm so proud of you, *papillon*."

"Thanks, Mom." She touched her hand and felt her own tears starting to form.

"Oh no, you don't." Millie wagged her finger. "No crying. It'll ruin your makeup."

Grace giggled as Millie sniffed at her own tears. Both women leaned forward and kissed Grace's cheeks.

"Go have fun tonight. That's an order." Millie pointed at her.

Her mother nodded. "She will. I just know it." After another kiss, Leola pressed their foreheads together and whispered, "You deserve all the good things life can give you. You're the kindest person I know, and tonight is just one of the many rewards you have so graciously earned."

"Aw, Mom." Grace shook her head. "I haven't earned anything. I've just been me. And who I am has been made possible because of you."

Her mother's affectionate smile said it all, and Grace sniffed and walked up the stairs before she started crying for real.

Stepping into the entranceway, she stopped short when she spotted Beau. He was pacing near the entrance to the dining room, and he looked so handsome that her belly did a backflip. His black suit fit him to perfection, his toned body highlighted in all the right ways, while his hair was styled and held in place with just the right amount of product. He looked like a supermodel... and it took her breath away for a moment.

He was... so dignified and princely.

My very own Prince Charming.

She nearly said it aloud, but then he turned and saw her... and the look on his face made her heart fly.

"Wow," he whispered, approaching her with an awestruck smile. "You are so beautiful."

She grinned. "So are you."

He let out an awkward, breathy kind of laugh, his fingers shaking as he struggled to open the corsage box.

"That's so pretty," she murmured as he slipped it around her wrist.

"Dad helped me pick it."

"He has good taste." She studied the miniature white roses and gave them a sniff just as Mr. Griffin walked down the stairs.

"Grace Bellamy." He shook his head. "You sure scrub up nice, young lady."

She laughed. "Thank you, sir."

"Pictures!" Leola walked in from the kitchen, holding up her phone and insisting the couple pose for way too many photos. Even Mr. Griffin got in on the action, snapping what felt like a hundred photos on his camera.

"Okay, that's enough." Beau raised his hand. "I need to take this beautiful girl to the prom."

The parents agreed with happy smiles.

"Your mom's already there, and I'm sure she'll want to take pictures too. You have been warned." Mr. Griffin raised his hand with a laugh. "Have fun, you two," he called just as they disappeared through the door.

"I hope my mom has the same reaction my dad did." Beau grinned as he opened Grace's door and helped her into the car. He was so careful with the fabric of her dress, it made her heart warm with affection.

She didn't care what Beau's mother thought. She didn't care what anyone thought.

The person who mattered the most was sitting right beside her, and he'd been blown away. That counted for everything.

As long as he was next to her, she was pretty sure she could handle anything the night would throw at her.

34

MY GIRL... MY BOY...

Grace was stunning. Her dress was perfect—the butterfly wings dancing over her body were so freaking meaningful, it nearly made him want to cry. Walking into the school with her on his arm was one of the proudest moments of his life, and he would never forget it.

He smiled down at her, and she grinned back, looking happy and maybe just a little nervous.

Stopping her just before they entered the main hall, he turned to face her and touched her cheek, running the tip of his finger along her deepest scar. "You'll be the prettiest girl in the room."

She shook her head. The blush lighting her cheeks was adorable.

He tipped her chin up so he could kiss her lips—just a soft brush that hopefully reinforced his claim.

Wrapping his arm around her waist, he guided her through the double doors and into the prom. The hall had been transformed into a fairy kingdom—a tribute to *A Midsummer Night's Dream*. It'd been his mother's idea, and she'd done an amazing job. He searched for her, catching her eye and giving her a thumbs-up.

She smiled, her eyes drifting to Grace. She looked pleasantly surprised and started walking toward them.

"Well, don't you two look handsome together." Again with the surprise.

Beau tried not to be offended by it.

"Thank you," Grace said. "You look amazing yourself. I love that dress."

His mother looked down at her gown, obviously enjoying the compliment, then laughed. "What? This old thing?"

Beau forced out a snicker, then spotted his friends. He pointed toward them, and his mother retreated back to the parents' corner. He wondered what she'd say to them. Would she go for her usual "showing off" about how great her kid was, or would she be more subdued now that Grace was with him? She'd have to somehow explain why Beau wasn't with Colette. That had no doubt been the expectation.

He shoved the thought aside and walked toward his friends. They were watching him, and he grinned, his chest expanding with pride as the girls noticed Grace's dress and pointed at it.

"You look amazing!" Colette said to Grace before smoothing her hand down Beau's jacket. "You look pretty good too." Her teasing was met with laughter, and Beau felt that sense of relief that they seemed to have turned a corner. Things were getting back to normal—thank God.

Since his argument with Colette after school, she seemed to have switched things up. He didn't know what he said—maybe it was the fact that he apologized for losing his temper, or maybe it was him practically begging her to give Grace a chance—but something had happened to soften his friends up. Over the past week, they'd allowed Grace into their circle. They'd never be besties, but at least they were talking to her, including her in conversations around the table and not saying nasty comments every three sentences.

They seemed to have come to a place of acceptance. It was a huge surprise and a welcome relief. He was sick of fighting the battle.

"Hey, guys. Looking hot." Julius eyed Grace up and down, wiggling his eyebrows.

Beau warned him off with a growl, which only made Etan laugh. "Get over yourself, man. We all know she's yours." The guy rolled his eyes, and Beau snickered, shaking his head with a silent apology.

"Let's dance!" Ella waved them to the dance floor.

Grace hesitated, but he put his hand on the small of her back and encouraged her forward. Her smile was nervous, more like a wince, so he put his arms around her waist and they slow danced, even though the song was a fast one.

He wanted to make her as comfortable as he could. She had good rhythm, and they swayed to the beat while his friends bopped around them. After a few minutes, he got a little creative and spun her beneath his arm. She laughed and went with it, starting to let the music take over. As she relaxed into the song, her laughter grew, and they danced straight into one song after another.

It was a blast.

Grace's smile was a sunbeam, lighting up his heart, and he reveled in her joy. He never could have imagined this for himself. She'd opened a doorway to happiness that he never expected, and he was almost struggling to get used to it. He loved it, but a small fear clung to him, wondering how long it could last.

When the music dropped down to a slow number, he pulled her close, resting his cheek against her head and enjoying the feel of her so close.

"You having fun?" he murmured against her ear.

She leaned back with a smile. "I didn't think this much fun was possible. I'm having the best time. Thank you." She touched his cheek, then leaned forward and kissed him.

He pressed his hand against her back, and they made out for a few bars before pulling away and smiling at each other.

"Thanks for being my girl."

She laughed and rested her chin on his shoulder. "Thanks for being my boy."

They swayed until the music stopped.

"Okay, guys, time to take a quick break before the next set." The singer of the band spoke into the mic. "Grab yourselves a drink and..." He stopped talking to hear what one of the teachers was saying to him. "Oh, I've just been told that the prom king and queen will be announced in about fifteen minutes!"

A loud whoop went up from the crowd. Beau joined in the cheering, hugging Grace against him.

Colette and Ella were jumping around with excitement. Colette would no doubt be named prom queen, and he wondered if he'd be king, or maybe it'd be Etan. He was pretty popular too. Zari and Amell were also contenders, although Beau knew one wouldn't want to win without the other. Those two were in love and did everything together.

Kissing the side of Grace's head, he was finally starting to understand Zari and Amell's relationship.

"I wonder who it'll be," Colette squealed.

"It's so going to be you." Ella rolled her eyes, looking just a touch jealous as she forced a smile at her best friend.

Beau shared a quick look with Grace, who bit her bottom lip, obviously fighting laughter. She probably thought that whole thing was ridiculous. And maybe she was right.

The whole king and queen ordeal... it was basically a popularity contest with people putting in votes, and he wished that others would win for a change. Why did the best-looking people always have to be up there? Why couldn't it be the smartest girl and the funniest guy?

For some reason, this school always voted for who they thought was the coolest. It made him sad that before Grace came along, he would have been strutting around with smug pride, assuming it'd be him.

Now he didn't even want it, especially if Grace wasn't going to be crowned queen alongside him.

"I'm so excited!" Colette squealed again. "I'm gonna go check my makeup."

"Me too." Ella threaded her arm around Colette's, then turned to Grace. "You want to come?"

Beau could have kissed his friends for asking. It was a huge deal.

Yes, it was only a makeup check in the bathroom, but they were including Grace!

He stepped away from her, allowing her space to move. She gave him a hesitant smile, and he bobbed his head.

"It's okay. I'll be right here." He winked at her, and she followed after the girls.

He watched her walk away, shaking his head in wonder.

Life was taking him down a path he never thought possible, and he couldn't believe how things were falling into place.

A feeling of overwhelming gratitude filled him as he followed his friends to a side table to grab some punch. Etan was already talking about how hot each girl looked tonight.

Beau internally rolled his eyes, knowing his buddy would never agree with him that Grace was one of them, but feeling quietly confident that he was the luckiest guy at prom.

35

BATHROOM BEAUTIES

Grace was a ball of nervous energy as she followed the girls out of the main hall. She felt untethered without Beau holding on to her, like she'd drifted away from her anchor and was about to get lost at sea.

"Are you having fun?" Colette asked over her shoulder.

Grace nodded, still adjusting to how friendly she was being. It had been a weird week. After months of what felt like pure hatred, to be treated like a friend was hard to wrap her head around.

They passed the bathroom with the female symbol on the door. "Aren't we…?" Her voice trailed off as she pointed to the sign the girls had walked straight past.

"Oh, we don't use that one." Ella giggled into her hand. "Don't tell, but we've been sneaking upstairs to the staff one all year. It's so much nicer than these."

Grace paused on the landing.

"Don't worry about it. We'll be fine." Colette snatched her wrist. "Don't be such a goody-goody. No one's going to catch us."

Forced to follow them up the stairs, Grace glanced over her shoulder, instinctively knowing that they had to be quick and quiet.

"It's fine." Ella rolled her eyes. "Seriously. Don't worry about it. The teachers are monitoring the dance. They won't be coming up here."

Grace wanted to argue that even teachers needed to pee, but she kept the thought to herself. She guessed the worst that could happen was they'd be told off and sent on their way.

But she'd never been told off by a teacher before.

She *was* a goody-goody… and she liked it that way.

With her heart in her throat, she slipped into the bathroom and was surprised to find a couple girls already in there. She didn't know them that well, but she'd seen them around. The girl with raven hair, applying a thick layer of lip gloss, had been a fairy in *A Midsummer Night's Dream.*

"Oh, hey, Colette." One of them grinned in the mirror.

Colette gave her a simpering smile and approached. "Hi, Cassidy. Looking hot tonight, girl."

"Thank you." She dipped her hip, sticking out her leg to reveal the extremely high split of her dress. With her plunging neckline, there hadn't been much fabric required to make the dress.

Grace averted her gaze, reminding herself that people could wear what they liked, and just because she didn't like to show all didn't mean there was anything wrong with it. Biting her lips together, she tried to ignore the uncomfortable squirming in her chest. She felt so out of place with these people, like an alien in a foreign world.

Looks aside, they were completely different girls to her, interested in things that didn't particularly inspire her—like the length of Cassidy's nails or the fact that some poor girl downstairs looked hideous in yellow, and what the hell was she thinking.

Ella cackled. "I bet her mom picked it out for her... or better yet, she probably handmade that repulsive dress. It's like she's puked blobs of yellow butter all over her daughter."

Colette snorted. "Is it really so hard to keep an eye on fashion trends? Honestly. She looks like she pulled it out of a recycling box at a thrift store."

Grace swallowed, a cold sweat breaking out on her skin as she waited for them to turn and start hassling her butterflies. Did she have the courage to admit that her mother had sewn them on, and she was beyond grateful? That she couldn't have felt more loved by her mother for taking the time to care enough to do that? They'd probably just laugh in her face. And she could only imagine the ridicule if she tried to stand up for the girl in the yellow dress. She hadn't seen her, but she was sure it wasn't as bad as they were making out.

Grace loitered by the stall doors, hoping to remain invisible and wondering if she should actually use the bathroom. A locked stall sounded pretty good right about now. But she didn't really need to pee, and her dress would be a mission to lift. The skirt section was so many layers of fabric, and who knew how hard the girls would laugh at her if she managed to pee on her dress or walk out with it tucked into her underwear.

Internally shaking her head, she quickly decided that

the effort to actually go just wasn't worth it. So, she smoothed down her gown, fidgeting with one of the butterflies while the girls primped and preened in the mirror. Thankfully, they'd moved on from the yellow catastrophe and were now talking about how gorgeous they all looked.

And then the conversation turned again...

"So, prom queen." The girl whose name Grace didn't know had a singsong voice. "It's definitely going to be you, Colette. I voted for you."

"Aw, you're so sweet. Thank you."

"I voted for me," Ella stated, causing the entire room to freeze and blink at her stupidly. She giggled. "Kidding! I totally voted for you, bestie."

Colette's look of indignation morphed to a proud grin.

Grace eyed Ella carefully, quickly figuring out that Ella had just lied. She'd totally voted for herself. Again, she stayed quiet, not wanting to cause any tension between the friends.

"Who did you vote for Grace?" Colette asked, eyeing her up in the mirror.

"Oh. I didn't." She shook her head, feeling the heat rush to her face. "I've never..." Her words petered out. Would these girls even get that she thought the whole prom king and queen was stupid? She didn't want to offend anyone, so she kind of winced instead.

"Hmmm." Colette spun to face her, her bright eyes flashing. Grace felt an instant spike of warning. She didn't know why, but something in her stomach pinched.

"Who do you think the king will be?" Ella asked, sharing a glance with Colette and Cassidy.

"I was assuming Beau, but I'm really not sure anymore. He may have lost a few votes in the last couple weeks." Colette's lips rose into a plastic smile. "No offense, Grace."

Grace swallowed, smiling off the sting and shaking her head.

None taken, she silently told them.

They probably wouldn't believe her if she said it anyway. And they probably shouldn't have.

How could she not be offended?

They basically just said that Beau had lost votes because he was dating *her*.

Colette ran a finger over her bottom lip and then adjusted her sparkling earrings. Her voice was sticky sweet. "But if he did win, you'd be okay with that, right?"

Grace nodded. "Of course. He deserves it."

"Yeah, but it's not like you'll be queen." Colette's eyes flashed, her lips curling into a smile that was anything but pretty. "If I win, he'll be dancing with me."

With a thick swallow, Grace nodded again. "I know. But... it's just prom queen and king. It won't change the fact that he's my boyfriend."

Colette's smile flatlined, and that internal alarm Grace was trying to ignore started blaring like a police siren.

This weird week was suddenly starting to explain itself. All those friendly smiles and sweet gestures the girls had been giving her... they were false.

It'd all been fake. A way to lure her away from Beau.

Bail! Bail now!

Grace turned for the door, but she'd barely made it two steps before she was surrounded.

"I don't want any trouble," she rasped.

"Neither do we." Colette clamped her hand around Grace's arm, her nails digging into her skin, while Ella grabbed her other side.

The two other girls, who were obviously in on this, snatched Grace as well, and the four of them overpowered her, dragging her out of the bathroom and down the hall. She tried to cry out for help, but a hand was clamped over her mouth.

Someone was yanking her hair, nails were biting even deeper into her flesh, and even though she fought against them, she wasn't strong enough to overpower four hellcats determined on making her pay for taking one of their own.

"Get her phone!" One of them was patting her down, looking for her device, but she didn't bring it.

Where was she supposed to carry it anyway? It wasn't like her dress had pockets.

"I don't think she has one."

"What? Don't be ridiculous. Check everywhere!"

Much to her humiliation, the girls took Colette's order literally, and she was felt up between both her legs and her breasts. She screamed and tried to twist away from the intrusion, but they were relentless.

"Nope. No phone."

Colette lurched to a stop in the hallway and grabbed Grace around the neck. "No phone? What the hell is wrong with you?"

"I didn't think I'd need it tonight," Grace rasped.

"Whatever. You're such a freak," she spat. Her look of hateful derision was brutal. "Let's go, girls."

"No," Grace whimpered, but they ignored her protests,

dragging her toward a cleaning closet, tearing at the fabric of her dress. Tears burned Grace's eyes when she saw a butterfly flutter to the floor. She dug her heels into the ground, but it was a pointless fight.

"No, please," she begged as the door was pulled open. Grace gaped into the dark shadows, the stench of cleaning supplies assaulting her nostrils as they tried to force her in there. "Please, don't do this."

They shoved her from behind and she landed in the closet, her knee hitting the edge of a bucket and a broom falling on her back. She struggled up and spun around to escape, but Colette was right there. She pushed her back, and Grace's dress caught on the edge of the metal shelving. The heartbreaking sound of irreparable damage made the girls titter.

Grace ignored it, gathering up the tattered gown and trying to squeeze past them.

But Colette blocked her.

"Where do you think you're going?" She laid a sharp slap across Grace's cheek before shoving her back so forcefully that Grace landed on her butt with a thud, the handle of a mop smacking her on the head.

She winced, her eyes watering as the girls laughed and Colette pointed at her.

"Stay down, mutt!" The look of disgust on her face hurt more than the slap did. "You don't belong at this prom. You don't belong in his life, you ugly beast!"

Colette slammed the door shut, and Grace heard the ominous click of a lock and then a cackle of laugher before feet scurried away.

She slowly got up, rubbing her sore head and fighting

tears. Of course this was all too good to be true. Girls like Colette didn't change their stripes so easily. Not everyone could grow a set of butterfly wings, even if Grace wished they could.

Grabbing the mop and broom that had landed on her, she rested them against the wall, then fumbled around until she found the light switch. An orange glow filled the room, and she squinted against it before checking her dress. It was torn down the back, but what did it matter now? Lifting the fabric, she looked at her throbbing knee. A bruise was already forming, but there was no blood.

She shuffled to the door and tried to open it. She knew it was futile. It was locked from the outside, and the only way free was to get help from someone. But who'd be able to hear her from up here?

Slapping the wood with her palm, she cried out in vain, "Help! Help me! Somebody, please! Help me!"

But no one came.

Her hand began to sting and she gave up, slumping down onto the floor and giving in to the tears shaking her belly.

Beau would come for her.

Wouldn't he?

The horrible thought that maybe he'd played a long con with her wriggled its way into her brain. Was this all some big prank?

Had Colette put him up to it?

Was that why he'd suddenly started being nice to her?

But... all those kisses. His gentle touches. The way he'd laughed and sang with her... taught her chess... opened up the way he did.

Had it all been fake?

He was a good actor, but…

She closed her eyes, picturing his tears in the bathroom after she took that prosthetic makeup off.

"You are the beauty… and I am the beast."

His face grew with clarity in her mind, and she whispered, "It's real. It has to be."

He'd come for her, because he cared about her. Because she was his girl.

MAKE A CHOICE

The girls were taking longer than Beau expected, and he couldn't keep his eyes off the door. He had a funny feeling in his stomach that he couldn't explain.

As soon as they swanned in, giggling among themselves, he rushed over to them.

"Where's Grace?"

"Oh, she's coming." Colette glanced over her shoulder, then leaned in to whisper, "I think she's stuck on the toilet, if you know what I mean." She rubbed her belly and winced. "I don't know what she ate, but she told us not to wait for her."

Beau cringed, gazing past Colette's shoulder to look out the door. Poor Grace. How embarrassing for her... and just when she was starting to make headway with the girls. No wonder he was feeling unsettled. Poor Grace was suffering, and he'd somehow sensed it.

"Don't tease her about it." He looked down at Colette, then eyed the girls who'd formed a semicircle in front of him.

"Of course not." Ella touched her chest, obviously mortified that he even thought they might.

With a simpering smile, Cassidy slipped past him and walked toward her boyfriend, Ricky. The tall guy wrapped his arm around her waist, and she whispered something in his ear that made him laugh, then kiss her.

Colette and Ella hung back. Ella was studying her nails, while Colette tapped her finger on her elbow, swaying to the music.

"I wonder if I need to go check on her." Beau moved for the door, but Colette quickly blocked him.

"Because that's not humiliating." She bulged her eyes. "Having your boyfriend lurking outside the bathroom while you…" She screwed up her delicate nose.

Beau let out a reluctant sigh but had to agree. He wondered about texting her, but then she'd know that he knew about her situation… and maybe she didn't want that. Maybe she wanted to him to act clueless so she didn't have to divulge her stinky situation.

"Come on." Colette took his hand. "Let's wait for her over here."

She tugged him farther into the room, and they milled around, sort of dancing to the music while they waited for the big announcement and then another set from the band.

Beau couldn't get into it. He kept checking the door, then his watch, wondering how much longer Grace could take. He couldn't help worrying about her and was about to go ask his mother to check when the principal stepped up to the mic.

"Hello, everyone." She grinned at the crowd below her.

"It is always my pleasure and privilege at this special occasion to announce the prom king and queen."

Beau stepped back, figuring now was a good time to slip away and make sure his girlfriend was okay. He scanned the room for his mother, but then Colette snatched his wrist.

"Where are you going?" she hissed.

"To find Grace."

"You can't." Her face puckered into an angry scowl. "They're about to make the announcement, and it could be you. It'd only be more embarrassing for her if you're out there and it draws everyone's attention to it."

He winced, hating that she was right.

Shoving his hands into his pockets, he stood beside his friends, dreading this moment. He didn't want to be prom king. He wanted Grace. She should be beside him.

He couldn't stop worrying about her, wondering what she'd eaten and why she hadn't shown any signs of not feeling well before.

Had he missed something? Guilt tugged at him. He should have watched her more carefully.

But you were. You were studying her like a hawk, desperate for her to feel safe and secure with you... to have a good time with you.

She'd been smiling and happy. This whole stomach thing had come on quite suddenly. Maybe—

"Congratulations, Beau Griffin!"

A cheer went up, and people started pushing Beau toward the stage.

Ugh. This was the last thing he needed right now!

He reluctantly walked up the side steps and forced

himself to smile when the principal placed the crown on his head.

"How fitting. Our Oberon is the prom king."

He stood on the stage and waved, spotting his mother in the back. She was clapping over her head and smiling like she'd won the crown herself.

"And now for our queen. Ladies and gentlemen, please give a round of applause to... Colette Winters!"

"Yes!" Colette screamed, pumping her arm in the air and practically running for the stage.

She was beaming as the crown was placed on her head. Stepping up beside Beau, she kissed his cheek, taking his hand and leaning into him.

The student body let out another cheer as she raised their joined hands above them.

"First dance!" someone started shouting.

Beau was relieved he didn't have to give a speech. He'd usually be up for that kind of thing, but he just wanted this moment over with so he could go and check on Grace.

"Dance! Dance! Dance!" the crowd chanted.

Beau gave them a good-natured smile and walked down from the stage with Colette clinging to him like they were a couple.

"It's just a dance," he murmured in her ear as she pressed her body against his.

"I know that." Resting her hand on his shoulder, she started to sway to the slow, romantic beat, letting out a dreamy sigh that told him she didn't.

It was hard to get into it. He kept looking up and around, searching for Grace. He really didn't want her walking back in to see him dancing with Colette. He wanted to be able to catch her eye and send a silent message that he didn't really have a choice.

The song ticked along, and there was still no sign of Grace. He started to worry that maybe she'd come back, seen him, and taken off.

The idea grew in his brain, like a parasite taking over, and soon he had to pull away from Colette and walk out of the circle.

"What are you doing?" She chased after him.

"Going to find Grace." He pulled out his phone, finding her number in his Favorites and lifting the device to his ear.

"Argh!" Colette threw her hands up. "Would you forget about her! She's not coming back!"

He stopped short, the words registering like a punch to the face. Spinning on his heel, he narrowed his eyes on Colette. "What did you just say?"

His friend blinked and shook her head, her lips pinching into a tight, guilty-looking frown. "Beau, you really—"

"What have you done with her?" He grabbed her arms and gave her a little shake. "Tell me where she is."

"Can't you just be in this moment with me and forget about *her*." The derisive tone, that haughty look on her face...

Alarm bells started blaring.

"*Where* is she?"

People nearby were starting to notice the altercation. Part of Beau didn't care. He wanted to jump on that stage and ask for everyone's help in a school-wide search, but Grace would hate that kind of attention.

Instead, he snatched Colette's wrist and pulled her outside so they could talk in private. But there were people in the corridor, so he kept walking, heading for the door leading outside.

"Slow down," she complained.

He ignored her protests, leading her toward a back door of the building. Pushing it open, he rushed her down the concrete steps. They were in a deserted, dark area behind the hall. It was filled with junk that the school caretaker hadn't gotten around to yet—old desks, metal piping, a broken chair.

Beau only knew about it because this was where kids came to smoke and drink sometimes. Or skip class and make out like crazy. He'd joined in once or twice. He and Colette had played a few rounds of tongue twister in the past, but not tonight.

Tonight, he wanted to be able to yell at her, and this was the perfect spot. He could shout right in her face if he needed to, and no one would be able to hear it.

"Colette, stop messing around." He spun her around to face him. "Where is Grace? What did you do with her?"

"I'm not doing this! I can't believe you've changed so much! What the hell has happened to you?" she practically screamed, wrenching the phone out of his hand and throwing it onto the ground.

"What the hell is wrong with you!"

"Let go of me!" She wriggled free just as Ricky and Etan came running down the steps.

Ella and Cassidy were right behind them.

"What's going on?" Etan asked.

"Colette's done something to Grace, and she won't fess up!" He went to reach for his phone, but she kicked it away. He watched with a growl as it skidded over the gravel and flipped onto its back. Giving her an incredulous glare, he started to shout, "I need to find her! So stop acting like such a bitch and tell me the fucking truth right now or I'll—"

"Or you'll what?" Colette's scorn deserved a sharp slap.

He curled his fingers into a fist, his nostrils flaring as he fought the temptation.

"C'mon, man." Etan jumped off the bottom step. "Grace doesn't belong in this place. We're just trying to help you see that."

He spun with a wounded frown. "You're in on this too?"

Etan lifted his hands, and Ella stepped in. "Of course he is. We had to make some kind of plan."

"We had to do something to make you see the light, you dumbass," Etan snapped. "We don't know what the hell you're on right now, but you need to snap out of it. This is an intervention, and the first thing we had to do was get Grace out of the way so you could start to see sense again."

"Where is she!" he bellowed, rushing Etan and tackling him to the ground. "Tell me!" He fisted Etan's collar and threw a punch at his friend. Etan's head snapped back, and he let out a pitiful whimper, blood spurting from his bottom lip.

Hands tugged at Beau, yanking him back. Someone

was fisting his hair while Ricky grabbed him and held him still.

"I thought we were friends!" Etan spat, wiping his mouth and landing a hard punch in Beau's stomach.

Beau lurched forward, fighting for air.

"That bitch has put a spell on you, man! Don't you see that?"

The door burst open, and Julius came rushing out. "What are you guys doing?"

"We're trying to talk some sense into this asshole." Etan pointed down at Beau, swiping blood off his lip.

Julius hung back, taking in the scene, then shaking his head. "This about Grace?"

"Help me," Beau rasped. "Help me find her."

His longtime buddy jittered on the top step for a moment, glancing around each of his friends before raising his palms. "This is way too much drama. There's a hall full of hotties just waiting for us in there, and you're out here beating each other up?" He tutted and shook his head like they were all crazy. "I'm out."

He spun on his heel and walked back inside. Colette and Cassidy jeered him, calling him a pussy, while Beau closed his eyes, hanging his head and wishing that he had just one loyal friend. Was that too much to ask?

Why had he tried so hard with these ignorant assholes?

The need to keep this friendship going evaporated, along with the fear of what they might to do him. He no longer gave a shit if they tried to make his school-life hell. He and Grace could handle whatever these douchebags tried to pull. As long as he could find her and be with her, their bullshit couldn't touch them.

"She's the best thing that's ever happened to me." Beau choked out the words. Struggling back to his feet, he shook Ricky off him with a growl, then pointed to each of his friends. "You've got nothing on her. She's gold. She's better than all of us, and you're just too blind to see it."

Etan scoffed, spitting out a string of curses, while Ella shook her head, looking hurt and wounded.

Colette's nostrils flared, and even in the dim light, Beau could make out the spark in her eyes. They flashed with scorn when she pointed her manicured nail at him. "We can't handle this version of you anymore, Beau. We want our friend back. It's either her or us!"

Beau shook his head. He hadn't wanted it to come to this, but the choice was a no-brainer.

"It's her," he rasped, then cleared his throat and spoke a little louder. "If you're making me choose, it's her. Every time, I will choose her, because I love her."

"Don't talk smack." Etan frowned.

Beau shrugged. "It's the truth, man. I love her."

"Psycho," Colette muttered, then stamped her foot. "Fucking psycho!" With an angry shout, she lurched toward him, pushing him back.

He barely moved. She wasn't the strongest, but she kept coming at him, whacking her fists into his chest. He took it, not wanting to hurt her. But when she wouldn't stop, he grabbed her wrists and lightly pushed her back.

An unexpected calm washed over him. He had no idea where it came from, but he channeled as much of Grace's dignity as he could muster, keeping his tone even but firm. "Tell me where my girlfriend is and we'll leave. You can enjoy the rest of the prom and—"

"Go to hell!" Etan shouted, lunging at Beau and getting his own back with a hard punch that sent Beau flying.

He stumbled backward, his feet tripping over a concrete block before he landed with a thud that didn't feel right.

His brain only just registered a squelching pain while his body went instantly numb.

Ella screamed and covered her mouth while Etan staggered back, his mouth agape as he stared at Beau's stomach.

Following Etan's line of sight, Beau looked down and felt like throwing up when he noticed the steel rod sticking right through his body. It was glistening with red paint...

No, that's blood, man. You've been impaled.

He blinked, still trying to figure out what that meant. All he knew was that it wasn't good.

"Help me," he whispered, but the words were so soft, he could barely hear them.

"Shit!" Colette started crying. "We gotta get out of here."

"What?" Cassidy squeaked. "We have to help him! Ricky!"

Her boyfriend shook his head, looking white with fear as he headed for the stairs.

Grabbing Etan's arm, Colette started pulling at him and shouting at Cassidy. "Run! You want to get busted for this? We have to go!"

"We killed him." Ella started blubbering and pointing at Etan. "You killed him."

"Shut up!" Etan growled, wrapping his arm around her waist and forcing her up the stairs.

"Help me." Beau reached out, but even Cassidy turned her back and ran away.

The door thudded shut behind them, and Beau was left with only the sound of muffled prom music and the night sky above him. He gazed up at the stars, wondering how this was going to end.

No one knew he was out here, and he doubted the others would run for help.

If they had any hearts at all, they might make an anonymous 9-1-1 call, but they seemed in shock, so the chances of that were slim.

His gaze was going fuzzy, but he searched the ground, spotting his phone face down on the ground. It was out of reach. Completely useless to him.

I could die out here.

The thought settled over him like a cold blanket.

He tried to wriggle free, instinct begging him to fight, but any movement hurt so badly that it threatened a blackout.

"Ahhh!" He panted, squeezing his eyes shut and willing the numb back over him.

"Help me," he whimpered, knowing it was futile.

"Grace," he whispered, wondering where she was and if she was okay. They must have locked her up somewhere, and all he could pray was that she found a way out and was safe. "Please be okay."

He murmured the words over and over again until his speech began to slur and the stars above him became fuzzy black spots.

37

STAY WITH ME

After a short break where she let a bout of futile tears take her, Grace resumed her door-hitting and yelling routine. She couldn't sit there moping.

Jiggling the lock a hundred times over, she tried to find a way out, but to no avail.

"Help me! Somebody! I'm stuck in here!"

She kept up her screaming, praying that a teacher might come along to use the bathroom. She yelled until her voice was hoarse and her throat was aching.

Until finally, she heard a faint…

"Hello?"

Grace gasped and began banging the door even harder. "In here! I'm in here! Help me!" She was rasping and coughing, but she powered as much volume into her voice as she could. "Help me! Please! HELP!"

There was a scurrying of feet and then a fumbling of keys.

Finally the door popped open, and Grace was facing Mrs. Gold, her beloved art teacher.

"Grace?"

"Thank you." Grace squeezed her hand, tears tumbling down her cheeks as she whimpered and bobbed her head. "Thank you."

Mrs. Gold's face was the picture of surprised horror as she took Grace by the elbows to steady her. "What are you doing in here?"

"I can't explain right now, but it was a prank." With a sniff, she quickly gathered herself and slashed the tears off her face. Anger was rapidly overriding her relief. Now that she was free, she could shake off her hopeless despair and allow something new and fresh to course through her.

Indignant rage.

That was it. Bright and potent. Foreign yet energizing.

"Thank you for helping me," she muttered as she pushed past her teacher.

"Grace?"

"I have to run," she called over her shoulder, lifting her tattered skirt so she could race down the stairs without tripping.

The sensible thing to do would have been to tell Mrs. Gold everything and get her support with disciplining Colette and her friends, but anger was driving her forward.

She knew if she was ever going to overcome this, she had to confront Colette on her own first.

That girl needed to know that Grace was not a total pushover. She'd put up with weeks of merciless bullying, trying to be kind and patient every step of the way. And what did they do?

They pranked her.

Colette was not going to ruin Grace's life this way.

It wasn't fair!

And even though kindness and love were the best places to start, tonight Grace was after a good showdown. She refused to be pushed around any longer. They needed to know she wasn't weak. She would not be a bully target anymore, dammit!

She popped out into the hall like a warrior woman about to attack and spotted her target racing toward her.

"Colette!" she screamed as the girl rushed past, heading for the front door like she was running from a ghost. "Get back here!"

The group ignored her, all of them chasing after one another as they headed out to the parking lot.

"Go, go, go!" a tall guy shouted, grabbing his girlfriend's wrist and pulling her faster down the hallways.

"Colette!" Grace shouted again.

The girl faltered, tripping over her dress and landing on her knees. She let out a squeak as the others ran past her, bolting out a side door.

"You can't treat me this way!" Grace barreled after her. "This bullying has to stop!" Grabbing Colette's arm, she helped her to her feet and made the girl face her. She looked scared, tears lining her lashes, and it took Grace by surprise.

Blinking, she nearly gave in to the compassion within her.

Are you okay? What's the matter? How can I help?

The words were on the tip of her tongue, but instead she shook her head and spat, "I will not be treated this way. Beau and I are together now, and you just have to live with it. You will *not* treat me like a second-class citizen, and you will *never* lock me in a closet again!" Grace was practically screaming the words, and she didn't even care.

Colette wrenched her arm free, glaring at her while her chest heaved as if she was on the verge of sobbing. Grace prepared herself for a catty reply, but all Colette did was lift her dress and run the other way. She looked petrified, and Grace didn't bother chasing her. She was acting weird. Grace couldn't imagine that a telling-off would upset Colette so much.

So, what was freaking her out?

Grace looked over her shoulder in the direction Beau's friends had come running from, and a knot formed in her stomach.

Something was wrong.

She walked back the way she'd come, wondering what was down that corridor.

"Grace?" Mrs. Gold appeared beside her. "Are you all right?" She touched Grace's arm. "I'm sorry this has happened, and on prom night too. Kids can be so cruel. I'd really like to help you. Can you tell me who did this?"

"I…" Grace stared down the hallway again, desperate to know what Colette and her friends had been running from. Had they pranked someone else?

She needed to find Beau. She needed his help.

"Grace?"

"I'm fine." She shook her head. "I don't want to deal with this tonight."

"But your dress." Mrs. Gold picked up the torn fabric.

"It's not okay that they did this. There needs to be consequences."

"And there will be, I'm sure. But I don't want to ruin the night for everyone else."

Mrs. Gold's expression turned soft. "You really are the most gracious…" She shook her head with a smile. "You have the perfect name."

Grace forced out a laugh, but it sounded awkward and weird.

"Now, you have to promise me that first thing Monday morning, you'll come to the art room and we'll deal with this situation. The school has a no-bullying policy. We can go and see the principal together."

Grace nodded, still distracted by the gnawing in her stomach.

"It's not your job to protect bullies. You need to tell the truth in order to protect yourself and other victims."

"I will."

Mrs. Gold looked dubious but nodded. "Okay. Well, can I call someone for you right now?"

"No, I just need to find my boyfriend." Grace spun and raced back into the main hall; anxiety was overwhelming her for reasons she couldn't even explain. The idea of some other poor girl trapped and crying behind a locked door spurred her on.

But the look of fear on Colette's face…

Maybe they'd taken it too far.

Maybe some poor girl was injured and locked away. Was it the one in the yellow dress?

Rushing into the main hall, she winced against the

blaring music and hunted for Beau. He'd know what to do.

She couldn't see him immediately and went onto her tiptoes, resisting the urge to shout his name. Why had she left her phone at home?

Idiot! Don't do that next time!

She spotted Julius and headed toward him, but he quickly turned and lost himself in the crowd of dancers. She frowned and nearly approached Zari and Amell, who were dancing so closely together they looked like one body.

But then she spotted Beau's mother on the other side of the room. Lifting her dress, she made a beeline for the elegant woman.

"Excuse me... sorry... please let me through." She was scoring a plethora of odd looks from those she passed, but she ignored them all, determined to get to Mrs. Griffin.

"Excuse me!" she shouted above the music to get the lady's attention. It took three tries, but finally the blonde woman spun. "Have you seen Beau?"

Beau's mother gave her a gushing smile. "He was crowned prom king."

"Oh really?" Grace wasn't that surprised, but it stung that she'd missed it. "Where'd he go?"

"Well, he was dancing with Colette, and then next thing I knew, they'd disappeared together." Mrs. Griffin winced, taking Grace's hand and gently patting it. "I'm sorry, dear, but those two have always had a special connection. I wouldn't go looking for them if I were you. They're probably out under the stars... well, being a king and queen together."

Grace's insides plummeted.

That didn't feel right.

Mrs. Griffin gave her a sympathetic smile and gazed over her. That was when her expression changed to one of confusion. "What happened to your dress?"

Grace couldn't speak.

Colette and Beau disappeared together?

But she just saw Colette and her friends running scared out of the—

Beau!

Ice-cold fear flooded her. The sensation was so forceful, she nearly lost her balance.

"Grace, are you okay?"

With a gasp, Grace fled, picking up her skirt and running for the door, nearly knocking over Mrs. Gold in the process.

"Sorry!" she shouted over her shoulder.

Shooting back into the corridor, she turned left, the way Colette had been running from.

There wasn't much down there, and she soon felt like she was in the deserted bowels of the school. Her shoes echoed on the polished floor, sounding like gunshots.

She nearly turned and retraced her steps, wondering if she'd missed something, but then she spotted a door leading outside.

She shoved down the metal bar and burst out into the open air. It was dark and hard to see, but the moonlight gave her a partial view. As her eyes adjusted, she began to make out pieces of junk. A broken chair. Some old desks.

"Beau!" she cried, horror tearing through her as she

practically fell down the steps and scrambled across to him.

He was lying on the ground at a weird angle, like his body was stuck in that position.

It wasn't until she was kneeling beside him that she noticed the metal bar jutting through his middle.

"Help!" she screamed, panic scorching her. "Beau?" Leaning over him, she lightly patted his cheek. "Beau, can you hear me?"

He stirred a little, letting out a moan before opening his eyes.

Blinking in the dim light, he gazed at her for a painful beat before rasping, "Grace."

"What did they do to you?" She started to cry, then whimpered, "Hang in there. I need to get you help."

"Don't leave me." He fumbled for her hand.

His fingers were slick, and Grace soon realized they were coated with his blood.

"You're bleeding," she whispered, horror tearing through her again as another layer of reality was added to this nightmare. This was real. Beau was badly injured. He could die! "Stay with me," she begged. "You have to... you have to be all right."

Her insides started shaking out of control.

Get him help!

Her logical voice was screaming at her, but she couldn't obey.

Leave Beau?

How?

Get him help!

"Help!" she screamed again. "I have to get you—"

"Hello?" The door swung open, and Grace glanced up.

"Help! Help us!"

"What is going on out here?" Mrs. Gold appeared on the stairs, using the light from her phone to guide her way.

"Call an ambulance!" Grace was still screaming, her voice pitching as a sob overtook her words.

"Grace? Is that you again? What is—" The teacher gasped. "Oh, Lord. Oh, please help us." She whispered the prayer as she took in the scene, then quickly went into action, dialing emergency services.

Grace leaned her head against Beau's shoulder, resting her cheek against his and whispering in his ear, "Stay with me."

"I'm here," he croaked. Touching the side of her cheek, he lightly caressed it. "Are you okay?"

"I'm fine," she hiccupped. "As long as you're okay, I'm fine."

She sat back so she could look down at him.

"They didn't hurt you?" His words were faint and wispy.

"No. They just locked me in a cleaning closet." Her hands shook as she lightly touched his stomach, wondering if there was more she could do to help him. "I can't believe they did this to you."

Beau closed his eyes while anger fired through her. How could they have left him like this?

"An ambulance is on its way," Mrs. Gold informed them. "Beau, I'll go get your mother." She rushed back inside.

Grace gripped his hand, pressing it against his cheek.

"It's gonna be okay." Tears trickled from her eyes and over his fingers.

He opened his mouth like he was going to say something, then couldn't.

Grace leaned closer to him. "Beau, stay with me."

His eyes slid shut.

"No. Beau!" Her voice hitched. "Stay." Her body shook with sobs as she curled over him, pressing her lips to his ear and whispering, "I love you. Don't leave me. Please. I love you."

38

TRUE LOVE

Grace loved him.

That was the only thought that got Beau through. It floated in his brain, three misty words he couldn't quite capture as he drifted into oblivion. He had no idea how he got to the hospital. There was a black space in his memory with only sounds—a hysterical woman weeping, rushed voices, ambulance sirens—but it was those three little words he chased. They kept him calm.

And they woke him up.

I love you.

His eyes eased open, squinting as they adjusted to the light before exploring the room. It looked more like a hotel than a hospital, with flowers by his bed and a painting on the beige wall. There was an armchair in the corner... and there was Grace.

She was curled up in it, her hands tucked under her chin as she slept.

"I love you too," he whispered, drinking her in and knowing it was true.

Licking his parched lips, he gently investigated the pain in his side. It was a dull ache that pounded right through his torso.

He shifted on the bed, wincing in discomfort and unable to hold back a hiss.

Grace's eyes shot open, and she bolted upright. "You're awake." Her face lit with a smile that was pure sunshine. "You're awake."

With a little sniff, she got up and came around his bed. Her hands were cool on either side of his face as she cupped his cheeks and drank him in like he was the most beautiful thing she'd ever seen.

"Hi," he whispered.

"Hi." Her giggle was soft and breathy. "How are you feeling?"

He swallowed, unable to describe the pain.

"I'll get the nurse." She fumbled for the buzzer, but he snatched her hand before she could.

Her skin was soft and smooth, and he explored it with his thumb while looking into her beautiful eyes.

"I love you too." His voice was weak and raspy, but she still heard him.

Those brown eyes that he adored so much glistened with tears. "I wasn't sure if you'd heard me."

"Those words kept me alive." It seemed kind of dramatic, but that was how he felt.

She pressed her forehead against his. "They're the truth."

"I know," he whispered. "I know it in my soul. They didn't understand."

"What do you mean?" She leaned back, her expression

darkening. "Are you talking about your friends?"

"They made me choose…" He swallowed, closing his eyes against the pain. "They didn't like my choice."

Tears spilled from her eyes, and she blinked rapidly, swiping them off her cheeks. "I didn't want that for you."

"This isn't your fault." He shook his head. "They're the ones with the problem. Not you. Not me." He squeezed her hand. "I told them I'd always choose you. It's a no-brainer." His lips curled into a smile, which he was hoping she'd kiss. He wanted to feel those lips against his again.

Her watery smile was gorgeous. He drank it in while she bit her bottom lip and sniveled, "You… honor me, my beautiful butterfly."

With a soft tug, he brought her back down to him, lifting his chin in a silent invitation.

She read his mind and pressed her lips against him, lightly kissing the corner of his mouth, his cheek, his chin, and then diving into a deep kiss.

He relished it. Cherished it. Soaked in it.

Cupping the back of her head, he extended their make-out session, even when she tried to pull away and he wouldn't let her. She got the giggles, and he sucked in the sound, smiling along with her and then making the mistake of laughing.

He groaned, his side protesting in earnest.

"Stop," Grace gently reprimanded him. "No laughing."

He winced and nodded, cradling his side.

"I'm getting the nurse." She rang the buzzer, and he let her.

Soon, a nurse was bustling in the door with his parents not far behind. They each carried a coffee mug and stood on the edge of the room, soaking in the sight of him. He felt like a newborn baby with those adoring, glistening stares but couldn't really complain with the nurse right there. She checked his wound, took his blood pressure, and helped him have a drink.

"The doctor will be in to check on you during his rounds. And I'll arrange some lunch to be brought in."

He wasn't hungry, but he didn't have a chance to tell her that before she left.

"How are you feeling?" his father asked.

"Like I lost a jousting match."

His father grinned, but the smile didn't last. He started to blink and looked ready to cry.

"I'm fine, you guys."

"You weren't," her mother squeaked. "We thought we were going to lose you."

His father wrapped a secure arm around his wife and pulled her in for a hug. She wept against him, and Grace took Beau's hand. Her fingers were shaking as she rubbed her thumb over his knuckles.

"But you didn't." He nodded. "I'm here. I'm gonna heal." He looked to Grace, that sweet stirring in his chest making him feel like he could fly. "I'm gonna be better than fine."

She grinned, placing a sweet kiss on his forehead.

He looked from her to his worried parents, and it suddenly struck him—he was blessed. He was beyond blessed. The people in this room, they loved him. They all had different ways of showing it, but that was okay. In that moment, he'd never been more certain of how much they all cared about him.

He'd never been more certain of how strongly those feelings were reciprocated.

For years, he'd fought so hard for the wrong people.

But the ones right here, they were his family, his true love.

They were the ones who gave him wings.

39

THE BUTTERFLY MAN

Grace nudged the sunglasses up her nose and rolled onto her stomach. She could get used to this.

Sun, sand, and a hot guy lying next to her.

She glanced at her boyfriend and grinned.

He'd dozed off with a book in his hands, and it was now resting open over his face.

Too cute.

Although, she'd have to wake him soon. She didn't want him burning to a crisp on their first full day of summer vacation.

After Beau had been released from the hospital, he'd spent a few weeks at home. He missed a lot of the end-of-year stuff, but he did return for exams. Julius, Zari, and Amell all tried to see him, but Mrs. Griffin wouldn't let them. She was furious with his circle of friends and made sure the entire town of Darien knew it.

It lost her a few of her richest acquaintances, but she was adamant that the people who hurt her son went down.

Colette, Etan, Ella, Ricky, and Cassidy were expelled. Mrs. Gold and the principal quickly learned the truth, and as much as Grace hated being a tattletale, she couldn't lie about what happened. It wasn't right. Julius eventually came forward to back up her story. He was ashamed that he hadn't fought for his friend and almost looked relieved to be suspended. His parents were outraged and disgusted with him, and he'd been permanently grounded and apparently had himself a job with his uncle in Nebraska for the entire summer.

Before he left, Mrs. Griffin allowed him and his parents into the house to apologize to Beau. Grace was proud of Beau's forgiveness and the way he was allowing Julius to start up a tentative friendship with him again. Things were going well so far… and Zari and Amell were tagging along for the ride.

They didn't know about the prank on Grace.

Zari had gotten wind of it beforehand and told Colette and Ella not to be so mean. That was why they'd recruited Cassidy and Ricky to help instead—a move the couple would regret.

All the parents were called in to the school, confessions were made, and it was decided that cruel, irresponsible behavior was not welcome at Lincoln Academy. There was even an article in the local paper about it.

Beau was told he could press charges if he wanted to, but he decided against it. Grace guessed it was his parting gift, in a way. They'd never see those people again. Colette's family had actually moved out of town.

Grace hurt for Beau. It was a loss. They'd been his best

friends for years, but her mom assured her he'd make new ones.

"I met my best friend in college." She grinned at Millie. "You don't always stay in touch with your high school buddies."

Grace knew that wouldn't be true in her case. She planned on staying in touch with Beau for the rest of her life.

High school sweethearts were a thing, and Beau was hers. She knew it in the very depths of her being.

Glancing at the scar on his stomach, she relived the nightmare of prom.

That metal pole had shot straight through Beau, nicking his small intestine. Thankfully, it missed his other vital organs, and the surgeon was able to sew him up in time. He lost a lot of blood, and that was what nearly killed him. By the time they reached the hospital, he was practically gray, and the ER team looked pretty grim as they rushed him into surgery.

It was the longest wait of Grace's life.

She paced a trench in that linoleum. Her mother came to sit with her, and her father called to comfort her. None of it helped. It wasn't until the doctor came out to tell them Beau would make it that she felt she could breathe again. Mrs. Griffin lost it, her legs buckling. Mr. Griffin caught her against him, and they cried together. In retrospect, it was a beautiful thing to witness.

Beau's near death had brought his parents closer together, and family time had really improved.

Grace was invited to dinner almost every night, and her mother usually joined them. The Griffins had embraced them like they were family, and she'd never felt more at home.

Reaching over Beau's naked torso, she brushed her finger over his scar. It was pretty gnarly, and Beau didn't like it very much. At first, he'd actually refused to take off his T-shirt, even when they were lying at home around the pool.

"How can you say that? You're gorgeous," Grace had argued.

She could tell he wanted to protest that the scar made him ugly, but he couldn't exactly say that in front of her.

She'd snickered and gone inside to grab a permanent marker off her desk. Walking back out to the pool, she stood over him and demanded, "Take off your shirt."

"What?"

"Take it off."

He'd eyed the marker dubiously.

"Trust me," she whispered, bending down to kiss him.

He'd given in, and she'd taken her time drawing butterfly wings around his scar. The gnarly line had become the butterfly's body, and she'd eventually stepped back with a proud smile.

He'd gazed down at her creation and laughed. "Fine. You win."

He'd kept his shirt off for the rest of the day, much to Grace's delight.

Her boyfriend was one fine specimen.

"That tickles," Beau murmured, his voice kind of sleepy.

She giggled and kept touching him until he grabbed her hand and splayed it over his stomach.

Leaning up on her elbows, she lightly kissed his shoulder.

"You ready to go swimming, sleepyhead?"

"Depends. Are you wearing that hot yellow bikini?"

A thrill raced through her. He always made her feel so desired and sexy. There was something very intoxicating about that.

"I guess you'll have to open your eyes to find out."

He threw his book down and sat up to look at her. She'd taken off her sundress while he was sleeping, and she enjoyed the way his eyes ran down her body.

He skimmed his fingertips over her stomach, and she shivered with pleasure.

"Come on, sexy. Let's get you wet." His wolfish grin made her laugh.

They jumped up together, and she let out a little squeal when he lifted her off the sand and ran them into the water. The cool salty ocean hit their skin, and she gasped at the sudden chill but was soon distracted by Beau's arms circling her waist.

She wrapped her legs around his hips and they bobbed in the water together, making out in the sunshine and reveling in each other.

Life had never been better.

Grace was aware that it wouldn't always be smooth sailing. To some, they were an odd couple, and they would never be understood by everyone.

But it didn't matter, because she knew that whatever storms came their way, they'd battle it out together—her and her butterfly man...

Once upon a time, there was boy who was broken...and then he met a girl who showed him what it truly meant to be rich, and that love was the most beautiful gift of all.

THE END

Thank you so much for reading Beau & Grace's romance. I really hope you enjoyed it. My favorite thing about this story is the transformative power of love. I believe every person on the planet has beauty inside of them... and I believe that real love can heal any hurt and turn someone's life around.

If you'd like to read another fairytale romance that is inspired by the power of love... and my favorite fairytale, Rapunzel...

You can check PAPER CRANES here:
www.jordanfordbooks.com/paper-cranes

NOTE FROM THE AUTHOR

Beauty and the Beast has always held a special place in my heart. It's the idea that beauty can be found in all things that really drew me to this romance. Belle was always so loving and kind, even when the Beast was so horrible to her and her father. But her gentle softness and tenacious spirit unearthed the Beast's inner beauty... and there's something so inspiring about that.

Our exterior shells hide so much, but when we let our inner beauty shine through... amazing things can happen. Whatever energy we put out there gets returned to us and Grace was amazing at putting out that loving, sweet energy... which eventually chipped away at Beau's hard exterior and let his butterfly wings come to life.

Even when she didn't always feel it, she held fast to her mother's mantra: *You are beautiful. You are worthy. You are enough.* And this is true of all of us. We won't always feel it everyday, but the fact remains... we have been created with love and that makes us automatically beautiful, worthy and enough. 🤍 How cool is that?

Thank you so much to all the people who continue to make this job so beautiful for me—you, my other readers, my editors, my proofreaders, my review team and my awesome Forever Love Crew.

Thank you to my amazing friends and family who show me their beauty every day.

And thank you to my creator, who crafted me into the person I am, gave me my own set of wings and helped me to fly with pure, unconditional love.

xx
Jordan

ALSO BY JORDAN FORD

THE BIG PLAY NOVELS

The Playmaker

The Red Zone

The Handoff

Shoot The Gap

THE BROTHERHOOD TRILOGY

See No Evil

Speak No Evil

Hear No Evil

THE BARLOW SISTERS TRILOGY

Curveball

Strike Out

Foul Play

Change Up

RYDER BAY SERIES

Over the Falls

The Impact Zone

Face of the Wave

Riptide

Wipeout

White Water

FOREVER LOVE SERIES

City Girl vs. Country Boy

Broken Girl vs. Fix-It Boy

Shy Girl vs. Popular Boy

Outcast Girl vs. Pretty Boy

Lost Girl vs. Wounded Boy

Fractured Girl vs. Reckless Boy

Wandering Girl vs. Torn Boy

BARRETT BOYS SERIES

The Runaway

The Fighter

The Protector

The Rescuer

The Warrior

MISFITS REMIX

Maverick Loves Londyn

Selah Loves Dante

Alexia Loves Troy

You can find information for the next Jordan Ford book release on her WEBSITE:

www.jordanfordbooks.com

ABOUT THE AUTHOR

Jordan Ford is a New Zealand author who has spent her life traveling with her family, attending international schools, and growing up in a variety of cultures. Although it was sometimes hard shifting between schools and lifestyles, she doesn't regret it for a moment. Her experiences have enriched her life and given her amazing insights into the human race.

She believes that everyone has a back story…and that story is fundamental in how people cope and react to life around them. Telling stories that are filled with heartfelt emotion and realistic characters is an absolute passion of Jordan's. Since her earliest memories, she has been making up tales to entertain herself. It wasn't until she reached her teen years that she first considered writing one. A computer failure and lost files put a major glitch in her journey, and it took until she graduated university with a teaching degree before she took up the dream once more. Since then, she hasn't been able to stop.

"Writing high school romances brings me the greatest joy. My heart bubbles, my insides zing, and I am at my happiest when

immersed in a great scene with characters who have become real to me."

CONNECT WITH THE AUTHOR

Jordan Ford loves to hear from her readers. Please feel free to contact her through any of the following:

Website:
www.jordanfordbooks.com

Facebook:
www.facebook.com/jordanfordbooks

Instagram:
www.instagram.com/jordanfordbooks

Email:
jordan@jordanfordbooks.com

Jordan Ford Newsletter:
Sign up and receive a free book!
www.jordanfordbooks.com/page/sign-up/